The Green Umbrella

Tree

bird home
leaf home
ant home
lizard home
twig
    branch
        caterpillar
            butterfly
    home

seed shade
sheep shade
cow shade
horse shade
wallaby shade
people shade
ground shade
sun shade

a tree is a green umbrella
with brown bits

Jenny Boult

The Green Umbrella

Stories, songs, poems and starting points for environmental assemblies

written and compiled by Jill Brand
with Wendy Blows and Caroline Short

Illustrations by Jane Ray

Published in association with
the World Wide Fund for Nature

A & C Black · London

CONTENTS

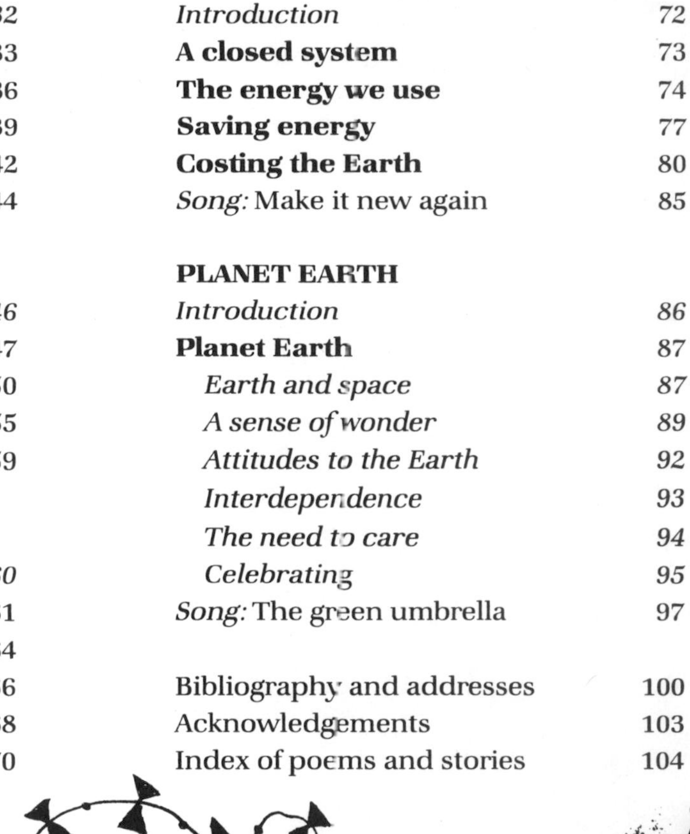

First published 1991 by A & C Black (Publishers) Ltd
35 Bedford Row, London WC1R 4JH

Poetry consultant Brian Moses
Story consultant Helen East
Religious consultants Elizabeth Brieully and Sandra Palmer (ICOREC)
Designer Dorothy Moir
Editor Sheena Roberts

ISBN 0-7136-3390-5

Typeset by ABM Typographics Ltd, Hull
Music set by Paul Heap Music Setting
Printed in Great Britain by Hollen Street Press

The text paper, supplied by Precision Publishing Papers of Yeovil, is Elk Offset, produced using an environmentally kind manufacturing process requiring less wood and only a fraction of the chlorine bleached pulp of many other papers.

INTRODUCTION

School assemblies on environmental themes have two main purposes: to foster in children a love for the Earth they live on; and to encourage them to want to take care of it. Unfortunately, the need for care is now pressing. There can no longer be any doubt that the global environment is under threat, and on many fronts.

Many people in industrialised societies live their lives out of touch with the natural world, which may seem to have little relevance for them. It has been all too easy to ignore the piecemeal destruction – a species of butterfly here, a drained marsh there. Even the slow deterioration in our own quality of life may be considered acceptable – a few more allergy sufferers in our inner cities could seem a small price to pay for the convenience of the motor car. After all, the Earth has constantly changed since its creation, and humankind has always altered it further.

But now the pace of deterioration is increasing faster and faster and the changes are on a larger and larger scale. Major disasters *are* happening, though not perhaps in our own back yards. People are dying in their millions from famine caused by soil erosion, deforestation, war and, probably, global warming. Animals are becoming extinct at the rate of at least one a day. Whole forests are being destroyed by the axe, fire or acid rain. Not only is the picture bleak for future generations, it is bleak now.

It is difficult for us to feel personal responsibility either for the devastation or for setting things right. Problems on this scale are so huge that individual effort might seem to be a waste of time.

We must help children to see that individuals *can* do something. Some might be able to make a considerable commitment, such as building an energy- and water-efficient house, for example. But we can all change our behaviour in small ways – remembering to switch off lights and buying environmentally-friendly products. It really is a case of 'every little helps'. Children are often very enthusiastic about investigating and putting into practice these small Earth-saving ideas, and spreading the word at home.

The second way we can help is by putting pressure on those in a position to take major decisions. Public pressure really does work, and our children are the public of the future. If they learn to care enough, they will take action.

The best way we can help them to care is by fostering a love of the Earth, its plants, its animals and its people. With the children, we must appreciate and celebrate all that is good. We must certainly let them know the dangers – and there are many appalling facts in this book – but they need to feel deep-down that it is all *worth* saving. This is the only home we have, and it is beautiful.

School assemblies are ideal occasions for encouraging this love, and for sharing the attitudes and beliefs of other people, past and present. But the assemblies should not stand in isolation. The whole school ethos needs to reflect this caring spirit, both on a practical level – the choice of materials used in school, energy saving, discouraging litter – and in the behaviour of the members of the school to each other and to the natural world.

Using this book

The book is divided into sections, each about one aspect of our environment (although there are considerable overlaps, of course). Each section, apart from *Planet Earth*, is divided further into individual themes, which could be the basis of one, or of several, assemblies. You might choose to use a section, or an individual theme, because it fits with work going on in school at the time; or because it is relevant to the time of year (e.g. during a cold spell requiring the use of extra energy), or to a particular festival, such as Sukkoth; or because of a current major news story. Alternatively, you may decide to have an entire term or year of environmental assemblies and use the whole book.

At the beginning of each theme is a set of purposes, followed by starting-points which are designed to capture the children's attention. The fact boxes provide information which can be presented directly to the children or used indirectly in discussion.

The discussion will often form the main part of the assembly. A number of different issues are suggested each time and you will know where you yourself wish to place the emphasis. Obviously, you will also need to adapt the ideas to suit the age and experience of the audience.

The suggestions for classroom activities indicate a few ways in which individual children, groups, or classes could follow up the assembly ideas. Sometimes these activities will provide material for further assemblies.

The last section, *Planet Earth* is organised somewhat differently (see page 86). Suggestions are given to help you to prepare a celebratory assembly or festival, in which the children can make their own commitment to caring for the planet.

Jill Brand

WATER

Water covers about 70% of the Earth's surface, and is the most common liquid. Without water, there would be no life on the planet. Indeed, the earliest forms of life originated in the seas, and it was millions of years before primitive species began to emerge onto dry land.

Humans and other animals have bodies which are largely composed of fluid, and, apart from a few species which get their liquid from food, they need to drink water regularly to maintain a healthy balance. Humans can live for weeks without food, but only a matter of days without water.

Water is also necessary for our food supply: many people depend on fish as a major food but, more importantly, plants, which are at the base of all food chains, need water to germinate, to photosynthesise and to grow.

Unfortunately, in many areas of the world, water is in short supply, or is poorly managed. Shortage of water means plants and livestock cannot thrive. People become malnourished and may die, either directly from thirst or starvation, or through lack of resistance to disease. In recent years, rainfall seems to have become more unreliable, and deserts are spreading. How much of this is due to human activity is a matter for debate, but some of it certainly is. Even in countries such as Britain, where there is fairly plentiful rainfall, fresh water can run low because of the enormous demands from domestic users, industry and agriculture.

For people and animals to thrive, they need not just adequate water, but clean water. Many organisms thrive in water, including some which are harmful to human life, like the cholera bacterium and the snails which are part of the bilharziasis cycle. Drinking water also needs to be free of poisonous mineral and chemical pollutants.

But water is more than just a matter of survival. We rely on it to clean ourselves and our possessions; we use it as a means of transport and as a source of energy for our mills and hydro-electric power stations; in industry it serves as a coolant and as a solvent; we extract vital minerals from it; and we often find ourselves spiritually refreshed just by looking at and listening to it. It is such an integral part of our lives, that it is a major symbol in many religions and often has a ritual significance.

Sadly, we also treat water as the world's rubbish bin – a convenient dumping ground for all kinds of waste, from human body wastes to radioactive material. Many other pollutants end up in our rivers, lakes and oceans inadvertently. We are in danger of making life impossible for vast numbers of diverse species which live in water, and of poisoning the water supplies on which our very lives depend.

WATER, WATER EVERYWHERE

Purposes

1 To understand that a large part of the Earth's surface is covered by water.

2 To think about the many different forms water can take.

3 To celebrate the beauty of water.

4 To think about the religious significance of water.

Starting-points

■ Show a large photo of the Earth from space (see the resource list on page 100). Ask the children why it is blue and white. If an alien ship orbited Earth, what sort of description might the aliens send back home? What name might they give the Earth? Is 'Earth' a suitable name?

■ Read the poems by Jonathan Kingsman and Nancy Byrd Turner. Ask the children what similar ideas the two poets have had. What are the main differences in the way they regard water? Are there any ideas Jonathan Kingsman has missed out? What does he mean by the last two lines?

■ Find two or three reproductions of paintings which feature water (for example, pictures by Turner, Constable, Monet or Canaletto) to share with the children. They can compare how different artists have treated water, how it fits into the composition, and why the artist might have chosen to paint the scene at all.

■ Invite someone from a local religious community to talk about the significance of water in their faith.

continued

Waterways

The ice-cap slowly melts and drips,
Tall icebergs float among tall ships.
From Arctic wastes the waters flow,
To make the seas and oceans grow.

Tempests and tides and roaring waves,
Have carved out arches, cliffs and caves,
Water creates and shapes the land,
From mountain range to grain of sand.

Up through the rivers water reaches,
Past headlands, deltas, cliffs and beaches.
From the rivers, little streams,
Spread through the land in glints and gleams.

The water-tank, up in the loft,
A liquid cube, pure, cold and soft,
Waits to rush out from tap to air,
And link you with the polar bear.

Leo Carey (aged 12)

Water

Send it cascading over waterfalls,
And break it with a roaring crash across rocks,
Wash in it, cook with it, drink it, heat with it,
Keep fish in it, kill people by the sheer force of
it.

Put out fires with it, rust metal with it,
Swim in it, wade in it, dive in it, splash in it,
open your eyes in it,
Journey across to France on it,
Freeze it and break glass as it expands,
Heat it and put it in radiators to warm the
body,
Or just make cement and build with it.
Let it pour from the sky in tiny droplets,
And leave it as dew to make daffodils sparkle
in spring.
Let it flow in rivers, make electricity from it,
Run it along the gutters, washing the stone,
and sail boats on it.
Water flowers with it, wash cars with it, make
fountains of it,
But most of all
Just leave it shimmering in a river or pool
And watch, but watch carefully or it will go
And never return.

Jonathan Kingsman

Fact box 1

Seventy per cent of the Earth's surface is covered by water.

Nearly all the water is salty. Only about 2.5% is fresh, and that is mostly in the polar ice-caps. Only about one-hundredth of a per cent is available for use by humans.

Each year 500,000 cubic kilometres of sea water evaporates, to fall again as rain.

Fact box 2

Water is such a vital and integral part of human life that it has become an important symbol in many religions, because of both its life-giving and its cleansing properties. For example, the Ganges River in India has always been a vital water supply but it is also revered for its purity by Hindus. All Hindus wish to bathe in the holy river at least once in their lives and to have their ashes scattered on its waters. For Sikhs in the Punjab, the coming of the monsoon rains is a time of celebration and rejoicing. The Christian ceremony of baptism can have different connotations, but essentially it signifies that a person is entering a new life. For both Jews and Muslims, ritual washing is an important symbolic act, which transcends a basic need to be clean. You can find out further information from particular religious groups, or from some of the many books about different faiths available for schools.

The sorcerer's apprentice

This version of the well-known story explains how the continents were separated, and people divided.

It so happens there was this young boy, probably about as young as yourself, who wanted to be a medicine man. So his parents found a medicine man living in a cave way up a steep hill, who agreed to teach their son. Straight away he handed the boy a broom, and said, 'If you want to learn the mysteries, this is where you start.' And he set him to work sweeping out the cave.

'Ugh!' complained the boy as he bent to his work. But while he swept, he watched, and while he watched, he saw strange mysteries performed. The medicine man had a conch to which he would utter these words, 'Conch, conch, tell me of the whispering, so I may hear.'

And the conch whispered long and low in words which only he could hear.

He had a large mirror standing against the wall. 'Mirror, mirror,' he would say, 'reveal to me the mysteries, that I may see.'

And the mirror would mist up, and then show him any part of the world that he wanted to see.

All his spells and medicines, the man wrote down in a huge book with a heavy cover.

Now, it so happened, that one day the medicine man had to go out. So he said to the boy, 'Stay here, and tidy up — sweep and clean and leave my things alone.'

The young boy did as he was told but as the day passed, he became more and more bored. As the afternoon drew on, he found himself dusting the big book of spells. Quickly he opened it, but was disappointed to see that it was filled with words he could not understand. He turned another page and found on it just one word, which he could not say, but which he spelled out loud.

Lightning flashed, thunder rolled, and clouds filled the cave. A demon appeared before him and roared, 'Give me a task!'

Shivering with fright, the boy stammered out, 'Well, um, er — there's a well over there, and there's a plant over there, and it's dying. Water the plant.'

The demon found a big hefty bucket, and went to the well. Swish, he watered the plant. 'Ha!' said the boy, 'that's got him busy.'

Swish, the demon watered the plant again. 'That's enough,' said the boy, 'you can stop now.'

But the demon just gnashed his teeth and went back to the well again and again, filling the bucket, and pouring it over the plant. The water spilled all over the floor and splashed around the boy's ankles. 'Stop, please, stop!' cried the boy.

But the demon gnashed his teeth again, and went back to the well for more water. Now the water was up to the boy's waist; soon it had reached his neck. 'Stop!' he cried, 'stop!' and with his last breath, as the water reached the ceiling of the cave, he called out to the medicine man to help him. Then he slid below the water and sank to the bottom of the cave.

The medicine man sat in deep meditation. But something told him the boy was in trouble. He woke up, saying 'I must go and find out what's happening.'

As he climbed up the mountain to his home, he saw the mouth of the cave covered like the curtain of a waterfall. Quickly he said some words, and, woosh, the water broke from the cave and tumbled down the hillside and out into the world. And there, coughing and gasping on the floor of the cave, was the boy, safe and well. 'Oh, master, master, I am very, very sorry.'

'Hey,' said the medicine man, 'you've been troubling my things, haven't you? Pick yourself up and let's see what wrong you've done.'

And he took up the conch, and held it to his ear. 'Conch, conch, tell me of the things I wish to hear.' But all that he heard was a babble of strange voices talking in many languages he did not understand. He put down the conch and looked into the mirror. 'Mirror, mirror, reveal to me the things I wish to see.' But all he could see was a shimmering expanse of water, dividing all the lands of the world from one another.

'Look what you have done,' said the master to the boy. 'You have made brothers not know their brothers, and sisters not know their sisters, for now they speak in many tongues and live in many lands. From this day onward I will teach you properly the ways of the mysteries.'

But from that day onward, water covered the Earth.

Traditional story, retold by Godfrey Tuup Duncan

Water is a lovely thing

Water is a lovely thing:
Dark and ripply in spring;
Black and quiet in a pool,
In a puddle brown and cool;
In a river blue and gay,
In a raindrop silver-grey;
In a fountain flashing white;
In a dewdrop crystal bright;
In a pitcher frosty-cold,
In a bubble pink and gold,
In a happy summer sea
Just as green as green can be;
In a rainbow, far unfurled,
Every colour in the world;
All the year, from spring to spring,
Water is the loveliest thing!

Nancy Byrd Turner

Discussion

● Why have so many artists and poets been attracted by water? What do the children think are the most beautiful forms water takes? Can they think of some good descriptive words? Is water always beautiful? Can it be harmful?

● Can the children imagine a world without water? Assuming they could find a way to survive, what aspects of water would they miss most? What else would disappear? If water is so essential to us, how should we treat it? Are people always careful about how they treat it?

● You could talk briefly about the water cycle, although most work would be done in the classroom. Help the children understand that it is a closed system – the same water goes round and round, although it may have a long journey. (See *Waterways* by Leo Carey on page 5, and *The stream and the desert*, on page 26.)

● Why should water be so significant in religion? Why would people at the time of the founding of some of the great religions regard water so highly? Some of the children might be able to share personal experience of the part water plays in their own religion.

Activities

♦ A group could work together to make a large collage of water, using a variety of paint techniques, fabrics, paper, foil, and other materials. It could perhaps be used as a background for words about water or other writings.

♦ Water is a good subject for the children to write their own poems about. They could try writing a haiku (five syllables in the first line, seven in the second and five in the third) or they could devise their own pattern. The tightness of the structure means they have to focus their thinking clearly to produce an effective image.

♦ A group could compose a piece of music representing the different moods of water – crashing waves, a bubbling stream, a dripping tap – using real or home-made musical instruments.

WATER AT HOME

Purposes

1 To appreciate how much we rely on water in our daily lives.

2 To consider the need to conserve water and think of ways of doing so.

3 To understand the necessity for clean drinking water.

4 To learn something about the lives of people who do not have access to enough water, especially clean water.

Starting-points

■ Line up enough buckets to show 100 to 150 litres capacity. (The average household bucket holds 9 or 10 litres.) Explain that this is the average amount of water each person in a 'developed' country uses in the home each day. How do the children think this is divided up?

■ Show 5 litres of water in a container, and explain that this is how much many people in developing countries have to survive on. Talk about how that might be divided up, pouring the quantities into appropriate measuring jugs. Alternatively, this could be used as a separate starting-point on another day.

■ Read the true account, *The long walk is over*. Talk with the children about all the ways life improved for the villagers.

■ Fill a bucket with water and see how far a child can carry it. Explain that in many countries, over half of all households have to fetch their water in containers. It is nearly always the women and children who do this.

Fact box 1

1 flush of a toilet cistern uses about	10 litres
1 bath uses about	80 litres
1 shower uses about	30 litres
1 washing-machine load uses about	100 litres
1 dishwasher load uses about	50 litres
1 garden sprinkler for 1 hour uses about	900 litres

I like water

Water from the tap
Like a tube of soft glass
Breaking. It chews round my fingers
Like waves breaking.

Water in the bowl
Smooth and sticking
Bubbles climbing down my arm
Like a leech.
I make a beard of bubbles.

Drinking water —
Clear and runs down the back of my throat
Slippery and slidey.
Undries my mouth.

Water in the bath
If Mum doesn't scrub me
It's warm and soothing.
I like water.

Edward Hawkesworth (aged 7)

The long walk is over

The UN Decade for Water planned to provide safe drinking water for everyone throughout the world. It failed to reach many of its targets, but in the instances where it succeeded, it brought enormous change to people's daily lives, as this account shows.

Mwanaisha Mweropia, a 23-year-old mother of six from Mwabungo village in the Kenyan district of Kwale, used to make seven journeys a day to a well some distance away. There was always a line at the well, even at dawn, and the rule was that no one might draw a second bucketful without joining the queue again.

Everyone quarrelled and women with large families — which was most of them — were constantly tired. Mwanaisha coughed perpetually and had chronic chest problems. Rainfall in this arid coastal area is seasonal and most streams and traditional wells dry up. Women were trekking long distances to dig in dry riverbeds. The picture is a familiar one in Africa where 60% of women spend hours of backbreaking labour collecting a few miserable buckets of water — which is often unsafe to drink.

In 1984 Mwanaisha's life changed when the Kenyan Water for Health Organisation installed an Afridev handpump in Mwabungo — part of a special project to drill boreholes and install pumps in more than 100 local communities. Not only is the Afridev handpump much closer to Mwanaisha's home and far less onerous to operate but the water is safe and her cough and chest pains have disappeared. The local project worker says that all water-related diseases have declined.

The strength of the project was the way it involved the community, and in particular the women, in the organisation and chose a small-scale pump appropriate to the local needs. Now that the pump is installed, each community collects five pence a week from each family for repairs and replacements. To Mwanaisha Mweropia it is a small price to pay for a better, healthier life.

Winnie Ogana

The house that Jack built

This is the house that Jack built.

This is the tea that everyone drinks
In the house that Jack built.

This is the water,
That makes the tea that everyone drinks
In the house that Jack built.

This is the kettle,
That boils the water,
That makes the tea that everyone drinks
In the house that Jack built.

This is the tap all shiny and bright,
That fills the kettle,
That boils the water,
That makes the tea that everyone drinks
In the house that Jack built.

This is the pipe — underground, out of sight,
That leads to the tap all shiny and bright,
That fills the kettle,
That boils the water,
That makes the tea that everyone drinks
In the house that Jack built.

This is the waterworks pumping all night,
That supplies the pipe — underground, out of sight,
That leads to the tap all shiny and bright,
That fills the kettle,
That boils the water,
That makes the tea that everyone drinks
In the house that Jack built.

This is the river — oh, what a delight!
That flows past the waterworks pumping all night,
That supplies the pipe — underground, out of sight,
That leads to the tap all shiny and bright,
That fills the kettle,
That boils the water,
That makes the tea that everyone drinks
In the house that Jack built.

These are the pesticides, herbicides, fungicides, nitrites, nitrates, trihalomethanes and polycyclic aromatic hydrocarbons . . .
That pollute the river — oh, what a delight!
That flows past the waterworks pumping all night,
That supplies the pipe — underground, out of sight,
That leads to the tap all shiny and bright,
That fills the kettle,
That boils the water,
That makes the tea that everyone drinks
In the house that Jack built.

Kevin Graal

The Prophet Muhammad was washing in a plentiful flowing river. He scooped up a small bowlful in which to wash. His companions asked him why he did this, since there was plenty of water in the river. He replied that even where there is plenty, one should not waste anything.

Muslim story

Fact box 2

About 70% of our body weight is water. We need to take in about 1.5 litres of fluid a day.

A healthy adult can live for many weeks without food, but only a few days without water.

In Britain, water supplies often break EEC regulations on permissible levels of impurities.

Millions of litres of water are used in industry as a solvent and as a coolant. For example, it takes 1600 litres to produce 1kg of plastic. Much of this is returned to the water supply.

Poisonous wastes, such as mercury from batteries, leach from landfill rubbish sites into the water supply, and are difficult to remove.

Tap water in London may already have been recycled six times before it reaches the capital.

In many countries only one person in five has access to clean water. Some families may spend half their income on buying water from a water seller.

It is estimated that 80% of all disease in the developing countries is caused by poor water supply and sanitation. Up to 20 million children die each year from lack of water or water-borne diseases. Many more are ill and weak.

Cholera and typhoid were two major killers in Victorian London. Improvements to water supplies and sanitation almost wiped them out.

Discussion

● Talk with the children about the need to conserve water, whether or not there is a drought. Even in countries such as Britain water tables are dropping, rivers are sometimes reduced to a trickle, and new reservoirs have to be built, flooding valleys, houses and farms. In addition, all the water which is piped to our homes has to be treated to make it safe, and this is expensive. Are there easy ways of saving water at home? Can we reuse any of it? Could we collect rainwater, and what could we use it for?

continued

The price of water

Should water be owned and sold? Gopaldas did not believe so, and this story tells what he did when someone tried to charge him for it.

There was once a good and honest merchant called Gopaldas. Every year he went on a pilgrimage, by foot, to the holy city of Kashi, on the banks of the Ganges. It was a long hard journey — over a thousand miles — and it was often difficult to find food or water along the way. The worst stretch was over the Rajasthani desert, across miles of shimmering dusty sand. Luckily for travellers, there was a well, halfway across, built by one Govindram, a generous man, who let people drink freely of the precious water.

Now, one year, Gopaldas was travelling with a group of people from his village. The sun was so fierce and the desert so hot, many people were falling sick, and crying out from thirst. But Gopaldas kept them going with promises of plentiful sweet water at Govindram's well. At last, late one night, the party arrived, more dead than alive. They turned to the well — but, to their horror, the entrance was fenced off and a guard watched over the water.

'The water costs two annas a glass. If you have no money, move along,' he said.

'What!' cried Gopaldas. 'But Govindram's well is always free to all.'

'Govindram is dead,' the guard said. 'Now the well belongs to his son, and water costs two annas a glass.'

Gopaldas was so outraged he demanded to see the new owner of the well. He was led to a beautiful house, where a richly dressed young man received him politely. When Gopaldas asked him about the well, he was charming, but firm.

'It is like this, sir,' he explained. 'My father spent 1000 rupees building this well in the desert. There has been no return whatsoever on this investment. Therefore, I have thought of a means to recover the money spent. It is simply a matter of practical business sense. I am sure you understand.'

Gopaldas almost choked but he knew it would be useless to argue. He thought for a while, and then he asked, 'Would you, then, young businessman, sell me the well for the price of 2000 rupees? That would more than cover your father's investment.'

The young man thought for a while. 'There is inflation to consider, too,' he said. But at last he agreed, the deal was settled, and Gopaldas handed over the money.

Then he went back to the well, got rid of the guard, tore down the fences, and allowed the travellers to drink freely.

'Let it be known, this water is for all who need it, once more without cost!' he cried.

Everyone cheered and thanked him, and called for blessings to be showered on his head. 'May you enjoy the best of life for ever!' they cried. 'May you have many daughters and twice as many sons!'

'Stop!' cried Gopaldas. Don't wish for many sons for me! Wish instead that I don't have any sons at all!'

Everyone was shocked. 'Why?' they asked. 'Every man wants sons! Are you mad?'

'No,' said Gopaldas, 'but supposing I have a son like Govindram's? A real modern businessman? When I am gone and he gets the well, you will be even worse off than before. For to recover my investment of 2000 rupees, he will have to charge four annas a glass!'

Indian story from the Puranas, retold by Helen East

Discussion *continued*

- Do the children have any experience of drought or water restrictions? What are the effects? How do people save water then?
- Why is it important that drinking water should be clean? What sort of diseases are carried by water and where do they come from? What prevents them?
- What other harmful things might be in water? Where does pollution come from? What should be done about it? Are there harmful things we ourselves pour down the sink, which may not be removed properly at the water treatment centre?
- Talk about the position of people in developing countries, who lack the basic human right of access to clean water. Encourage the children to exchange their own ideas about how the people themselves, the authorities in those countries, and we in the richer countries could all help.
- Help the children to see that it is not only lack of rain which causes the problems, but factors such as who owns the land and water sources, the expense of piped water, the knowledge of how to trap and conserve water, and the need to keep domestic water and sanitation separate.

Activities

♦ Children could devise their own methods for finding out about the use of water in their homes. For example, how much water is used each day for flushing the toilet? How much water is used if they clean their teeth with the tap left running?

– Do the results give any clues about how water can be saved? Some children could work out figures for the whole class/school/country.

– They could also collect literature about household appliances which use water. Do the brochures say anything about how much water is used? If not, they could write to the manufacturers to find out. Is there much difference between different makes?

♦ Some children could make up a drama or story about what would happen in a family if all the water had to be carried from a standpipe. How would it be carried? Who would do it? What differences would it make to their lives?

WATER AS A HABITAT

Purposes

1 To appreciate the enormous diversity of plants and animals which live in, on or near water.

2 To begin to find out how such species are affected by pollution.

3 To consider some of the causes of that pollution and how it can be remedied.

Starting-points

■ Describe a creature, which has water as a habitat, for the children to guess, using perhaps just three clues. Individual children could then do the same. Try to ensure a good variety – octopus, whale, snail, duck, shrimp, otter . . . You could show the 'describers' a picture to help them.

■ If you or the school has any water creatures in tanks or aquaria, make them available for the children to look at, or show some large pictures. How are these creatures different from land animals? How do they get oxygen? How do they move through the water? Which live underwater all the time?

■ To demonstrate the effects of oil pollution, fill a tall glass container, such as a spaghetti jar, with water. Pour in some engine oil and hold it up so the children can observe the result. You could also use a container with a greater surface area, and get some children to spray it with detergent. Try dipping bird feathers in it to see what happens.

■ If there is a local firm which uses water from a nearby lake, river or the sea, invite someone in to talk about how the water is used and what happens to it afterwards.

Fact box

Penguins in the Antarctic have been found with large accumulations of DDT in their bodies.

Millions of fish, more than 30,000 birds and nearly 1000 sea otters were killed when the tanker *Exxon Valdez* spilled oil off Alaska in 1989.

continued

In the beginning there was only darkness and emptiness, but the darkness and emptiness were not cold or lifeless. There was a warmth and a dampness and a soft breathing. Gradually the breathing became a whisper and the whisper grew and grew until it filled all the space. The first word was created, 'Om'.

The first word had power. It created a deep ocean, and in the depths of the ocean lay a seed. Long, long years passed and the seed floated to the surface and became a huge golden egg. Gently the waves rocked it and the light from within reached out to light up the world.

The years passed and everywhere was heard the sacred word 'Om'. It nourished the life within the shell and created Brahma, himself Creator of Worlds. One day the egg broke open with a loud crack. Brahma was born. From one half of the shell he created the sky; from the other he created the earth, and to keep them apart he created air.

Hindu creation story

Baby dragonfly

Jaw snapping creature looking for food.
Living among slime.
Waiting to turn into a creature with wings.
Brown creature looks like it's jumped into a jar of Marmite.
Eyes sticking out on end as though it's seen a ghost.
Feelers that move around like worms.
Jaws bounce out as he catches his prey.
Next year he's a beautiful dragonfly.

Kerry Sibbett (aged 9)

The fish leave the sea

The fish are growing feet
and walking on the land:
they're fed up getting wet
while we're all getting tanned.

They look a bit unsteady —
like babies when they walk.
No doubt in several days
you'll hear them start to talk.

And after that, I wonder,
what will their spokesmen wish?
Well, first of course, a ban
on people eating fish,

and then, amongst the next
of several major laws,
that cats must be on leads
or else stay locked indoors.

But after several weeks
of travelling in trains,
of watching television
and falling down the drains,

the very clever fish,
or so it seems to me,
will quietly stroll away
and slip back in the sea.

Charles Thomson

Fact box *continued*

The USA banned drink cans with detachable ring pulls because so many ducks starved to death after getting their bills caught in them.

The 50,000 ships sailing the oceans put at least 6 million tonnes of metal, glass and plastic in the sea *each day*.

Phosphates in the water encourage algae to grow. These then suffocate and poison water creatures. Phosphates come from some detergents, fertiliser on farmland and slurry from cows.

Over 3000 square kilometres of Britain's coastline habitats have been lost to roads, factories, housing and other developments.

In 1986 a fire in a factory in Switzerland spilled chemicals into the River Rhine, killing all life in a 320km stretch of the river.

Raw sewage from millions of people is pumped directly into Botany Bay in Australia.

Grey seals in the Baltic have declined from 100,000 in 1900 to about 2000, because chemicals in the water affect their capacity to breed.

Discussion

- Encourage the children to think more about how beautifully water creatures are adapted to their environment. An obvious example is streamlining in those creatures that need to move fast through the water. Point out that creatures as different as penguins, sharks, goldfish and seals have a similar shape under water.
- Talk about different kinds of water habitat. Do the same creatures live in the sea as in fresh water? Why don't whales live in rivers? What lives in marshland? What sort of birds live in or on the water? Could fish from the Great Barrier Reef survive in the Arctic? Help children realise that some creatures are very adaptable, while others occupy very particular niches.

Seal

Down the wet strand lumbering,
heaving, shoving the great
sloppy sack of his guts across
a grit of pebble, shingle . . .

now, shuffling faster, he meets
the salt sea's fraying edge as if
he's being dragged there
by herring-smell, mackerel-smell . . .

suddenly he's dissolved in waves
and two minutes later is
a tennis ball bobbing half-a-mile out.

Matt Simpson

Jetsam

Foaming wave . . . aftershave
Plastic comb, brittle bone
Bottle top, building block
Wooden spar, plastic car
Thermos top, can of pop
Salt-stained shoe, tin of glue
Tennis racket, empty packet
Car tyre, coil of wire
Pram wheel, rubber seal
Tar-blacked stone, fir cone
Rusty lid, twisted grid
Chipboard, orange cord
Empty and faded
Almost forgotten
On a winter beach.

Nigel Cox

Children watching the seagulls

Silver gulls with moon bright eyes
who ride the winds in cloud grey skies
screaming prehistoric screams,
diving where the ocean gleams,
fly heaven high and out of reach
of death black oil upon the beach.
When we grow up, we'll make quite sure
we keep the living ocean pure.

Marian Swinger

The pool in the rock

In this water, clear as air,
Lurks a lobster in its lair.
Rock-bound weed sways out and in,
Coral-red, and bottle-green.
Wondrous pale anemones
Stir like flowers in a breeze;
Fluted scallop, whelk in shell,
And the prowling mackerel.
Winged with snow the sea-mews ride
The brine keen wind; and far and wide
Sounds on the hollow thunder of the tide.

Walter de la Mare

The river's story

I remember when life was good.
I shilly-shallied across meadows,
Tumbled down mountains,
I laughed and gurgled through woods,
Stretched and yawned in a myriad of floods.
Insects, weightless as sunbeams,
Settled upon my skin to drink.
I wore lily-pads like medals.
Fish, lazy and battle-scarred,
Gossiped beneath them.
The damselflies were my ballerinas,
The pike my ambassadors.
Kingfishers, disguised as rainbows,
Were my secret agents.
It was a sweet time, a gone-time,
A time before factories grew,
Brick by greedy brick,
And left me cowering
In monstrous shadows.
Like drunken giants
They vomited their poisons into me.
Tonight a scattering of vagrant bluebells,
Dwarfed by those same poisons,
Toll my ending.

Children, come and find me if you wish,
I am your inheritance.
Behind the derelict housing-estates
You will discover my remnants.
Clogged with garbage and junk,
To an open sewer I've shrunk.
I, who have flowed through history,
Who have seen hamlets become villages,
Villages become towns, towns become cities,
Am reduced to a trickle of filth
Beneath the still, burning stars.

Brian Patten

Ducks' ditty

All along the backwater,
Through the rushes tall,
Ducks are a-dabbing,
Up tails all!

Ducks' tails, drakes' tails,
Yellow feet a-quiver,
Yellow bills all out of sight
Busy in the river!

Slushy green undergrowth
Where the roach swim —
Here we keep our larder,
Cool and full and dim.

Everyone for what he likes!
We like to be
Heads down, tails up,
Dabbling free!

High in the blue above
Swifts whirl and call —
We are down a dabbling
Up tails all.

Kenneth Grahame

● Objects thrown in the water cause great harm to wildlife. What examples can the children think of? What should be done?

● You can introduce other issues about pollution, using the fact box. Help the children see that there are not necessarily any easy answers. For example, we have all benefited greatly from increased food production, which has depended on the use of fertilisers. If sewage is to be treated more efficiently, the public will have to pay more for the sewage service. How should industry be helped to be more caring about pollution? Again, are we prepared to pay more for products?

● The overall moral question is, of course, that if pollution is an unavoidable result of human development, should the needs of wildlife take second place?

Activities

♦ If there is a stretch of water near you, children could make a survey to find out what litter or other pollutants are in it. How could these pollutants harm wildlife? How did they get there? How could people be stopped from dumping rubbish there? Is it serious enough to be reported to anyone? Could the children start a local campaign or organise a clear-up themselves, or even 'adopt' it on a permanent basis?

♦ Encourage children to make an inventory of all the things in their homes which end up going down the drain. They can look at the ingredients on the packaging and try to find out if any of them are likely to be harmful to wildlife. Could they be used more sparingly? Are there any alternative products their families could switch to?

♦ If children become interested in the issue of the human need or desire to develop waterside land versus the needs of wildlife, you could set up a role-play activity. Groups could represent the developers, whose scheme will bring work to the area; a bird protection group; local fishermen; the council; and so on. The drama could be presented at a later assembly with the audience acting as arbiters.

♦ A group could write a letter or speech from a delegation of water creatures to the human world, reporting the effects on them of pollution and suggesting what might be done.

WATER FOR PLANTS

Purposes

1 To understand that all plants need water to survive.

2 To gain an insight into the lives of people who live in drought areas.

3 To think about some of the problems of water management.

Starting-points

■ With the help of one class, prepare a display of plants which have been given varying amounts of water. Quick-sprouting plants like mung beans or cress will provide clear evidence that water is needed for both germination and growth; busy Lizzies respond quickly to over- or under-watering. Ask some children to examine the plants and describe exactly what they see – not just that the plants are dead or dying, but what signs tell them that.

■ Display a large world map and establish where the major deserts and areas of low rainfall are. What sort of lives are led by the people who live there?

Fact box

Areas which get less than 25cm of rain per year are officially recognised as deserts. Such areas cover at least one-fifth of the world's land surface and are spreading.

Sometimes when rain does fall, it is torrential and quickly runs away, especially on hard, sun-baked surfaces.

Some desert plants can survive on dew; others have very long roots to reach water supplies underground.

In India 93% of the water supply is used for irrigation – in Britain only 3%.

For years the rivers which fed the Aral Sea in the USSR were diverted to irrigate vast areas of crops. Gradually the Aral Sea has been turning into a dried-up chemically polluted, dust bowl.

Prayer for rain

O God, make it rain!
Loose the soft silver passion of the rain!
Send swiftly from above
This clear token of Thy love.
Make it rain!

Deck the bushes and the trees
With the tassels of the rain.
Make the brooks pound to the seas
And the earth shine young again.
God of passion, send the rain!

Oh, restore our ancient worth
With thy rain!
Ease the heartache of the earth;
Sap the grain.
Fill the valleys and the dales
With thy silver slanting gales;
And through England and wild Wales
Send the rain!

Lord, restore us to Thy will
With the rain!
Soak the valley, drench the hill,
Drown the stain;
Smite the mountain's withered hips,
Wash the rouge from sunset's lips,
Fill the sky with singing ships.
Send the rain!

Herbert Palmer

Summer drought

Do you remember rain?
Do you remember summer rain falling steadily from grey clouds, covering everything with a soft film of raindrops?
Do you remember wet grass and dripping leaves and roses, heavy, bent with rain?
Do you remember the smell of those first raindrops hitting the dry, dusty, parched ground? How everything turns green again with the rain and begins to grow afresh? How new it feels, after the rain?
Can you imagine no more rain?
The leaves are falling already. They lie crisp and brown on paths and pavements. Apples wither on the trees, tired of trying to grow fat and rosy. Flowers droop. The straw-coloured grass is burned and brittle. The glorious sun shines, and shines. The sky stays blue, always blue, except for sometimes a few wispy, white clouds.
A perfect summer.
Yes — but for the want of the rain. The beautiful, cool, thirst-quenching rain.

Ann Bonner

The greedy Heron

When drought came and the plants all died, the animals had to learn how to help each other by managing the water supplies stored in the Earth. The greedy heron thought that he had enough water for his needs, and so refused to help.

Once, before before, there were no wells on the Earth. Plants, birds, and beasts alike relied on the rain, and the pools and rivers it formed on the surface of the Earth as it fell.

But a time came when the rains failed. The sun grew hotter and hotter. The rivers and ponds shrank to slimy puddles. The grass scorched brown and dry, moss crumbled, flowers withered, fruits and grains shrivelled, and even the water weeds lay dry and lifeless. Still there was no rain. The earth turned to dry dust and blew away in the wind, and the ground baked hard and cracked. The birds and the beasts grew thin and thirsty and sick.

Only the Heron was happy. As his pond water dwindled, the fish, who had nowhere to go, grew easier and easier to catch. And the Heron still had just enough water to stand in – after all he could balance on one leg.

Then at last the Creator took pity on the Earth, and called all the creatures together. 'My children,' said the Creator. 'Great and small alike, you must all dig. Dig down into the Earth and you will find water.'

Weak and thirsty as they were, the creatures obeyed. They burrowed and bored, and scratched and scraped with tusks and hooves, and beaks and claws. The robin worked as hard as the elephant, the worm and the eagle worked side by side, and everywhere they dug, water began to bubble up out of the earth, until each had a well of water sufficient to his own need and the needs of all.

Only the Heron did nothing to help. At last the Creator noticed and asked gently, 'Heron, my child. Why do you stand idle? Why don't you help all the others?'

'Why should I?' said Heron. 'I have enough water for myself. What is the point in dirtying my beak for nothing?'

'Very well,' said the Creator, angrily. 'You may keep your rainwater. But that is all you will ever get. Well water you may not touch – now and forever.'

And so it is today. The Heron lives in marshy land where rainwater collects, and when there is a drought, and the surface waters all dry up, he cannot go to the wells to enjoy the water from the depths of the Earth. Then you can hear him, calling, calling, with his harsh croak. He is crying to the sky to send water to cool his parched tongue. And now you know why.

Rumanian folktale, retold by Helen East

It is He who sends down
Rain from the sky,
From it ye drink,
And out of it grows
The vegetation on which
Ye feed your cattle.

With it He produces
For you corn, olives,
Date-palms, grapes,
And every kind of fruit:
Verily this is a Sign
For those who give thought.

from the Qur'an

Discussion

● Establish with the children some of the reasons why plants need water, for example: it physically supports the stems and leaves; it contains nutrients or it dissolves them from the soil and distributes them to where they are needed; it is necessary for germination, and for photosynthesis.

● The children will probably know from the news media something about famine caused by drought. How does it affect people? How must it feel to leave home and walk for maybe hundreds of kilometres for food and water – to see your livestock dying, and eventually many of your people? How can we help?

● While arousing the children's sympathy, you also need to help them realise that such tragedies are due not only to lack of rain. A severe drought in Australia causes hardship and the death of many animals, but not starvation for the people. In countries like Ethiopia where millions may die, rich people still eat and the country still exports food.

● Hardly anywhere gets exactly the right amount of rainfall at the right time, so what ingenious ways have people found to conserve water and transport it to the plants? What harmful effects might result from badly planned schemes? What are the main differences between the way rich and poor communities conserve water? Which are the least environmentally harmful methods?

Activities

♦ Children can devise tests to see what happens when plants are given varying amounts of water. They could also weigh fruit and vegetables when fresh, and again after allowing them to dry out for a few days.

♦ Putting cut flowers in coloured water allows children to see how the water travels. Do all flowers react the same way? What happens if you don't put flowers in water at all? What happens to celery in coloured water or no water?

♦ A good atlas will provide information about rainfall. Which parts of the country/the world get most/least rainfall. When does most rain fall? Is it the same pattern in every country? There are some interesting figures in *The Guinness book of records.*

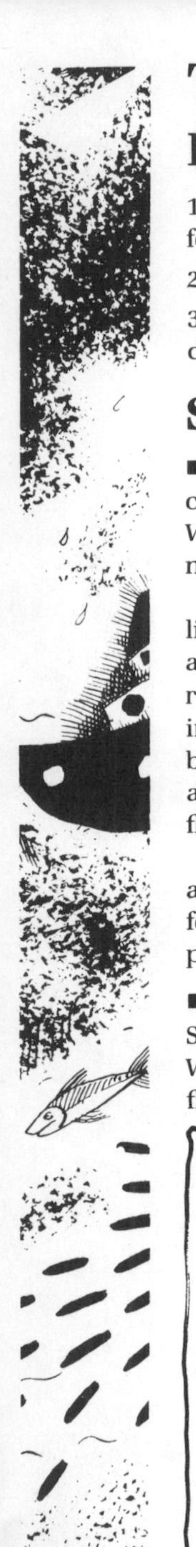

THE POWER OF WATER

Purposes

1 To appreciate that water can be a very powerful force.

2 To consider ways people harness that power.

3 To empathize with people caught up in the destructive force of water.

Starting-points

■ Start telling a simple story about a flood, with children acting out in mime what your words suggest. When you pause, they can role-play what they think might happen next. For example:

'It was a stormy night in March, and from their living room window, Mr and Mrs Jenkins were anxiously peering through the rain to the river which ran along the bottom of the garden. The children were in bed. Suddenly, the television programme they had been watching was interrupted by a special announcement giving a warning about approaching floods . . .'

As the drama proceeds, you can step in as narrator again, as you feel it appropriate, or ask the audience for suggestions about what should happen. A few props would probably help things along.

■ Read *Shiva and the Ganges* and talk about how Shiva's hair (the forests) broke the force of the water. What will happen if we cut down forests? How can floods be controlled?

Fact box

A French proposal to build flood defences in Bangladesh would cost $10,000 million; 20,000 hectares of land would be requisitioned and thousands of people displaced.

As a defence against flooding, many Bangladeshis live in houses on stilts. They have devised floating hen-coops, and mesh fences to stop fish from escaping.

The first textile mills which heralded the start of the Industrial Revolution were powered by water-mills. They were replaced by steam, another form of water power.

Shiva and the Ganges

India's particular dependence on water is reflected in its ancient religions. Temples were often dedicated to rivers and their sources, and the mighty River Ganges is renowned for the holy regard in which it is held by the people of India. But the powerful monsoon rains which swell the descent of the Ganges make it a frightening force as well — one which can tear away everything in its path and wash the precious topsoil out with it to the sea. The ancient story of Shiva and the Ganges tells how Shiva's hair breaks the force of the rains and the river: even in those days it was recognised that forests — Shiva's hair — were essential in controlling the power of water.

Long, long ago, the sons of King Sagara so angered Indra, King of the Gods, that with a mighty roar and a single terrible thunderbolt, he blasted them to ashes.

Sagara wept for his lost sons and gathered the ashes together to wash them. But his sons could go to heaven only if the ashes were cleansed in the sacred waters of the river-goddess, Ganga. Ganga at that time was living far off in the heavens and could not be found.

At last Sagara's grandson, Bhagirathu, went into the mountains to live as a hermit and pray to Brahma, the father of the gods. After a thousand years Brahma was so impressed by Bhagirathu's faith that he told him that he would send Ganga down to Earth so that the ashes could be cleansed. But he warned Bhagirathu that the waters of Ganga were so powerful and had so far to fall, that they would wash the Earth away.

Bhagirathu appealed to the god Shiva to help him and after even more prayer, Shiva agreed to stand between heaven and Earth to break the fall of the water.

Then Ganga cast herself down from heaven, thinking secretly to herself that she would wash Shiva away too. But it took her many years to find her way through Shiva's long thick hair that filled the skies. On the Earth below, all watched with wonder and delight. The falling waters sounded like thunder and the heavens were filled with flakes of white foam, fishes, porpoises and turtles glistening in the sunlight.

The locks of Shiva's hair divided Ganga into seven streams that came pouring down onto the Earth, running apart over the mountains and then joining into a great torrent. As the ashes of Sagara's sons were washed by her waters, they were cleansed of all their sins and their spirits rose to heaven. The people on Earth rushed to dip themselves in the sacred waters as Ganga flowed down to the sea.

Hindu story

When the Arno broke its banks

It rained and it rained and it rained. I am very, very tired. For the past two days I have been up to my knees in slime, mud and water, in the icy wind looking for the jewels that were in the shop that was.

You could not possibly imagine the havoc and destruction that has been wrought here. The city seems to be in ruins; it is only a miracle that more people were not killed, but it happened that Friday was a national holiday so everybody was at home. If the shops had been open, goodness only knows how many would have died.

The Arno broke its banks at about five on Friday morning and within a few hours practically the whole of the city was under water. Not only this, but half the streets had turned into raging torrents twelve feet deep. The street where we live was at least six feet

Next morning our street was free of water but about two feet deep in mud. We walked to the Lungarno and looked. I have never been so shocked in the whole of my life. The bridges were still standing, but with whole trees and steel girders wrapped round the supports. The river wall had been torn away and whole sections of the road had been ripped up and hurled into the shops, all of which were quite ruined. Cars were piled one on top of another as if the victims of some ghostly crash.

Vivien Flaxman

The moon and gravity

water water on the move
tides high and low
chuckling streams and river run
always on the go

thank the moon and gravity
for making water rumble
we can whizz the turbines round
with water's rush and tumble

powering cities round the world
with watts and amps and ohms
piping the moon and gravity
straight into our homes

Matt Simpson

A seashore breakfast

Early morning,
and the sea is breakfasting.
Chewing hungrily on the seashore
with its sharp teeth of white waves.
Biting deeply into crunchy rock pools
and lapping up a cereal of golden brown sand.
Occasionally it spits the bits
that are inedible
The pollution of human leftovers.
Until finally it licks its salty lips
and slides back down the shore,
shouting, 'I'll be back later, for more!'

Ian Souter

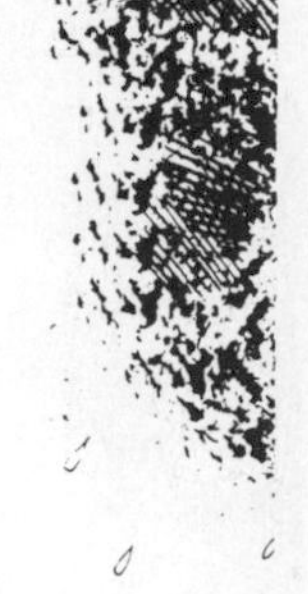

The Narmada Sagar dam in western India would provide much-needed hydro-electricity. Unfortunately, it would mean the displacement of 11,000 people.

A tidal barrage across the River Severn could produce as much power as four or five conventional power stations, but would cause enormous environmental damage.
(See also *Energy and waste*.)

Discussion

- Despite their ingenuity, humans do not completely control the natural world. How do people cope with disasters such as floods? How do they feel? What can outsiders do to help? Some children might have experiences to share of a minor flood, such as a burst water-pipe. Even this can have very disruptive effects.
- Talk about some of the human-related causes of floods, such as deforestation, perhaps with reference to *Shiva and the Ganges*.
- How have people harnessed the power of water for their own use? What effects do these methods have on the environment? What might be the human costs?
- Another area of discussion is the power of water at sea. Talk about the bravery of people who defy the elements for the sake of others.

Activities

- ♦ A flood makes a good subject for a painting. Children could concentrate on the plight of a small group of people, or paint a flooded landscape.
- ♦ A group could make up a drama about a shipwreck.
- ♦ Set children a problem of devising a means of using water power; for example, using a running tap to power a conveyor belt.
- ♦ Using reference books, personal experience and other source material, children could make a group book about ways of harnessing water power.

Ocean of mystery

A big blue giant cloaks the land;
He sprays the cliffs and hugs the sand,
With a mighty roar he crashes down,
And laughs from under his foamy crown.
Ocean of mystery,
Deep your secrets lie.
Ocean of mystery,
Where the seagulls fly.

Cold as castles, fathoms down,
Tossing tears, yet always proud,
Sometimes making us afraid
Yet calming us on windless days.
Ocean of mystery . . .

Swelling with his stormy power,
Waves as tall as any tower,
With a mighty roar he crashes down,
And laughs from under his foamy crown.
Ocean of mystery . . .

Words and music: Niki Davies

Chorus
GLOCKENSPIELS
Am Em7 Am Em7 Am Em7 Am Em7
O - cean of mys - te - ry, Deep your sec - rets lie.
Am Em7 Am Em7 Dm7 G7 C E7
O - cean of mys - te - ry, Where the sea - gulls fly.
Am Em7 Am Em7 Am Em7 Am
Coda

AIR

The Earth's atmosphere extends upwards about 2400km, but what we usually think of as 'air' is an inner layer of about 80km. The further away from Earth, the thinner the air is. The atmosphere is in a number of different layers, each with a different composition of gases.

Air is essential for life: animals, including humans, need the oxygen to help convert food to energy; we can live for weeks without food, days without water, but only a few minutes without air. Plants need carbon dioxide to photosynthesise, and plants and animals which live wholly in the water need the gases dissolved from the air.

Unfortunately, humankind is polluting the air to the extent that breathing it can actually be harmful. There are the terrible accidents which make the headlines, like Soveso, Bhopal and Flixborough, but people are being made ill, and even dying, all the time from the effects of day-to-day air pollution.

One of the biggest culprits is the motor vehicle, which produces lead, carbon monoxide, nitrogen oxide, sulphur dioxide and other gases which react to form ozone — all lethal. Power stations and many manufacturing processes are equally guilty. The good news is that pollution can be controlled, if we have the political will and are prepared in some cases to spend money on the problem.

On a global level, three kinds of air pollution pose a major threat. Ozone — deadly at ground level — is necessary to protect us from harmful ultraviolet rays, and the evidence suggests it is being destroyed by a variety of gases, mainly chlorofluorocarbons (CFCs). The problem is being tackled, again due in part to public pressure, but CFCs have by no means disappeared from the market, and are still being manufactured. Acid rain and global warming, two totally different problems, have a common cause — once again, the waste gases from motor vehicles, aeroplanes, fossil fuel power stations, heating systems and industry.

If we continue to destroy the air, we destroy life. We must help the next generation to care enough to find ways of cutting down the use of cars and of electricity, and to make safer the processes we do use.

Finally, a form of pollution connected with air which does not receive nearly so much publicity is noise. Intrusive noise — not necessarily loud — is an irritant which causes bad temper and frustration; loud noise is a real health hazard. Continued exposure to loud noise causes deafness, and there is evidence that it can also affect the digestive system, blood pressure and the nervous system. There are controls and safeguards in industry, and individuals can take up particular issues with various authorities, but there is not enough protection for the public against more general noise pollution, such as continual traffic noise. Music is often played at levels which would be banned in industry, and at schools near Heathrow airport, communication is impossible for fifteen seconds in every two minutes. We are in danger of producing a whole generation who are hard of hearing, unless we add this to the list of issues we want our children to care about.

AIR ALL AROUND US

Purposes

1 To understand that air is all around us.
2 To appreciate that we depend on air for life.
3 To celebrate the pleasure air can give us.
4 To consider the issue of air pollution.

Starting-points

■ Read the story of *Hanuman*, and talk about how important air is for all life.

■ Ask the children to put their hands lightly on their chests, fingertips just touching, and then to breathe really deeply. Talk about what is happening. Send a few children off to run round the playground. Time the breaths per minute of those left behind. Take a rough average. When the runners return, time their breathing and compare it with that of the non-runners.

■ Get some children to blow streams of bubbles – you could make it a surprise, by having the bubble-blowers hidden. Use it to introduce a discussion about the pleasure air can give us.

■ Light some indoor fireworks – the sort that make a lot of smoke. Ask if any children have been near a bonfire when the wind blows the smoke at them. How do their bodies react? Get them to talk about their reactions to tobacco smoking. Or hold a saucer above a burning candle, to demonstrate how much solid pollution there is just in candle smoke. Ask the children to brainstorm their ideas about air pollution.

Fact box

Air is about 20% oxygen and just under 80% nitrogen. About 1% is made up of helium, neon, krypton, argon and xenon, and a tiny proportion is carbon dioxide. There are varying amounts of water vapour and, increasingly, there are manufactured gases.

– Water creatures, other than those which come up for air, get their oxygen from the water.

continued

Hanuman

The Lord of the Winds left the Earth, taking the air with him, when his son Hanuman was killed. Soon the Earth began to die, and Indra, King of the Gods, set out to find him and bring him back.

Long, long ago in India lived the Lord of all the Winds. He had a son, whose name was Hanuman. If you or I looked at Hanuman, we might think he was just a little monkey, because that is what he looked like. But he was really a prince, a god, the Son of the Wind.

Hanuman grew up in the forest. He played with the deer and the elephants on the ground, and he played with the monkeys and the squirrels in the treetops. Because he was the Son of the Wind he even learnt to fly, so that he could play with the birds and the butterflies in the air.

But one morning he sat at the top of a tall tree and he saw someone he had never played with before. It was the sun, shining like a golden ball as it rose over the trees and sailed through the sky.

'It's lovely! I want it! I want to play with it!' cried Hanuman, and stretched out his arms. He jumped from his tree, and flew towards the sun, shouting, 'Play with me! Play with me!'

But the sun did not hear what he was saying, and was frightened. The sun ran away from Hanuman, and ran all over the sky, calling, 'Save me! Save me!'

The great god Indra of a Thousand Eyes was passing by and he saw the sun running all over the sky.

'Who has frightened the sun?' he roared. He threw his spear at Hanuman, and Hanuman fell down, down, down to the Earth below. The birds and the butterflies, the monkeys and the squirrels, the deer and the elephant all cried as they saw him fall.

But saddest of all was his father, the Lord of the Winds. He rushed down to the place where Hanuman had fallen. And as he passed, the waters were lashed into great waves, the trees bent and broke, and the animals hid in their caves. The Lord of the Winds gathered up his son in his arms and flew far, far away to the ends of the Earth. And wherever he flew, you could see where the terrible wind had passed.

When the wind had gone, peace came back to the Earth. The waters became smooth again and the trees stood upright.

But something was wrong. With no wind, nothing could breathe. There was no air on the Earth. The trees died, the birds and butterflies died. The squirrels and monkeys died, the deer and the elephants died. All was quiet. Nothing moved.

Once again Indra of a Thousand Eyes, King of the Gods, passed by. He knew that he had made a terrible mistake. What could he do?

He travelled to the east and the west, the north and the south, looking for the Lord of the Winds until at last he found him, sitting in a dark, dark cave underneath the earth, crying over the body of his son.

'Forgive me!' cried Indra, 'and do not be sad. Hanuman is not dead. Return to the world and his life will return.'

The Lord of the Winds took his son's body in his arms and flew upwards to the Earth. Gentle breezes followed him. Gradually the trees and flowers, the animals, the birds, the insects came to life again. Men, women, boys and girls yawned and stretched and looked around with delight. Hanuman too returned to life, and began to play with his friends again as his father breathed gentle breezes over him.

Hindu story, retold by Elizabeth Breuilly and Sandra Palmer

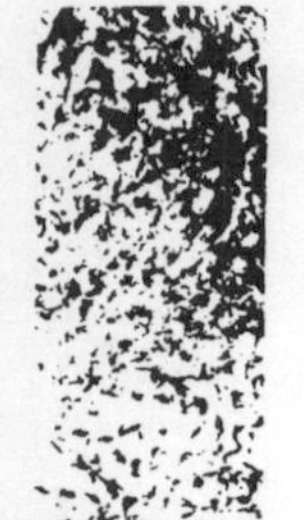

Fact box *continued*

– Animals, including humans, need oxygen to help break down the sugars and fats stored in the body to give energy. Carbon dioxide is a waste product.

– Plants need carbon dioxide, water and light to photosynthesise. Oxygen is a waste product.

Inhaling smoke from other people's cigarettes may cause serious illness.

Sunlight reacts with vehicle exhausts, and other pollutants, to form photochemical smog.

Lead in petrol fumes can cause kidney disease and brain damage, particularly in young children.

In Cubatao, Brazil, industry is uncontrolled. The fumes are so bad that hardly anything grows, and there is terrible illness and deformity amongst the people living there. The area is called the Valley of Death.

In 1984 an American-owned factory in Bhopal in India accidentally released toxic fumes and killed over 2500 people (some estimates are much higher) and injured 200,000. Safety standards were lower than permitted in the USA.

Plants which are covered with dust and other pollutants are prevented from photosynthesising and transpiring properly.

Discussion

● Ask if the children know of places where there is no air. Why did the astronauts who landed on the moon have to wear space suits? Why do climbers of high mountains have to wear oxygen masks? What do people mean if they are in a small, crowded room and say 'there is no air'? How can you feel air? Why does a balloon eventually burst if you keep blowing it up? How can you put fires out, and why do the various methods work?

● Why do our bodies need oxygen and how do we get it? Why do we get short of breath when we exercise? Perhaps some children have experience of asthma and how it affects people.

Every morning

Every morning
I awake
full of dust
and odours

As if
no one has
lived in me
for years

And
every morning
I throw open
all my windows
and doors

Clean
and fumigate
myself

As if
I were just
moving in

George Swede

Facts about air

Scientists say
That air consists
Of about 78% nitrogen and 21% oxygen,
Plus some carbon dioxide
And small amounts
Of the rare gases — helium, argon and neon.

These are facts, I know.
But I also know
That when I go outside
On a spring morning
The air tastes as crisp
As a fresh lettuce
And that when I sit
On the patio
On a summer evening
The cool night air
Brushes my cheeks like a feather.

John Foster

Wings

If I had wings
  I would touch the fingertips of clouds
    and glide on the wind's breath.

If I had wings
  I would taste a chunk of the sun
    as hot as peppered curry.

If I had wings
  I would listen to the clouds of sheep bleat
    that graze on the blue.

If I had wings
  I would breathe deep and sniff
    the scent of raindrops.

If I had wings
  I would gaze at the people
    who cling to the earth's crust.

If I had wings
  I would dream of
    swimming the deserts
      and walking the seas.

Pie Corbett

The air is precious
to the red man, for all things share the same breath — the beast, the tree, the man, they all share the same breath.

Chief Seathl

An experiment

For this you will need a goldfish bowl,
a ball big enough almost to fill it but also
squashy enough to fit easily inside,
some water,
and, unfortunately,
one small fish.
Now take these to the largest, emptiest room
you can find,
and placing the bowl at its centre, put in the
ball.
Then add the water, carefully, to cover.
Darken the room, turn out all lights but one.
Now
slip the small fish into the bowl, so it can swim
between the ball and glass, round and round
the narrow water.
Does the fish hope
that the whole room could be flooded? Does it
wish
that there was another bowl, another fish, in
sight?
Round and round, round and round,
in the dark room, under the one strong light,
in the only water there is,
which it hopes is clean,
because it must have water
and this water, trapped between
the rough surface of the ball
and the edge of vast waterless space,
is where it has to live,
whatever its dreams may be.

Now you can try this experiment. You sit
down
and watch the fish.
And watch the fish. And imagine
what the water means to the fish. You imagine
the water drying up or spilling out. Imagine
the water filthy or poisonous. You sit
and watch, and when you feel the time is
right,
when you feel you understand
this moving round and round
with a small world
in the one
and only
possible
place
you bow to the small fish
and go outside
and look at the sky
and breathe in deeply. Now
how does the air taste?

Dave Calder

Air

It's what it does that shows it's there.
It probes our clothes and scuffs our hair.

It tumbles pollen in the breeze
And shuffles clumps of leaves on trees.

It pushes mountain clouds away
And smacks the wave tops into spray.

It fills our lungs and feeds our blood.
It pops up in a soapy sud.

It panics litter down the street.
It fans a sea from fields of wheat.

So when it seems that nothing's there,
Remember there is always air . . .

Charles Thomson

- What do we mean by 'fresh air'? We breathe all the time – when are we most conscious of what we breathe? What smells do the children like? How else does air give us pleasure?
- What do the children know about air pollution? What should be done about factories which discharge pollutants? How can people be encouraged to use unleaded petrol? Tell the children how effective public pressure was in getting unleaded petrol introduced.
- You could use this opportunity to initiate a discussion about tobacco smoking.

Activities

- Children could devise their own tests to show the presence of air and/or its power to move things.
- A display could be mounted to illustrate some of the ways in which we use air, as in tyres, airbeds and inflatables; hair dryers, fan ovens and tumble dryers; windmills and washing lines . . .
- There are many possible investigations into breathing. For example, how long does it take for breathing to return to normal after exercise? Does the rate of breathing relate to size? How fast do pets breathe? How long can children hold their breath? Can they improve with practice? How can they measure lung capacity? Why do fire-fighters need a chest expansion of 5cm?
- Suppose the children were staying on the moon for a while, safely enclosed in their space suits, but living out in the open. Ask them to write about what the lack of air around them would mean to them. What would they miss? What wouldn't they be able to do?
- A local survey could be conducted into unleaded petrol. How many people use it? How available is it? How much cheaper is it? Why was lead put in petrol?
- If you are in an industrial area, children could monitor local factory chimneys. How often do they smoke? What colour is the smoke? Is there any smell? You could perhaps contact local firms to try to arrange for children to do some more detailed investigations.
- Children could research into the harmful effects of smoking, and design posters or leaflets to discourage it.

AIR AND WEATHER

Purposes

1 To begin to understand the part that air plays in weather patterns.

2 To explore how our feelings are affected by different kinds of weather.

3 To learn a little about the causes and effects of acid rain, the greenhouse effect and the depletion of the ozone layer, and consider ways of combating them.

Starting-points

■ Tape-record a weather forecast or gale warning from the radio and play some of it, or video a weather forecast or enlarge a newspaper weather map. Use this to introduce a discussion about the part air plays in producing different kinds of weather.

■ Individual children can choose some of the weather poems to read aloud. Ask the audience which ones they like best, and why. How do the poems make the children feel?

■ Screw up some newspaper, put it in a metal tray and set light to it. Why does the smoke rise? To introduce the idea of light gases rising, show a helium-filled balloon and an ordinary one. Why does the helium balloon float and the other one not?

■ Boil a kettle of water and ask the children to talk about what they see. Establish that the steam they see is water vapour condensing into tiny droplets. Relate this to their breath on cold days. You could hold a tin tray above the steam so they can see the condensed water.

Fact box

Sulphur dioxide and nitrogen oxides in the air react with water to form acid rain, snow, fog and hail. These gases come from fossil fuel power stations, from industry, from heating systems and from vehicle exhausts.

– Fifity-six per cent of the acid rain which falls in Canada originates in the USA.

Storm

Bursting on the suburbs with relentless gusts of energy
And concentrated fury comes the mad March gale,
Blowing off the roofing felt which lies across the garden sheds
And patterning the window with a splash of sleet and hail.

Distending all the trousers on the wildly waving washing-line,
Drumming on the window like a hanged man's heels,
Swaying all the sculpture of the television aerials,
Muddying the roadway underneath the turning wheels.

Ear lobes reddening at the slashing of the hailstones,
Nose tips deadening at the coldness of the sleet,
Eyelids wincing at the brightness of the lightning,
Wet stones glistening beneath the hurried feet.

White marbles bouncing on the flat roofs of the garages,
Black sky paling as the storm dies down.
Wet folk emerging from the haven of a doorway
As the sun comes out again and smiles upon the town.

Nick Bartlett

Owl and Hurricane

Owl knew that his friend the wind was there by the way the grass bent as he passed, but he could not see him. One night his curiosity got the better of him.

A long time ago, Owl, and his best friend Hurricane, the wind, lived in the Australian desert. The part of the desert where they lived was dry and flat, with only a few gum trees and bushes clustered around the places where there was any water. Owl and Hurricane used to hunt together. They were good hunters: Owl used to fly on ahead, and hide behind a rock, or a clump of spiky spinifex grass, whilst Hurricane would blow as hard as he could, driving maybe a kangaroo, or a goanna, or a flock of wild duck, towards where Owl was hiding. Then Owl would jump out and kill the animal with his spear, after which the two friends would make a fire, roast the meat, and then lie in their sleeping blankets under the stars, and tell stories until they fell asleep.

But Owl was continually troubled by one thing. Because Hurricane was a wind, he was invisible. Owl always knew where he was because Hurricane used to carry his spear on his shoulder, and Owl could see it travelling alongside him as they searched for food. And he could see how the trees and the bushes bent back as they passed by, but it still troubled him.

'How do I know if you really exist?' Owl asked.

'Of course I'm here,' said Hurricane. 'Don't I always run alongside you when we're hunting, carrying my spear on my shoulder?'

'I can see your spear, and hear your voice,' replied Owl, 'but I wish I could see you as well. It's strange to have an invisible friend.'

'But we're better hunters: none of the animals can see me sneaking up behind them!' laughed Hurricane.

Owl couldn't be satisfied. He desperately wished that he could see his friend, but however hard he stared in the direction of Hurricane's whistly voice, he saw nothing, except perhaps the grass bending back, or the grey-green leaves of a white ghost gum gently stirring.

One night, after a particularly successful hunt, the two friends lay down as usual under the stars by the glowing embers of their fire. Hurricane quickly fell asleep: Owl could hear him snoring! But Owl lay awake, thinking. Perhaps Hurricane had a special spell to make himself invisible. Maybe the magic wore off in the night when he was asleep! There was definitely the shape of a figure wrapped snugly in the blanket next to him on the other side of the fire. Owl decided that he would sneak up to Hurricane and take a peep at him whilst he was asleep.

Quietly, Owl slipped out of his blanket and tiptoed around to the other side of the fire. He carefully drew back the edge of Hurricane's blanket, and opened his eyes as wide as he could. He could see only darkness, so he strained to open his eyes even further, trying to catch a glimpse of his friend. But just at that moment he stepped on a twig.

Crack! Hurricane awoke. All he could see was a pair of horrifying, huge, white-rimmed eyes staring at him out of the darkness. He thought he was being attacked by a ghostly creature unlike anything he had seen before! He let out a wailing shriek, flew out of his blanket, and raced off across the desert. As he did so, he blew up a wind that got fiercer and fiercer, becoming first a gale, then a whirling storm, then a howling wind stronger and more terrifying than any previous desert storm. Trees were uprooted, bushes bowled over, stones and rocks hurled away to either side. All of the animals — the lizards, the kangaroos, the emus, and even the frogs sleeping on the edge of the watersoaks — awoke and scurried for shelter. The birds — sulphur-crested cockatoos, grey-pink galahs, paintbox-coloured budgerigars — desperately tried to hide from the dreadful wind, but many were blown out of the trees and had to find their bedraggled way home once it had passed. And for hours after he had travelled on, Hurricane's howls and wails of fear still echoed along the creeks and swirled among the desert's few trees.

And that is why the hurricane, when it comes, brings with it a trail of destruction; if you listen carefully, you can still hear his moans as he remembers the frightening sight of those *huge* staring eyes. It's also why the owl has got wide white-rimmed eyes, as if they are forever trying to make out the form of the invisible wind.

Aboriginal story retold by Alan Howe

Fog in November

Fog in November, trees have no heads,
Streams only sound, walls suddenly stop
Halfway up hills, the ghost of a man spreads
Dung on dead fields for next year's crop.
I cannot see my hand before my face,
My body does not seem to be my own,
The world becomes a far-off, foreign place,
People are strangers, houses silent, unknown.

Leonard Clark

– In Sweden over 18,000 lakes are now so acid that they support very little life. What fish there are can be poisonous for birds – and humans – who eat them.

– Acid rain damages buildings by dissolving the stone. The Parthenon in Athens has suffered more damage in the last 30 years than in the previous 2000.

– Over half of Germany's forests are dead or dying. Most scientists say this is because of acid rain.

Holes are appearing in the 'ozone layer', a thin mixture of gases about 30km above the Earth which absorbs ultraviolet light. Too much ultraviolet light could lead to an increase in skin cancer. It may also destroy plankton, which produces large quantities of oxygen and absorbs carbon dioxide, and is the main food for many fish and whales.

– Chlorofluorocarbons (CFCs) are one of the main causes of ozone depletion. They are used in some aerosols and as a refrigerant, and in the manufacture of fast food packaging and foam padding.

Scientists generally agree that the atmosphere is warming up, but disagree about why, and how long it will go on. Many believe it is because we produce too much carbon dioxide and other gases. In the upper atmosphere these gases act like the glass of a greenhouse – they let some of the sun's heat through and then stop it from escaping back.

– Carbon dioxide comes from the burning of many things. Fossil fuel power stations and vehicles are the worst culprits. Burning the rainforests is doubly harmful because it not only produces carbon dioxide, but also destroys trees which would otherwise absorb enormous amounts of the gas.

If the polar ice-caps melt, low-lying areas like London and large parts of the Netherlands and Bangladesh would be flooded, unless expensive defences are built.

continued

Discussion

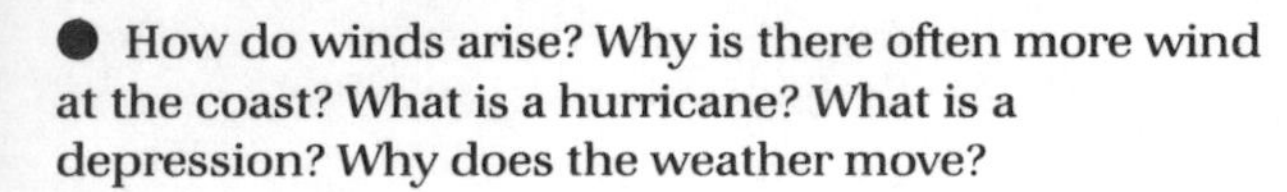

- How do winds arise? Why is there often more wind at the coast? What is a hurricane? What is a depression? Why does the weather move?
- What is fog? How do clouds form, and why does it rain? What are snow and hail?
- How are we affected by the weather? What is it like to be out in mist or fog? Have the children got any good stories? In what ways can fog be dangerous? Can they think of some good words to describe fog?
- How does it feel to be out in a strong wind? Why do children get excitable when it is windy? Do the children know of occasions when the wind caused damage? What happens to the sea when it is windy? Could we make better use of wind power? How far do the winds blow? What implications should that have for countries which produce pollution?
- Do the children like hot weather? How does it affect their behaviour? What are the main differences in people's lifestyles in summer and winter, or in hot countries and temperate ones? What strategies do people use to help them cope with very hot weather?
- If the children are to do any work on acid rain, they need to know a little about how it forms, and what it does (see the fact box). They need to understand the basic principles of the water cycle – water evaporates, rises, condenses in colder air high up, and falls again as rain. They also need to realise that pollutants in the air rise, either because they are warm or because the gases are lighter than air.
- Move on to discuss their ideas about how we can reduce acid rain, both on a personal and global level. Are we willing to pay more for products if that helps to prevent pollution? How could we cut down our use of electricity? And cars? (See *Energy and waste* section). Who should pay for the damage already caused?
- If you discuss the thinning of the ozone layer, let the children know how effective public pressure was in reducing the use of CFCs in aerosols. Manufacturers are trying to find harmless replacements, but meanwhile what can individuals do to help? What could be done about the fast food containers? What about people in the developing countries who would also like refrigerators and aerosols?

The stream and the desert

The stream learns how to cross the hot desert in the arms of the wind and fall again as rain on the other side.

High on a mountain was a spring. It bubbled out of the earth, flowed into a little stream, and ran away downhill. On it went, weaving its way through every kind of countryside — past trees and bushes, over plants and rocks and stones. As it flowed on, it grew larger and larger and stronger and stronger, and it seemed that nothing could stop it — until it reached the desert. And there the stream ran into the sand, trying to cross the desert. But of course the sands soaked up the water and the stream ran dry. Yet still it tried to go on and cross the desert.

Then a voice spoke from the sand. 'The wind crosses the desert; so can the stream.'

'But the wind has wings,' said the stream. 'I have none. I cannot fly.'

And still the water tried to flow into the sand and still it got dry. Again the voice from the sand spoke. 'You cannot cross the desert as you are.'

'So then how can I cross the desert?' said the stream.

The voice replied, 'You must let the wind take you across.'

'But if I let the wind take me across, I won't be a stream anymore and then I won't be who I am.'

'If you continue as you are,' said the voice, 'you'll no longer be a stream anyway. You must let the wind take you across.'

And so the stream gave itself up into the arms of the wind, and the wind carried the water vapour from the stream across the desert until it came to its destination on the other side. And there it fell gently as rain which gathered together in rivulets and made a stream again. And the stream flowed on downhill until it became a great river.

And the voice from the sands said, 'We see this every day because we stretch from the mountain to the river and back again. And so they say that the stream of life's journey is written in the sand.'

Raymond Chatlani

Graveyard scene

There are no names on the gravestones now,
They've been washed away by the rain.
The graveyard trees are skeletons now,
They will never wear leaves again.

Instead of a forest, the tower surveys
A bleak and desolate plain.
Those are not tears in the gargoyle's eyes,
They are droplets of acid rain.

John Foster

Workings of the Wind

Wind doesn't always topple trees
and shake houses to pieces.

Wind plays
all over woods, with weighty ghosts
in swings in thousands,
swinging from every branch.

Wind doesn't always rattle windows
and push, push at walls.

Wind whistles
down cul-de-sacs and worries
dry leaves and old newspapers to leap
and curl like kite tails.

Wind doesn't always dry out
sweaty shirts and blouses.

Wind scatters
pollen dust of flowers, washes
people's and animals' faces
and combs out birds' feathers.

Wind doesn't always whip up waves
into white horses.

Wind shakes up
tree-shadows to dance on rivers,
to jig about on grass, and hanging
lantern light to play signalman.

Wind doesn't always run wild
kicking tinny dustbin lids.

Wind makes
leafy limbs bow to red roses
and bob up and down outside windows
and makes desk papers fly up indoors.

James Berry

What's the weather on about?

What's the weather on about?
Why is the rain so down on us?
Why does the sun glare at us so?

Why does the hail dance so prettily?
Why is the snow such an overall?
Why is the wind such a tearaway?

Why is the mud so fond of our feet?
Why is the ice so keen to upset us?
Who does the weather think it is?

Gavin Ewart

Calendar of cloud

A springtime cloud is
    sudden grief
    a sneak-thief
squeezing the morning dry.

A summer cloud is
    a wishbone
    a fishbone
filleted clean from sky.

An autumn cloud is
    a broomstick
    a doomstick
chasing cobwebs into night.

A winter cloud is
    a bucketful
    a ducking-stool
dowsing everything in sight.

Moira Andrew

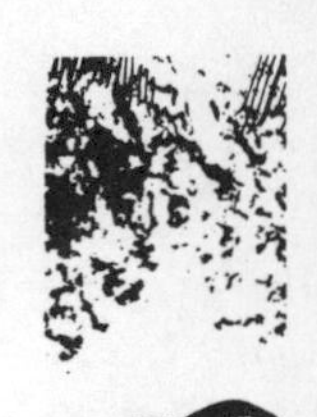

● What might be the effects of global warming? Would anyone gain? Who would be most likely to suffer? Are we prepared to cut down our use of cars and electricity? It costs a lot of money to clean up power stations – would people pay more for electricity? What alternative sources of power are there? (See also the section *Energy and waste*.)

Activities

♦ Children can write their own poems about weather, which could be mounted on a large background picture of a foggy day, or a collage of a high wind.

♦ To celebrate the air, have a kite festival, with home-made or bought kites. This would reflect a Chinese tradition of making large and colourful kites, which they take on a particular day to the top of the highest hill. There they all fly the kites together in celebration of the wind and the pure, clean air.

♦ How many ways can the children think of for saving electricity, so cutting the emissions of acid rain gases, and decreasing global warming? They could make a list of resolutions for themselves and their families at home; they could survey the use of electricity in school and put up posters to persuade people to cut down; and some children might go on to think about energy saving in the wider world. (See also *Energy and waste*, which has ideas about alternative sources of energy.)

♦ Car exhausts also contribute to acid rain, so children could work out ways of cutting down on the use of them. It could be a personal list, or they could devise a whole transport policy for their area. (See also *Energy and waste*.)

♦ Children can investigate air as a source of power. They might design and make a working model of a wind-powered machine, using scrap materials or a construction set.

♦ From books, magazines and the news media children can find out a lot more about global warming, acid rain and the ozone layer. They could design campaign posters addressed to individuals, and they could also write to relevant companies and authorities, and perhaps to local papers and radio stations.

SOUND

Purposes

1 To celebrate the pleasure sound can give us.

2 To think about noise as a form of pollution, and consider ways of improving matters.

Starting-points

- Display different kinds of musical instruments, and arrange a 'recital' with a few bars played on each – perhaps one class could compose a suitable piece. Or invite a musician – child, teacher or guest – to play an instrument for the children. Ask about favourite instruments, and why the children like them.
- Read *Pleasant sounds* to introduce a discussion about sounds that give us pleasure.
- Set up a conflict scene about noise for a group of children to act out; for example, people playing music very loudly with the window open, while the neighbours are trying to enjoy the peace of their gardens. Involve the children watching in working out a resolution.

Fact box

Sound is measured in decibels; roughly, an increase of ten decibels means a doubling of loudness:

A whisper is about 30 decibels.
A fairly noisy classroom is about 70 decibels.
A busy road is about 90 decibels.
A pneumatic drill is about 110 decibels.
A disco – 1m in front of loudspeaker – can be about 120 decibels.

Loud noise can interfere with our vision, blood pressure, digestion and concentration. Prolonged exposure to sound levels over 90 decibels can permanently damage our hearing.

Noise is one of the main causes of argument, and even violence, between neighbours.

Be quiet, down there!

The ancient Babylonian gods were so tired of the ceaseless noise the people on Earth were making that they sent famine and flood to silence them — with little success.

In ancient times, when the world was young, there was a lot of work to be done on Earth. So Entil and Enki created mankind to do the work, so the gods could sleep.

That was fine for a while, but mankind multiplied. There were more and more people — working, and talking and laughing and crying. Soon there was so much noise coming from Earth that the gods were disturbed in their sleep. And they couldn't get back to sleep either. So they ordered Entil to make mankind quieter. And Entil sent down a drought and a famine to reduce mankind's numbers and so their noise as well. The drought dried the Earth and turned soil to dust and rivers to slime. Crops withered, and famine came. Mankind grew thin. Old and young died. Now there were few people. But the hunger and the sorrow made people cry out from their hearts. And the sound of their tears and sufferings was so loud that once again the gods were disturbed in their sleep.

'Entil,' they stormed, 'silence mankind at once.' So Entil prepared a great flood, that would still mankind for ever . . . But Enki, his brother, could not bear his creation to be completely destroyed. He wanted to warn man, but of course he could not give away his fellow gods' secrets and tell mankind directly. Instead Enki came down to Earth one night and wandered through Shurruppak, the capital city of Arkah. He came to King Atrahasis' house, a beautiful mansion built of strong reeds. No one was about.

'Build a ship,' he whispered softly to the reeds. And then he left.

The reeds picked up the whisper and echoed it gently up and down their long shafts. The King, lying on his couch, heard them murmuring their message — a haunting tune.

'Build a ship, build a ship, build a ship.' The words and the tune ran round his head all night and a picture came into his head of a ship of ships — a ship of reeds. In the morning he gathered his carpenters and boatbuilders, his shepherds and his hunters.

'Build a ship,' he said. 'Build it now — build it like this.'

And it was done.

'Gather animals, wild and domestic, a pair of each kind.'

And it was done.

'Furnish the ship with comforts and foods of all kinds.'

And it was done.

Then King Atrahasis and all his family, and all the animals, wild and domestic, went onto the ship of reeds. And that is how they escaped the Great Flood, and that is why mankind, and animals too, survive to this day. And the reeds still whisper that tune, 'Build a ship, build a ship, build a ship.'

As for Enki, Entil and the other gods — how much sleep do you think they are getting these days?

Ancient Babylonian myth, retold by Helen East

Pleasant sounds

The rustling of leaves under the feet in woods and under hedges;
The crumping of cat-ice and snow down wood-rides, narrow lanes, and every street causeway;
Rustling through a wood or rather rushing, while the wind halloos in the oak-top like thunder;
The rustle of birds' wings startled from their nests or flying unseen into the bushes;
The whizzing of larger birds overhead in a wood, such as crows, puddocks, buzzards;
The trample of robins and woodlarks on the brown leaves, and the patter of squirrels on the green moss;
The fall of an acorn on the ground, the pattering of nuts on the hazel branches as they fall from ripeness;
The flirt of the groundlark's wing from the stubbles — how sweet such pictures on dewy mornings, when the dew flashes from its brown feathers!

John Clare

Noise

I like noise.
The whoop of a boy, the thud of a hoof,
The rattle of rain on a galvanised roof,
The hubbub of traffic, the roar of a train,
The throb of machinery numbing the brain,
The switching of wires in an overhead tram,
The rush of the wind, a door on the slam,
The boom of the thunder, the crash of the waves,
The din of a river that races and raves,
The crack of a rifle, the clank of a pail,
The strident tattoo of a swift-slapping sail –
From any old sound that the silence destroys
Arises a gamut of soul-stirring joys.
I like noise.

Jessie Pope

Discussion

- What makes some sounds pleasant to hear? Why do people find the sound of a stream or the sea soothing? Are there sounds which make us feel excited? Or sad? What sounds give the children pleasure?
- What do people get from listening to music? Do different kinds of music have different effects? Why is music sometimes played so loudly?
- How is sound useful to us, apart from speech?
- What is noise pollution? What noises do the children dislike? Are there sounds which are in themselves unpleasant, or is it only the context or the loudness we object to? When might even quiet sounds be annoying? Teachers probably tell children off for being noisy more than for almost any other reason – why should that be? How are people's lives affected by living near an airport? What sort of jobs require the wearing of ear defenders? Why?
- What can we do about noisy neighbours? What about noise from a factory? How can traffic noise be cut down? Is your area bothered by aeroplanes, helicopters, hovercraft . . .? What should be done? Should we have stricter laws about noise pollution, or are there other ways of controlling it? How can we be considerate to other people in our own lives regarding noise?

Activities

- Children could make tape recordings of sounds they like, perhaps putting together a piece of music with a mixture of natural and musical sounds.
- Encourage children to write their own poems with the title 'I like noise' or 'I hate noise'.
- If there is a serious noise nuisance in your area, help the children to take appropriate action. Information can be obtained from the local authority environmental health office about local by-laws, and from the Noise Abatement Society or the National Society for Clean Air for more general information and advice (see page 100).

Air is the world that we all of us share

Come where the trees grow tall
and the air is clear,
And the smell of new spring grass
is everywhere,
Feel how the wind blows the dust
from the old dead year,
And breathe in deep the life-embracing air:

Air is the water in which we swim,
Air is the life that we light
with our very first breath.
Dancing on air, floating on air,
Air is the world that we all –
we all of us share.

But what is this land where the lakes
are dying,
Overhead a poison cloud?
Why are those breathing forests burning,
Turning the air to a blackened shroud?
And why do those voices cry out
their warning,
Beware, take care?
Air is the water in which we swim . . .

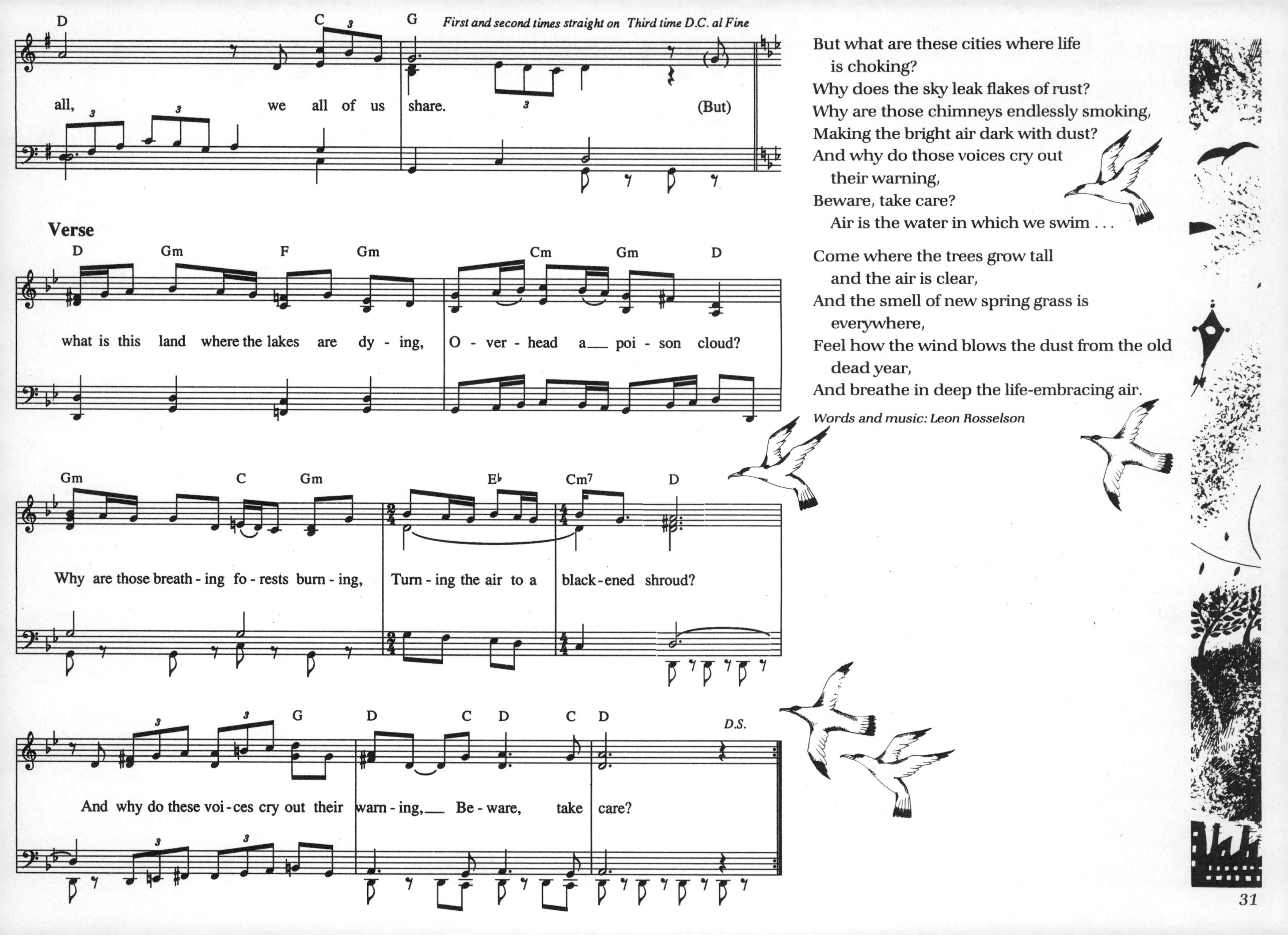

But what are these cities where life
is choking?
Why does the sky leak flakes of rust?
Why are those chimneys endlessly smoking,
Making the bright air dark with dust?
And why do those voices cry out
their warning,
Beware, take care?
Air is the water in which we swim . . .

Come where the trees grow tall
and the air is clear,
And the smell of new spring grass is
everywhere,
Feel how the wind blows the dust from the old
dead year,
And breathe in deep the life-embracing air.

Words and music: Leon Rosselson

LIVING THINGS

As far as we know, the Earth is the only planet in the solar system, and maybe in the universe, where conditions are exactly right for life to occur. It is miracle enough that life exists at all, but there are *millions* of different species, from the minute bacteria to the huge blue whale. They have found ways to live in a wide variety of habitats, from the incredibly lush rain forests of the tropics to seemingly hostile environments like the very depths of the sea, the freezing wastes of the Antarctic or the searing heat of the Sahara. But they are all – plant, animal and microscopic organism – bound together in one great ecosystem.

Human beings are just one of these species, but we have a disproportionate effect on the others, both plant and animal. We cut, burn and flood plantlife, destroy it with herbicides and manipulate its genes. With the destruction of the mighty rain forests we are exterminating hundreds of entire species.

Our record with animals is perhaps even worse. We domesticate and restrain them for our own purposes – to serve us as pets, as a means of transport, as a source of power for our machines, to provide clothing material and for food. We also use them as a form of entertainment: as exhibits in cages, as trained performers of tricks, or worse, as fighting animals. It must also be said that many humans and animals enjoy a very harmonious life together, and children may well wish to discuss their feelings and opinions on this issue, as well as on the pros and cons of vegetarianism. More contentious, perhaps, is our practice of experimenting on animals to find cures for human illness and to test the safety of manufactured products.

Not content with keeping animals in captivity, we also interfere greatly with animals in the wild, to such an extent that many have already become extinct and many more are endangered. We hunt and trap them for food, and for their fur – perhaps excusably in very cold countries, but less so in warmer climes where fur coats are just a symbol of wealth. We kill them for their tusks and horns, their bones and even their scent glands. We even hunt them simply for the fun of it.

Increasingly, we are also putting animals at risk just by the way we live. They are accidentally poisoned by our effluents, pesticides and other chemicals; and their habitats are being sharply eroded by human encroachment on their natural territory.

Some cultures and religions specifically teach that we should respect other forms of life, and live in harmony with them. Traditionally, 'Western' cultures have not taken this position so strongly, and now, with the human population increasing so rapidly, wildlife is even more in danger as our needs and theirs conflict. Fortunately, attitudes and practices *are* changing, both at an individual and at a governmental level. Certain species have international protection, reserves are being set up, animal experimentation is slowing down and, in many countries, both more humane farming methods and vegetarianism are on the increase. It is public pressure which has brought about these changes and we must help the next generation to care enough to keep up the pressure to balance human and animal needs more fairly.

THE DIVERSITY OF LIFE

Purposes

1 To celebrate the vast number of species and the enormous variety of life.

2 To understand the interrelatedness of living things.

3 To learn a little about how living things are adapted for particular habitats.

Starting-points

■ A class can prepare *The Albatross and the Equator* for choral speaking. Encourage the children to talk about why the albatross was unhappy and wanted to return home. Use it to introduce a discussion about how animals are adapted for particular ecological niches.

■ Read Gerald Durrell's account of his first visit to a rainforest. You could ask the children to close their eyes and try to picture the scene, or, if any classes are studying the rainforest (see the activity below), they could display their pictures and models as a backdrop. This could be done very effectively if the room were semi-darkened, and a spotlight shone on appropriate parts of a large mural as you read.

Fact box

The African lungfish, which lives in pools which frequently dry up, can enter a state of suspended animation which allows it to survive well over a year without food and water.

The giant saguaro cactus of North America stores hundreds of litres of water.

Some wasps lay their eggs inside caterpillars. When the grubs hatch out, they eat the caterpillar from the inside.

The mallee-fowl of the Pacific islands lays its eggs in volcanic ash, and the heat of the lava far below keeps the eggs warm.

continued

Yhi brings the Earth to life

Life on Earth lies dormant and frozen until Yhi awakes from the dreamtime.

In the beginning there were no stars, no sun, no moon. The Earth lay waiting, silent in the darkness. Nothing moved, no wind blew across the barren plain or the bare bones of the mountains. There was neither heat nor cold, alive or dead . . . nothing but waiting. Who knows how long?

Beyond the Earth, Yhi lay waiting too, sleeping the long sleep. It was Baiame the great spirit who broke her sleep. His whispering filled the universe: 'Yhi, awake. Yhi, awake.'

In her dreams she heard him. Her limbs stirred, her eyelids flickered and opened, and light shone from her eyes, flooding across the plain and the mountains.

Yhi stepped down to Earth and from that moment, where there had been nothing, there was everything — sound, movement, light.

The Earth felt all these things and it woke at that first footstep. At each new step Yhi took, the Earth showed what it had dreamed throughout that long dark time. Flowers, trees, shrubs and grasses sprang up wherever she walked and where she stopped to rest, the barren plain was lost under a sea of blooms.

Then Baiame whispered:

'The ice caves in the frozen mountains — take your light there.'

It seemed that Yhi had met her match in the cold blank silence of the ice caves. But somewhere there began the steady drip, drip, drip of water, free at last. Then, a cracking and crashing as great slabs of ice lost their freezing hold on the cave walls. The surface of the ice lakes splintered and fish, snakes and reptiles were swept out to join the living Earth outside as the lakes overflowed.

Yhi pressed on deeper but this time as she moved from cave to cave it was not solid, resisting ice she met but the touch of fur and feather. Birds and animals gathered to her and she led them out to add their voices to the new world.

'It is good. My world is alive,' Baiame said.

Aboriginal creation story

Fuelled

Fuelled
by a million
man-made
wings of fire —
the rocket tore a tunnel
through the sky —
and everybody cheered.
Fuelled
only by a thought from God —
the seedling
urged its way
through the thicknesses of black —
and as it pierced
the heavy ceiling of the soil —
and launched itself
up into outer space —
no
one
even
clapped.

Marcie Hans

Fact box *continued*

A shrew-like animal called a desman lives in water and has developed a long, mobile nose which it uses like a snorkel.

A flower called a stapelia relies on flies to pollinate it. Instead of having a sweet fragrance, it smells like rotting meat.

The following figures give the total number of species known to Western scientists of some life forms. In reality, there are likely to be far more, especially of insects. One estimate suggests 30 million!

Plants	
flowering	250,000
others	130,000
fungi	50,000
Vertebrates	
fish	18,924
birds	9120
reptiles and amphibians	8892
mammals	4000
Invertebrates	
insects (and other arthropods)	1,000,000
arachnids (spider family)	65,000
molluscs	47,000

Discussion

- Do children know the basic groups of living things (mammals, insects, etc.)? What are the main differences between them? Ask children to guess how many species of mammal they think there are. Use the figures in the fact box to talk about the amazing number of species. How many fish/birds/flowering plants . . . can they name in one minute? How long would it take to name them all?
- Use the fact box to introduce the idea of species occupying particular niches in nature to which they are specially adapted.
- Which animals eat only plants, and which are carnivores? What is the food chain for an animal such as a fox? Help children to see that at the lower end of any food chain there is always a plant.

I remember vividly the first time I entered a tropical rainforest.

I spent a whole day bewildered and enchanted by all the sights, sounds and scents. The leafmould alone contained hundreds of insects I had never seen or heard of before. Roll over any rotting log and I found a world as bizarre as anything thought up by science fiction. Each hollow tree was an apartment block containing anything from snakes to bats, from owls to flying mice. Every forest stream was an orchestra of frogs, a ballet of tiny fish, and from the canopy high above came a constant rain of fruit, twigs and pirouetting blossoms thrown down by the great army of creatures — mammals, birds, reptiles and insects — that inhabit this high, sunlit, flower-scented realm. I did not know where to look next. Every leaf, flower, liana, every insect, frog, fish or bird was a lifetime's study in itself, and I knew that there was another hidden, secretive army of creatures that would emerge at night to take over. As any naturalist knows, there is nothing like a tropical rainforest for replacing arrogance with awe.

Gerald Durrell

Spider

I'm told that the spider
Has coiled up inside her
Enough silky material
To spin an aerial
One-way track
To the moon and back;
Whilst I
Cannot even catch a fly.

Frank Collymore

Voices

Every forest has its own voice
Unlike any other.
In Rathnaphur
Birds like flames burn in the trees
Their sharp cries
Etching light onto green shade.
A cosmic hum
Grows in the tiger's throat,
Sunlit content
Resonating like a drum.
High in the tree-tops
Monkeys shake down brittle shards of sound
That pierce harsh insect atonalities.
Every lightest breath
Imprints the air,
Patterning sound shapes
Only configured here.

Smaller than a forest
My city wilderness speaks too.
Above the hubbub
Of thrush and blackbird
Blackcaps bubble and spill melody.
While under leaves
With delicate cobweb sounds
Spiders are busy
Parcelling insects up.
Foxes whose barking tears the night
Whose paws crisp the snow
Lie hidden here.
Moth movements
Brush sounds as faint as seeds
Falling, from dusty wings.

Zoë Bailey

The Albatross and the Equator

'Albatross, Albatross, why do you fly
Under my blue equatorial sky?
Albatross, Albatross, why do you roam
So far from your icy delectable home?'

'Capricorn warned me to turn to the right,
But I strayed from my course in the dead of
the night;
And the stars of the tropics, so many and new,
Led me by long ways and weary to you.'

The kindly Equator arose with a yawn
To the green and the gold of the tropical
dawn.
He called his Leviathans, little and large,
And handed the Albatross into their charge.

And he said to his Porpoises: 'Cease from your
play,
And listen to me for the rest of the day:
I never have seen and seldom have heard
Of such an amazingly beautiful bird.

'She has flown from the far impossible South,
And strange are the sounds that come out of
her mouth;
But the white of her breast and the spread of
her wings
Are both surpassingly wonderful things.'

So they crowned her with seaweed Queen of
the Birds
And humbly addressed her with flattering
words;
And they gave her oysters and elegant fish
Daintily served on an amethyst dish.

They gave her a coral isle set in the calms
With long white beach of coconut palms.
'Deign with your delicate feet,' said they,
'To tread this shade in the heat of the day.'

But the Albatross smiled with a tear in her
heart,
As she said: 'I will walk for a little apart.'
And she paced by the echoing ocean alone,
Crooning a sorrowful song of her own:

'Fair are the tropical seas in the noon,
And fair is the glistening path of the moon.
But, oh, dearer to me are the storms of the
Horn
Where the grey world-wandering waves are
born.'

One moment they saw her, the next she had
fled
Like a dream in the dawn or a shaft that is sped;
And all that she left on that desolate strand
Was the print of her foot and a tear in the sand.

She flew through the day and she flew through
the night
With a heart that was bursting with hope and
delight,
As the changing horizons came up with a
swing
And the long leagues of ocean slipped under
her wing —

Into the far incredible South,
Till she tasted the smell of the snow in her
mouth
And fluttered to rest in the land of her birth
On the ice that envelopes the ends of the
Earth.

E. V. Rieu

● What sort of habitat do children think the giant saguaro cactus lives in?

● Help them to build on their knowledge about animal adaptation. For example, they will know a seal has flippers, not legs, but may not have thought about its streamlined shape or know it can close its nostrils. They will know camels can go long periods without water, but why do they have such large, flat feet and such long eyelashes?

● Do they know of any plants or animals which are highly specialised (such as the giant panda, which eats little except bamboo)? Which animals are the most adaptable? Why are rats and humans found in so many different places? Why did rabbits spread so rapidly when introduced into Australia?

● What examples of camouflage do the children know about?

● Ask for examples of how animals and plants depend on each other in other ways, as in plants being pollinated by insects, seeds being dispersed by mammals and birds, dung acting as fertiliser and animals using plant matter for shelter.

Activities

♦ Children could make illustrated food webs and chains.

♦ A class book could be made about animal or plant adaptations, with groups each researching a particular one.

♦ A metre quadrant or a PE hoop can be used for making a detailed survey of life in and on different types of ground, such as a lawn, waste ground, a vegetable garden, woodland . . . Long-term studies could also be done. If you have a suitable mini-ecosystem such as a pond or hedgerow, children could make a detailed study of what species live there and how they interrelate.

♦ Animals can be categorised in many different ways: herbivores and carnivores; water or land dwellers; domestic and wild; native or foreign . . .

♦ Give the children some world maps which show vegetation and climate, or some pictures of particular habitats, and ask them to think what animals might live there.

LIVING TOGETHER

Purpose

1 To consider our relationship with domestic and captive animals.

Starting-points

- Read *The gift of the sacred dog*. Talk about the way the Native Americans regarded the horse as a great gift to be looked after. What care did the horses need? How did they help the people? How do we use horses now? Do we regard them 'as relatives'?

or

- Invite someone who owns or works with a working animal to talk to the children about how he or she trains, looks after and uses the animal.
- Children could prepare readings, paintings and photographs about their own pets.
- Have some children role-play a conflict about an animal rights issue. For example, start to tell a story about protesters picketing a circus. What do they say to potential customers? How does the situation develop? Other subjects might be someone beating a dog, or setting laboratory animals free.

Fact box

In 1987 the RSPCA in Britain found homes for 108,336 cats and dogs, destroyed 65,007 healthy cats and dogs, and received 85,419 complaints of cruelty.

In the wild a hamster can travel up to 8km a night.

The vaccine which has eradicated smallpox from the world could not have been developed without testing on animals.

The LD_{50} (lethal dose, median) test, used when testing new products, involves increasing amounts of a substance being given to a batch of animals until 50% of them die.

Heart attack patients are likely to recover more quickly if they have a pet.

The gift of the sacred dog

Horses were brought to North America by the Spanish. To the tribes of nomadic buffalo hunters who lived on the Great Plains, horses were truly miraculous. This wonderful animal could not only carry and drag far heavier burdens than the dogs they had used before, but could also carry a rider and run faster than anyone ever imagined was possible. They tell factual accounts of the first horses they saw, but the story is told as well in ways which remind them that Sacred Dogs were also a gift from the Great Spirit. This version tells how the people were suffering from a great famine:

There was a boy in the camp who was sad to hear his little brothers and sisters crying with hunger. He saw his mother and father eat nothing so that the children could have what little food there was.

He told his parents: 'I am sad to see everyone suffering. The dogs are hungry too. I am going up into the hills to ask the Great Spirit to help us. Do not worry about me; I shall return in the morning.'

He reached the top of the highest hill as the sun was setting. He raised his arms and spoke: 'Great Spirit, my people need your help. We follow the buffalo herds because you gave them to us. But we cannot find them and we can walk no further. We are hungry. My little brothers and sisters are crying. Great Spirit, we need your help.'

As he stood there on the hilltop, great clouds closed across the sky. Wind and hail came with sudden force, and behind them Thunderbirds swooped among the clouds. Lightning darted from their flashing eyes and thunder rumbled when they flapped their enormous wings. He felt afraid and wondered if the Great Spirit had answered him.

The clouds parted. Someone came riding toward the boy on the back of a beautiful animal. There was thunder in its nostrils and lightning in its legs; its eyes shone like stars and hair on its neck and tail trailed like clouds. The boy had never seen any animal so magnificent

The rider spoke: 'I know your people are in need. They will receive this: he is called Sacred Dog because he can do many things your dogs can do, and also more. He will carry you far and will run faster than the buffalo. He comes from the sky. He is as the wind: gentle but sometimes frightening. Look after him always.'

The boy did not remember going to sleep, but he awoke as the sun was rising. He knew it was something wonderful he had seen in the sky. He started down the hill back home again to ask the wise men what it meant. They would be able to tell him.

When the boy had reached the level plain he heard a sound like far-away thunder coming from the hill behind. Looking back, he saw Sacred Dogs pouring out of a cave and coming down a ravine toward him. They came galloping down the slopes, neighing and kicking up their back legs with excitement.

The leading ones stopped when they were a short distance away. They stamped their feet and snorted, but their eyes were gentle too, like those of the deer. The boy knew they were what he had been promised on the hilltop. He turned and continued walking toward the camp and all the Sacred Dogs followed him.

The people were excited and came out from the camp circle when they saw the boy returning with so many strange and beautiful animals. He told them, 'These are Sacred Dogs. They are a gift from the Great Spirit. They will help us to follow the buffalo and they will carry the hunters into the running herds. Now there will always be enough to eat. We must look after them well and they will be happy to live with us.'

Life was good after that. The people lived as relatives with the Sacred Dogs, together with the buffalo and all other living things, as the Great Spirit wished them to live.

Native American story, retold by Paul Goble

Tiger

He stalks in his vivid stripes
The few steps of his cage,
On pads of velvet quiet,
In his quiet rage.

He should be lurking in shadow,
Sliding through long grass,
Near the water hole
Where plump deer pass.

He should be snarling around houses
At the jungle's edge,
Baring his white fangs, his claws,
Terrorising the village!

But he's locked in a concrete cell,
His strength behind bars,
Stalking the length of his cage.
Ignoring visitors.

He hears the last voice at night,
The patrolling cars,
And stares with his brilliant eyes
At the brilliant stars.

Leslie Norris

The circus elephants

What are they thinking?
The circus elephants,
As they tramp round the ring each night.

Do they wish that they
Were far away
In the forest's leafy light?

Where they'd roam at will
And could eat their fill
Far from human sight.

As the gentle giants
Perform their tricks,
The children stare with delight.

But is it fair?
Should they be there?
Is keeping them captive right?

John Foster

Ari and the chickens

A Jewish story tells how one of the great holy men, Ari, pointed at one of his disciples one day and said, 'Go away, you have angered God.'

The disciple fell at the feet of the holy man and begged to be told what he had done wrong so that he could set it right.

And Ari said to him: 'It is because of the chickens you have at home. You have not fed them for two days and they cry out to God in their hunger. God will forgive you on condition you see to it that before you leave for prayers in the morning you give food to your chickens. For they are dumb animals and they cannot ask for their food.'

Jewish story

Several big cosmetic firms have now stopped animal tests.

Dolphins live about 25 years in the wild, but only about 3½ in captivity.

'Sniffer' dogs are better than any machine for detecting drugs.

Discussion

● Why do people keep pets? How do the children feel about their own pets? Why do people keep vicious dogs? What do the children feel about caged pets? How can we best look after our pets? Are there some animals which shouldn't be kept? Should people have to pass a test to keep a pet? What should be done about cruelty to pets?

● Have we the right to experiment on animals? Is there a difference between experimenting for medical reasons and testing the safety of consumer products? What alternatives are there? Can we draw a line about how much suffering is permissible? Do mice suffer less than chimpanzees? What do the children think about people who set laboratory animals free, or, in extreme cases, plant bombs to injure or kill experimenters?

● What sort of work do animals do? It is right for animals to work for us? Do they enjoy their work?

● What are zoos, safari parks and aquaria for? Are people more likely to care about the fate of elephants if they have been near enough to touch one, or is it more effective to watch films of animals in their native habitats? If we do have zoos, how can we produce the best conditions?

Activities

♦ Animals seem to arouse strong feelings in people. Children are likely to have their own ideas about what they would like to do; for example, writing poems or stories, making up plays, designing posters, finding out about animal testing, improving the living conditions of school pets and writing rules for their care, drawing up a code of conduct for themselves and their families on issues such as buying free-range food, cruelty-free cosmetics and so on.

Fifth rabbit

He rode in triumph on the carrier of our bike,
His ears giving the streets the victory salute,
Death and dissection cheated at the eleventh hour;
The future — silly names, tickling, and food the like
No rabbit, even in nursery-land, had the right
To expect in the run of luck. The other four
Had now gone to the gas and the experiment,
Their futures cut and dried, needing no sentiment.

Yet he, his bacon saved, is hopping mad
That we should wire him in and make him fat;
And, no doubt, will soon try to burrow out
From salvation, and, alone, lose his head
To whatever preys on innocent things
Which, being blest with scuts, never grow wings.

Julian Ennis

I'm a parrot

I'm a parrot
I live in a cage
I'm nearly always
in a vex-up rage

I used to fly
all light and free
in the luscious
green forest canopy

I'm a parrot
I live in a cage
I'm nearly always
in a vex-up rage

I miss the wind
against my wing
I miss the nut
and the fruit picking

I'm a parrot
I live in a cage
I'm nearly always
in a vex-up rage

I squawk I talk
I curse I swear
I repeat the things
I shouldn't hear

I'm a parrot
I live in a cage
I'm nearly always
in a vex-up rage

So don't come near me
or put out your hand
because I'll pick you
if I can

pickyou
pickyou
if I can

I want to be free
CAN'T YOU UNDERSTAND

Grace Nichols

The exile

The fool said to the animals:
'You are merely my chattels,
With one lesson to learn —
That what happens to you is not your concern
But mine; for a just God has set
You on earth for my profit.'

The animals answered the fool
Nothing at all,
But for a single moment
Turned on him their wild, true, innocent
Eyes, where an Angel of the Lord
Holds Eden's flaming sword.

Frances Bellerby

The magnificent bull

My bull is white like the silver fish in the river,
White like the shimmering crane bird on the river bank
White like fresh milk!
His roar is like thunder to the Turkish cannon on the steep shore.
My bull is dark like the rain-cloud in the storm.
He is like summer and winter.
Half of him is dark like the storm cloud;
Half of him is light like sunshine.
His back shines like the morning star.
His brow is red like the back of the hornbill.
His forehead is like a flag, calling the people from a distance.
He resembles the rainbow.
Drink, my bull, from the river;
I am here to guard you with my spear.

Dinka praise song, Africa

My puppy

It's funny
my puppy
knows just how I feel.

When I'm happy
he's yappy
and squirms like an eel.

When I'm grumpy
he's slumpy
and stays at my heel.

It's funny
my puppy
knows such a great deal.

Aileen Fisher

ATTITUDES TO WILDLIFE

Purposes

1 To examine our behaviour and attitudes to wildlife.

2 To consider ways in which we can help wildlife to survive.

Starting-points

■ Children can alternate reading the short quotations about how we should behave towards animals with the facts in the first fact box.

■ Invite a speaker from a local religious group to talk about their religion's teachings on attitudes to wildlife.

■ Set up a debate, with a panel of teachers taking sides, on the proposition, 'This house believes shooting wild birds should be banned', or a similar topic. Conduct it on formal lines, with questions and comments from the floor at a set time. At the end, take a vote.

Fact box 1

Around 13,000 foxes are killed every year in Britain by hunts with horses and hounds.

An animal trapped for its fur is held in the trap for an average of 15 hours.

Badger baiting still goes on in Britain although it is illegal.

Thousands of dolphins die every year because they are trapped in tuna fishing nets.

Field voles die because they get trapped in bottles carelessly thrown away.

continued

One should treat animals

such as deer, camels, asses, monkeys, mice, snakes, birds and flies exactly like one's own son. How little difference there actually is between children and these innocent animals.

from the Hindu scriptures

There is not an animal

that lives on the earth, nor a being that flies on its wings, but forms part of communities like you . . . and they shall all be gathered to their Lord in the end.

Islamic: from the Qur'an

Not to hurt our humble brethren

is our first duty to them, but to stop there is not enough. We have a higher mission to be of service to them whenever they require it.

St Francis of Assisi

The time will come

when men such as I will look back upon the murder of animals as they now look upon the murder of men.

Leonardo da Vinci

Whether they belong to more evolved species

such as the human or to simpler ones such as animals, all beings primarily seek peace, comfort, and security. Life is as dear to the mute animal as it is to any human being; even the simplest insect strives for protection from dangers that threaten its life. Just as each one of us wants to live and does not wish to die, so it is with all other creatures in the universe, though their power to effect this is a different matter.

The Dalai Lama

Hurt no living thing

Hurt no living thing,
Ladybird nor butterfly,
Nor moth with dusty wing,
Nor cricket chirping cheerily,
Nor grasshopper, so light of lea,
Nor dancing gnat,
Nor beetle fat,
Nor harmless worms that creep.

Christina Rossetti

Birdfoot's Grampa

The old man
must have stopped our car
two dozen times to climb out
and gather into his hands
the small toads blinded
by our light and leaping,
live drops of rain.

The rain was falling,
a mist about his white hair
and I kept saying
you can't save them all,
accept it, get back in
we've got places to go.

But, leathery hands full
of wet brown life,
knee deep in the summer
roadside grass,
he just smiled and said
they have places to go to too.

Joseph Bruchac

Fact box 2

Many firms no longer use animal products in the manufacture of cosmetics.

The EEC ban on importing fur from harp and hooded seal pups reduced the annual kill in Canada from about 180,000 to 24,000.

In Britain, an area which is particularly important for wildlife can be given a measure of protection as a Site of Special Scientific Interest.

Ramps are often put in cattle grids to give hedgehogs a means of escape.

Local conservation groups are springing up everywhere, and there is an increasing number of wildlife parks and gardens.

Discussion

- What contact have children had with wild animals? How do they feel about them? Can humans have any real relationship with them? Do we have any responsibility towards wildlife?
- How different religions and cultures regard animals? For example, Native Americans used to say prayers to the buffalo to thank them for providing meat. Australian Aborigines can survive only by eating the species that share the land with them, but they have very strict rules about when they can hunt and gather the different species, so they never wipe them out.
- Have we the right to kill animals for our own pleasure – for sport, for luxury clothes such as furs, for ornaments made of horn? Should we pick wild flowers to beautify our homes? Chop down trees for Christmas? Does it make any difference whether or not the species is endangered? Does it matter if we tread on ants? (See also *Endangered species*, pages 42-43.)
- What about people who have traditionally relied on animals, such as the Inuits (Eskimos) who kill seals to provide themselves with food, clothing, light and heat? What about animals which eat our food, or endanger our livestock or crops, or hurt or even kill people?

The killer of seals

Once there lived in the North of Scotland the cleverest and quickest of seal-fishermen. He had killed more seals than anyone could keep count of, but one day he stopped, put his spears and clubs aside, and never again killed a seal.

When people asked him why he had given up his work, this is what he told them.

One night a stranger came to his door. 'Am I at the door of the man whose fame for catching seals is known wherever the sea meets the land?'

'You are,' said the fisherman.

'I have business for you, then. I come on behalf of someone who wishes to buy your sealskins. You must come with me, to discuss the price to be paid.'

'Say no more,' said the fisherman, and although the hour was late, he leaped up behind the stranger on his horse, and they set off at great speed through the night. The horse's hooves hardly touched the ground, and in no time they were at the edge of the sea, at the very brink of a high cliff. Below them, in the dark, the waves crashed and crashed unceasingly on the rocks.

'Hold tight now!' the stranger cried, and the fisherman had no time to do anything but cling to the stranger's waist, before they were plunging through the air and crashing into the sea.

Down, down they went. 'I shall drown!' the fisherman gasped. But the next surprise of that strange night was that he found he could breathe under water. As soon as the horse's hooves struck the floor of the sea, the stranger leaped off and made a sign to the fisherman to do likewise. Then they walked through a maze of rocky caves and corridors into a large cave, where several seals seemed to be waiting for them. One of them came forward and handed a large knife to the fisherman.

'Did you ever see this before?' the stranger asked him.

'Indeed I did. It's mine. I lost it earlier today.'

It was truly his own knife. He had stuck it into the side of an especially big seal, but the beast had flipped over and, with a powerful thrust of its flippers, slipped into the sea, taking the knife with it.

'Yes, it's my best knife. What do you intend to do with it?'

He was feeling very nervous now, and fairly sure that they were going to stick him with his own weapon.

'The seal you slashed at is my own father,' the stranger said. 'You are here to cure him.'

'But how? What can I do?' the fisherman spluttered.

'All you need to do is to lay your hands on him and wish him well. Simply will him to get well. That will be enough.'

Then the stranger led the fisherman to a corner of the cave where the great old seal was lying quietly, a terrible wound in his side. The fisherman was nudged forward until he stood shamefully before the old seal. All eyes were on him: they didn't look accusing, but seemed to express a terrible sorrow.

So he raised his hands slowly, placed them gently on the wound, and let them rest there quietly for a moment. And he found himself willing the old seal to recover. Not only to recover, but also to forgive him.

Suddenly he felt relieved. He looked around, and it was as if all the seals were smiling. Then he met the eyes of the old seal, his very own victim. 'I'm going to recover,' the old beast's eyes seemed to say, 'but only because you willed it. And you, too, are going to recover from your blood-lust, your craze for killing, because we all will it.'

Then the stranger, his guide, nudged his elbow and led him away. So they retraced their steps through the labyrinth of caves and passages. Then the stranger lifted him onto the horse again.

A great surge of water and air, and he felt as if his lungs were going to burst, and they were on the cliff-top. Then a wild rushing across the hills, and he stood once more at his own door. He rubbed his eyes, and the stranger and his horse had disappeared into the night.

Then he fell into his bed, knowing that his life would never be the same again.

Traditional British story, retold by Geoffrey Summerfield

A fly

If I could
See this fly
With unprejudiced eye,
I should see his body
Was metallic blue — no,
Peacock blue.
His wings are a frosty puff;
His legs fine wire.
He even has a face,
I notice.
And he breathes as I do.

Ruth Dallas

Moss-gathering

To loosen with all ten fingers held wide and
 limber
And lift up a patch, dark-green, the kind for
 lining cemetery baskets,
Thick and cushiony, like an old-fashioned
 doormat,
The crumbling small hollow sticks on the
 underside mixed with roots,
And wintergreen berries and leaves still stuck
 to the top —
That was moss-gathering.
But something always went out of me when I
 dug loose those carpets
Of green, or plunged to my elbows in the
 spongy yellowish moss of the marshes:
And afterwards I always felt mean, jogging
 back over the logging road,
As if I had broken the natural order of things
 in that swampland;
Disturbed some rhythm, old and of vast
 importance,
By pulling off flesh from the living planet;
As if I had committed, against the whole
 scheme of life, a desecration.

Theodore Roethke

If I were a doe living in the forest, eating grass and leaves, with God's grace I would find God. If I were a cuckoo living in a mango tree, contemplating a singing, God reveals through his mercy. If I were a female snake, dwelling in the ground, let God's word be in my being, my dread would vanish. Eternal God is found, light meets light.

from the Sikh scriptures: the Guru Granth Sahib (Sikh)

● What can we do to help wildlife and, specifically, what can the children do? Is there some action they could take at local level, or a local group they could join? How can children get their views known? How can people's attitudes be changed? What should be done about people who break the laws which protect wildlife?

Activities

♦ Again, children will probably have their own ideas about what they would like to do. Different groups might research issues such as fox hunting, shooting, fur farming and trapping, the use of animal products in cosmetics and so on, and present their own assembly.

♦ One activity you might suggest is making up a board game based on a specific issue, or on human behaviour towards wildlife in general. It could have simple instructions: 'You hear the hunt in the distance. Miss two turns while you wait for it to pass.' Or it could incorporate discussion cards: 'You find an injured bird. What do you do?'

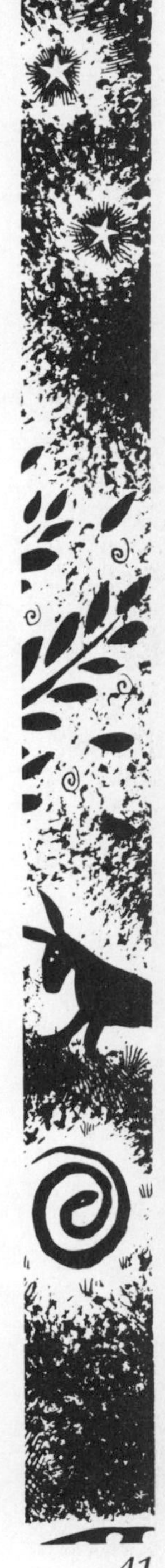

ENDANGERED SPECIES

Purposes

1 To understand the variety of causes which can lead to species being endangered or becoming extinct.

2 To consider the moral issue of human involvement.

3 To investigate how people are tackling the problem and how children can help.

Starting-point

■ Show some pictures of dinosaurs. Ask if anyone has ever seen a real one. Talk briefly about some of the possible reasons for their extinction, but the focus should be on the fact that they can never come back. Show a picture of an endangered animal the children are likely to have seen (see *Fact box 1*). Emphasise that unless we do something now, *their* children may only ever see a picture in a book.

or

■ A group of children could recite *The flower-fed buffaloes*, to introduce a discussion on some of the reasons animals become extinct.

Fact box 1

Since the year 1500, humans have been responsible for the extinction of about one species per year. At present, animals are dying out at the rate of about one species per day, and plants at 100 to 200 a year.

Rhinos have been around for about 40 million years, but they are now in danger of extinction because people want their horns – as a medicine, or to make ornamental daggers. A rhino horn can fetch up to £50,000.

The American robin almost died out through eating worms poisoned with DDT.

In 1066 there were still wolves in Britain. They died out partly because so much forest was cut down, and partly because they were killed to protect livestock.

In Britain, the following are under threat: bat, barn owl, peregrine falcon, red squirrel, natterjack toad, otter, common dormouse and orchid.

World-wide, these are just a few of the species under threat: giant panda, Indian rhinoceros, snow leopard, blue whale, California condor, cheetah, mountain gorilla, Galapagos giant tortoise, giant earthworm and the African violet.

Fact box 2

In 1973 the Indian government set up nine reserves as part of 'Operation Tiger'. The tiger population figures tell the story: 1900 – 40,000; 1972 – 2000; and 1989 – 5000.

In Zimbabwe, the elephant is protected, and numbers are steadily growing.

The osprey became extinct in Britain in 1908, through shooting and egg collecting. In 1954, a pair nested in Scotland, and, with strong protection from the RSPB, there were 50 or 60 pairs by 1989.

UK membership of the World Wide Fund for Nature increased from 106,000 in 1986 to 227,000 in 1990.

The flower-fed buffaloes

The flower-fed buffaloes of the spring
In the days of long ago,
Ranged where the locomotives sing
And the prairie flowers lie low:—
The tossing, blooming, perfumed grass
Is swept away by the wheat,
Wheels and wheels and wheels spin by
In the spring that still is sweet.
But the flower-fed buffaloes of the spring
Left us, long ago.
They gore no more, they bellow no more,
They trundle around the hills no more:—
With the Blackfeet, lying low,
With the Pawnees, lying low,
Lying low.

Vachel Lindsay

Why?

Sand Lizard
I can't live in a factory,
I can't live in a flat.
I only need my heathland;
Why take that?

Otter
I can't live on your poisons,
Can't eat polluted fish.
I only need my river;
Why spoil this?

Butterfly
I can't live with your chemicals
In every flower that grows.
I only need my grasslands;
Why spray those?

Judith Nicholls

Tree

'What's that?'
The little girl asked,
As she sat in the machine.
'I think,' said the man,
'It is a tree,
A relic from
The time of flowers.'
The machine sped on,
Cutting its way
Through the artificial air
In the artificial town.
The tree was trapped,
For tourists' eyes,
In a plastic cage,
Among a mass
Of plastic towers,
Its branches bare;
Its leaves long dead.

Patricia Cope (aged 13)

The greedy monster

A greedy monster
came and ate
the leaves from the trees.

The wind was sad.
He had no one
to tickle with his breeze.

The greedy monster
came and ate
the branches, every bit.

The birds flew sulky
in the sky;
they had nowhere to sit.

The monster
ate the forest,
trunks and roots, in a day.

Now houses stand
where the forest stood,
and the birds have gone away.

Irene Rawnsley

If only elephants

If elephants were Man's Best Friend
and slept in wicker baskets by the fire,
ate supermarket forest
cooked and canned,
came when we called,
wore fur we could admire,
we wouldn't see them massacred for tusks.

We'd paint their toenails,
show them off at Crufts.

Irene Rawnsley

Discussion

● Children need to understand that it is human activities which are hastening the process of extinction at unbelievable speed, through destruction of habitat; hunting and trapping for food and other animal products; accidental poisoning and other man-made disasters (such as the contamination of reindeer after Chernobyl). And extinction is *final*. (See also *Attitudes to wildlife*, pages 39-41.)

● The children can share their ideas about how the destruction can be halted, and what we in our society can do. Help them not to be too simplistic: for example, can we expect poor nations to set aside vast areas of land as wildlife reserves, when some of their people are desperate for food? What should be done about an ivory poacher who needs the money to feed his hungry family? How can we balance the need to preserve an area of woodland to protect a rare orchid against the need for a development which would bring much-needed jobs?

Activities

♦ A group could research into one particular endangered species, and organise their own campaign. They might produce posters and leaflets, and large background paintings of the habitat; make models; set up an exhibition; prepare talks or even a whole assembly . . .

♦ Some brave children might like to write a 'letter to an unborn grandchild' describing an elephant, a blue whale, an otter . . . and explaining why they no longer exist.

Nowhere else to go

They're pulling down our house to build
a supermarket,
The bathroom will be full of tins of beans,
Somewhere there's a man with a special
master plan,
I think this is what progress means.
I'll have to find a new place for the budgie,
I'll have to find a new place for my bed.
A JCB was waiting, I'd no time for hesitating,
So I went up to its driver and I said,
And I said –

Your place is my place,
It's nothing very fancy, sir, I know,
But it's all that I have got
So I'm asking you to stop,
'Cos there's really nowhere else that I can go,
No, there's really nowhere else that I can go!

They're pulling down the forest with their
diesel chainsaws,
Tearing down the bushes and the trees,
Filling in the holes which give shelter to the voles,
And burning all the shady leaves.
The foxes and the badgers will be homeless,
The spiders, ants and every living thing.
The weasels were all worried until out a rabbit
scurried,
He said, 'Gather round the lumberjacks and sing!'
And they sang:

Your trees are our trees,
They're nothing very fancy, sir, we know,

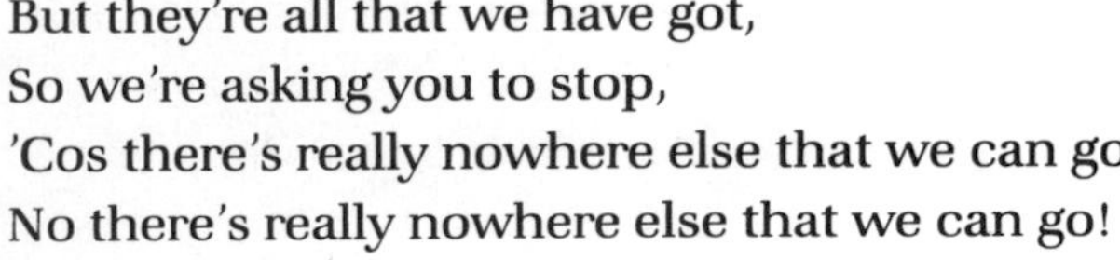

But they're all that we have got,
So we're asking you to stop,
'Cos there's really nowhere else that we can go,
No there's really nowhere else that we can go!

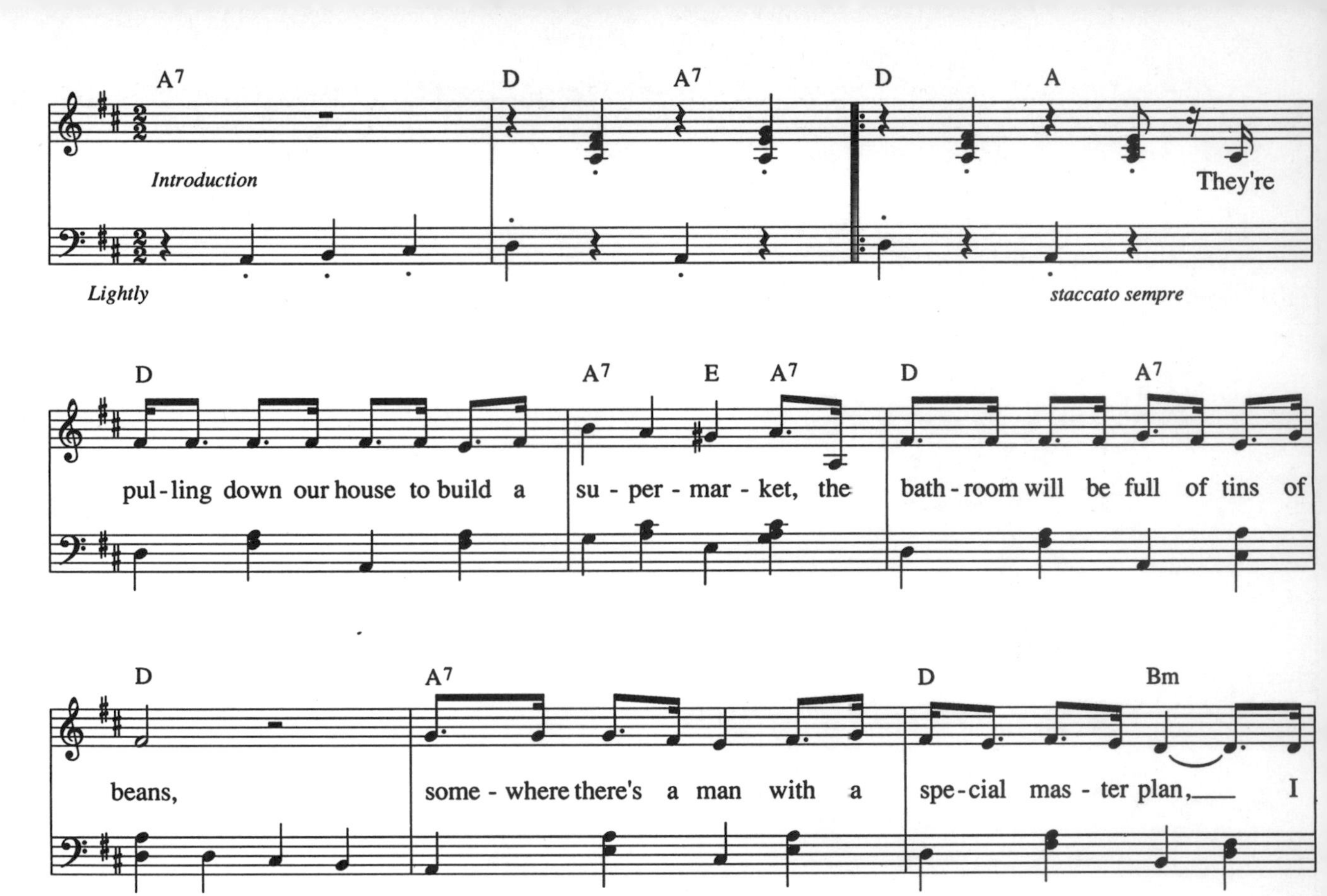

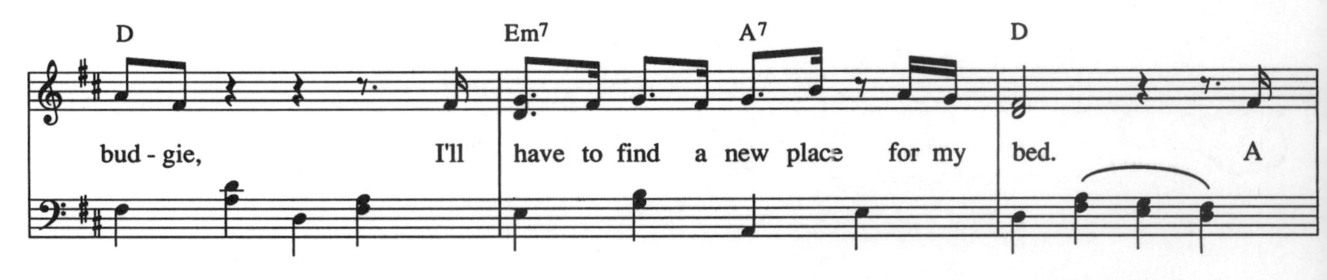

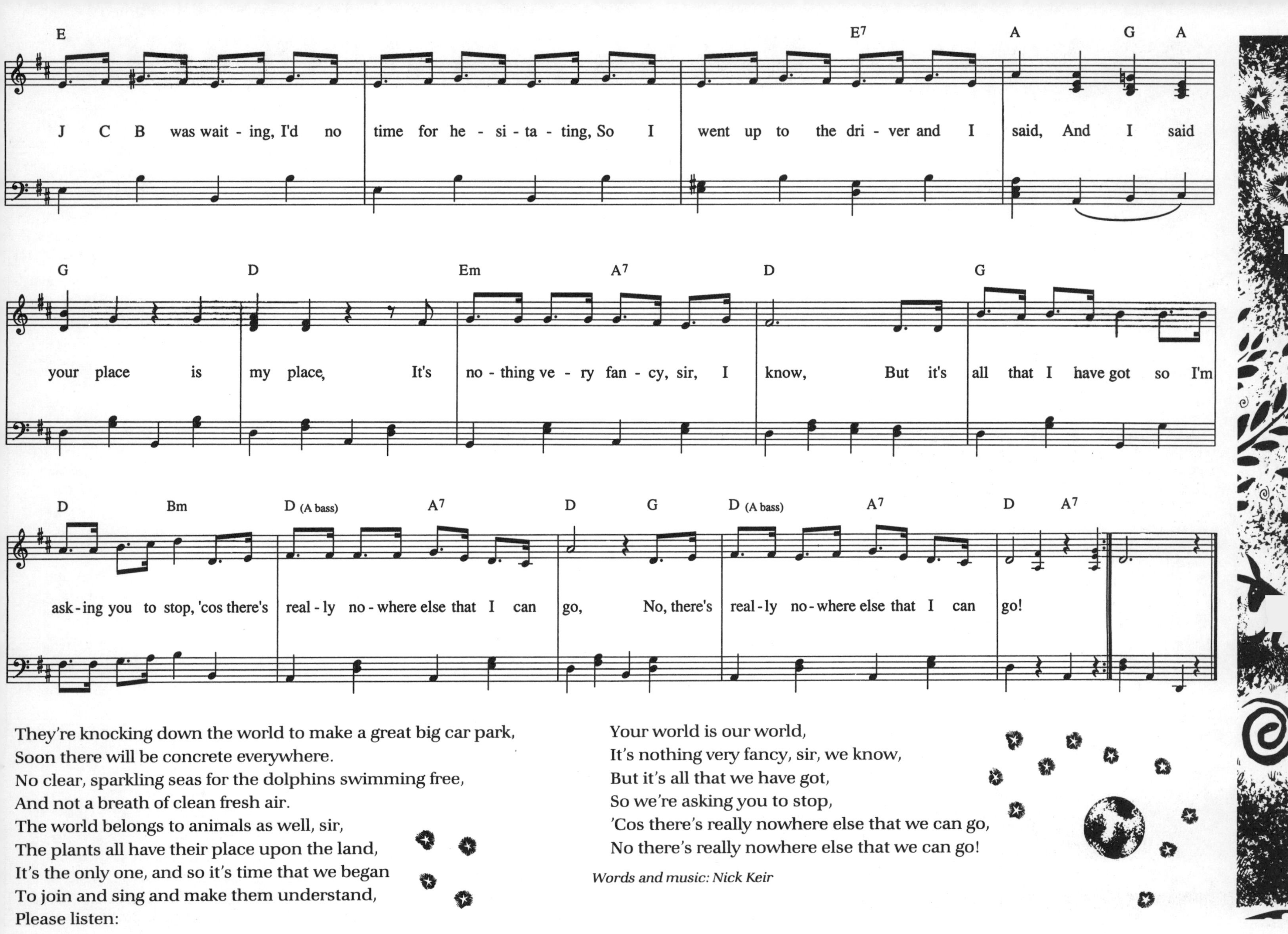
E E7 A G A
J C B was wait - ing, I'd no time for he - si - ta - ting, So I went up to the dri - ver and I said, And I said
G D Em A7 D G
your place is my place, It's no - thing ve - ry fan - cy, sir, I know, But it's all that I have got so I'm
D Bm D (A bass) A7 D G D (A bass) A7 D A7
ask - ing you to stop, 'cos there's real - ly no - where else that I can go, No, there's real - ly no - where else that I can go!
They're knocking down the world to make a great big car park,
Soon there will be concrete everywhere.
No clear, sparkling seas for the dolphins swimming free,
And not a breath of clean fresh air.
The world belongs to animals as well, sir,
The plants all have their place upon the land,
It's the only one, and so it's time that we began
To join and sing and make them understand,
Please listen:
Your world is our world,
It's nothing very fancy, sir, we know,
But it's all that we have got,
So we're asking you to stop,
'Cos there's really nowhere else that we can go,
No there's really nowhere else that we can go!
Words and music: Nick Keir

PEOPLE AND PLACES

All over the world, except in the very harshest environments, people have found ways to live. In fact, people have now found ways to live, on a temporary basis at least, in that most inhospitable of environments, space. But there, and in places such as Antarctica and on the high seas, humans have to take with them everything they need for survival. Elsewhere in the world, they have shown remarkable ingenuity in living off the land, eating the plant and animal food which flourishes in that particular spot, and making use of whatever natural resources there are to supply them with clothes, shelter, transport, heating, energy and recreation.

In some cases, human habitation has had little effect on the land; people live in harmony with their environment, feeling themselves part of it. But, increasingly, people all over the world have come to control and adapt their environment to suit themselves, often with no real sympathy for the land and its other inhabitants.

In Western Europe, there are few places untouched by human influence, as people seek to improve their lives. Motorways and railways criss-cross the continent; Britain's native forests have almost disappeared; even the once remote mountains of the Alps are now dotted with ski resorts. In Australia, mining and quarrying are permanently changing the face of the landscape; the deserts of North Africa were once fertile lands, denuded by overgrazing as far back as Roman times.

Living in the countryside often sounds idyllic to town dwellers, but life is often far from easy and all over the world people are migrating to the towns. They may be enticed by the many attractions of city life, or they may be driven by desperation. Large numbers of people living together puts enormous pressures on resources; food and other necessities must be brought in from the surrounding countryside, and the larger the conurbation, the further afield the resources must come from to supply the increased numbers. Power supply, water, waste disposal — all these have to be organised, in many cases, for millions of people living in one comparatively small area. Urban living can bring many problems, such as overcrowding, homelessness, unemployment, alienation, crime, violence, racism, pollution . . . but for many, slum-dwelling is the only alternative to starving in the countryside.

Changes in the environment and in people's lives are often highly desirable, but now they are happening at a faster rate and on a larger scale than ever before. In addition, it is becoming harder and harder for ordinary people to have control of their own lives, as decisions which vitally affect them are often made hundreds, or even thousands, of kilometres away, by people they have never seen. Whole valleys may be flooded by dams, vast areas of forest cut down, huge tracts of land fenced off for missile testing . . . Even where changes are not on such a huge scale, people's lives are being disrupted without their consent by the decisions of local councils, government or big business.

We must try to help children feel a sense of identity with their neighbours and their local territory, not to foster small-scale nationalism, but to give them a reason to want to protect what is good and improve what is bad, and to play an active part in what goes on there.

PEOPLE EVERYWHERE

Purposes

1 To think about the basic requirements of human beings.

2 To understand that all over the world groups of people have lifestyles which enable them to live in harmony with nature in their particular local environment.

3 To consider problems caused by *not* living in harmony with nature.

4 To celebrate the diversity of human life.

5 To celebrate the diversity of environments in which we live.

Starting-points

■ Ask the children to imagine that they are stranded out in the countryside somewhere in their own country. How would they survive? What wild food might they find? How could they make a shelter? Do they think it would be possible for anyone to survive for long? Read *The Old Man makes the world*. How did the Old Man help the humans?

■ Some children can prepare and read the poems. How do the different poets feel about where they live? What sort of country is it? How do the people live? How does it compare with the children's own environment? (See also *Where you live*, pages 55-58.)

■ If a class has been doing some extended work about a particular group of people, they could present their work at assembly. See the activities below.

Fact box

The following are brief examples of ways some communities have found of living in a particular environment. For any extended work you will need further information (see *Resources*, page 00). You might include desert herding tribes, Bushmen, Inuits (Eskimos), Tibetan mountain dwellers. . .

continued

The Old Man makes the world

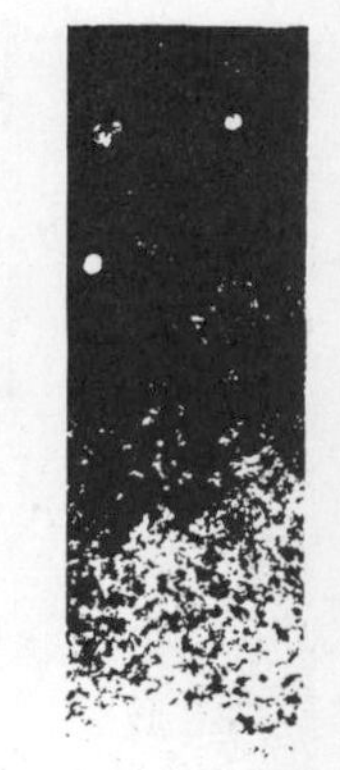

According to the legends of the Blackfeet tribe of North America, the world was shaped by the Old Man. First he created the mountains, prairies and forests, and then the land animals, birds and fish. He scooped up some clay to form the first people and stayed for a while to teach them how to make a good life for themselves.

He took the naked and helpless man, woman and child to the river to bathe. Next he showed them the roots and berries he had planted, saying: 'These are good to eat.' Then, pointing at certain trees, he added: 'And you can also eat the bark of these — you just peel it away when it's young and soft.'

The Old Man then decided to show the three new people where to find the herbs, leaves and roots which they would need to cure illnesses. So they went on a long journey across the prairies, the swamps and the forests.

'You have to pick all these at the right times of the year,' the Old Man explained.

By now the man, the woman and the child had seen the animals which the Old Man had made not long before. He said: 'They're good to eat too.' After a moment, he added: 'And so are the birds.'

So the Old Man cut a short strong shoot of a serviceberry plant. 'You'll need weapons,' he said. 'First you peel off the bark . . . there — now you tie on a string and you've a bow.'

He split a feather and fixed four pieces on the end of another smaller stick. 'There, this is an arrow,' he said, smoothing the feathers of the flight.

'Now you'll need good points for the arrows,' muttered the Old Man, looking around. He tried all sorts of stones, breaking them up into sharp pointed pieces, 'Black flint seems best,' he said, after a while. 'And some of the white isn't bad either.'

Then the Old Man taught the three human beings how to hunt with the bow and arrows.

'You can't eat meat raw; it'll be bad for you,' he told them next. Picking up some dry scraps of rotten wood, the Old Man shredded it into soft pieces. Then he found a lump of very hard wood and, using one of the stone-tipped arrows, drilled a hole in it.

'You take this,' he said to the man, giving him a stick of hard wood, 'and put it in the hole and then twirl it between your hands . . .'

The man did so and soon smoke came from the hole. The Old Man said to the woman: 'Quick, you drop in some pieces of the bark.'

The woman did so and, within moments, they had caught fire.

'There you are,' said the Old Man, smiling.

He watched the three humans as they tried to cook their meat. They were not sure how to do it.

continued

Fact box *continued*

The people of Lapland use their reindeer to provide milk and meat for food, hides for clothes and shelter, bone and horn for tools, and power to pull their sleighs. They follow their herds to find new grazing land when necessary.

The Yanomami people of the Amazon rainforest produce 85% of their food by growing vegetables. The rest they obtain by hunting and gathering. They also grow tobacco and cotton. Although they have to cut down the forest, they continually move their fields so that it recovers. Their villages are built of wood and palm fronds, and when the buildings deteriorate after a couple of years, the people move to a new location and start again.

Australian Aborigines who live in the traditional way have such an intimate knowledge of the land, plants and animals that they can live well in country that would appear to others to be almost barren. They find berries, dig for root plants, gather grass seed to make into flour, collect insects and small mammals, and catch larger creatures such as wallabies and emus. They have very few possessions, and those they do have are largely made from wood, bone and plant fibres. They rarely settle for long in one place. They believe that you do not own the land, but that the land owns you.

Discussion

- Compare the ways that people live together – in families, tribes, village communities, etc. What contact do the children have with their own extended families? Who are the people they know best? How is work organised – co-operatively or individually? Is it divided by gender? Do the children work? What about leisure?

The Old Man makes the world continued

'You need some dishes,' the Old Man said. 'Look!' He searched about and found a flat slab of soft rock and then a pointed lump of hard rock. 'It takes a while,' he said, starting to hollow out the first piece with the second piece. 'Patience, that's another thing that you'll need.' He passed the pieces of stone to them.

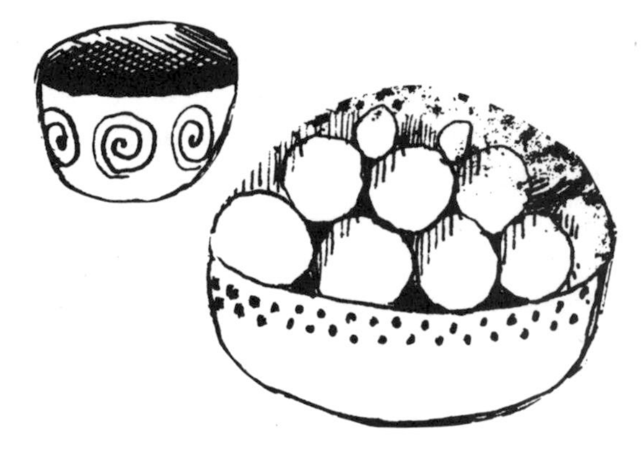

The Old Man now decided that he would move on the next day. So in the evening after the man, the woman and the child had enjoyed their first supper, he told them how a person could call for help from the spirits.

'You must first go away and sleep on your own somewhere. Then, in a dream, there will come a messenger to you, perhaps an animal: do as it says. In the same way, if you are travelling alone and need help, cry out aloud to the spirits and, through perhaps an eagle or a buffalo or a bear, help will come.'

The Old Man then set off northwards, making more people and animals as he went. Finally he reached a high mountain and, looking down over all he had created in the region, was very pleased.

Native American story, retold by John Mercer

The vast grassland is my beloved home

The vast grassland is my beloved home;
Here my white-haired mother was born.

The grassland waves like the green sea;
The scent of the grass floats over the misty hills and mountains.

Horses cannot reach the ends of the grassland;
Birds cannot fly to the edge, it is so vast.

Here thousands of animals graze
In the beautiful valleys of my beloved home.

Mongolian song

Composed upon Westminster Bridge, September 3, 1802

Earth has not anything to show more fair:
Dull would he be of soul who could pass by
A sight so touching in its majesty:
This City now doth, like a garment, wear
The beauty of the morning; silent, bare,
Ships, towers, domes, theatres, and temples lie
Open unto the fields, and to the sky;
All bright and glittering in the smokeless air.
Never did sun more beautifully steep
In his first splendour, valley, rock, or hill;
Ne'er saw I, never felt, a calm so deep!
The river glideth at his own sweet will:
Dear God! the very houses seem asleep;
And all that mighty heart is lying still!

William Wordsworth

Glorious it is

Glorious it is to see
The caribou flocking down from the forests
And beginning
Their wanderings to the north.
Timidly they watch
For the pitfalls of man.
Glorious it is to see
The great herds from the forests
Spreading out over plains of white.

Glorious it is to see
Early summer's short-haired caribou
Beginning to wander.
Glorious to see them trot
To and fro
Across the promontories,
Seeking for a crossing place.

Glorious it is
To see great musk oxen
Gathering in herds.
The little dogs they watch for
When they gather in herds.
Glorious to see.

Glorious it is
To see the long-haired winter caribou
Returning to the forests.
Fearfully they watch
For the little people,
While the herd follows the ebb-mark of the sea
With a storm of clattering hooves.
Glorious it is
When wandering time is come.

Translated from the Inuit by Dr Edmund Carpenter

Roses round the door

In the month of June the grass grows high
And round my cottage thick-leaved branches
sway.
There is not a bird but delights in the place
where it rests
And I too — love my thatched cottage.
I have done my ploughing:
I have sown my seed.
Again I have time to sit and read my books.
In the narrow lane there are no deep ruts:
Often my friends' carriages turn back.
In high spirits I pour out my spring wine
And pluck the lettuce growing in my garden.
A gentle rain comes stealing up from the east
And a sweet wind bears it company.
My thoughts float idly over the story of King
Chou
My eyes wander over the pictures of Hills and
Seas.
At a single glance I survey the whole Universe.
He will never be happy, who such pleasures
fail to please!

T'ao Ch'ien (AD 365–427)

● What damage is done to the environment by different lifestyles, including ours? What can we learn from other people's lifestyles? What can they learn from ours? To what extent are traditional lifestyles changing and what is our part in this? Is it important that different ways of life should be preserved? What do the children find most/least attractive about a particular lifestyle? What might a Yanomami Indian find most/least attractive about our lives?

● Compare your own and the children's way of life with the lifestyle of another group of people. Or discuss differing lifestyles in general, using a variety of examples.

● How does the climate affect the way people live? What different *kinds* of food are there and how do people get them? Where does *our* food come from? What are shelters built from and why are those materials used? What possessions do we and other people have and who makes them? Emphasise the wonderful ability of people to make use of whatever is at hand, including modern technology.

● Children can also consider how modern technology helps people to live in difficult environments. (For example, many Inuits have found snowmobiles very useful.) How do scientists survive in Antarctica and even, for short times, on the moon?

Activities

♦ Perhaps different classes could each study one particular group of people and how they survive in their environment. Using information books, they can discover facts about climate, vegetation, wildlife and so on. The results could be presented as a series of exciting 'follow-up' assemblies, with painted backdrops, music, poetry and drama.

♦ Children could make lists of things they 'couldn't do without', 'would find hard to give up' or 'don't really need at all'. What measure of agreement is there? Is an adult's list the same? Children with experience of boating or camping holidays could talk about the joys or otherwise of more basic living.

♦ Suppose there was an expedition to Mars to set up a small colony. What would the expedition need to take? Children could work in a group to compile an inventory.

CHANGES, CHANGES

Purposes

1 To think about the advantages and disadvantages of both rural and urban life and consider how the drawbacks might be alleviated.

2 To be aware of changes in the local neighbourhood and why they happen.

3 To think about the causes and effects of change in a more global way.

Starting-points

■ Invite someone who has lived in the area a long time to talk about how it has changed. Alternatively, make a display of old local photographs, and encourage children to talk about the changes.

■ Ask children who have moved house to describe for the others what it was like to leave all that was familiar and move to a new place.

■ Choose a development issue suitable for your area, such as the building of a by-pass or a new shopping centre, and present the basic proposition, maybe in the role of a planner at a public meeting. Prime different teachers around the hall to interrupt with arguments for and against. The children can join in and perhaps, at the end, give a judgement.

■ Ask some children to prepare a role play. They are a family who are going to move to a different part of the country to be near their grandparents, who live on the very edge of a large town. They have to decide whether to live in the town itself or out in the country.

■ Read the true account *I'm not going to be a bum*, and ask the children for their reactions. How was Victor trying to improve his life? Is it right that children should work? Apart from working to earn money, is there anything children in your school could do to improve the quality of life for themselves and others?

The town mouse and the country mouse

The two mice try out each other's life styles, but neither is much impressed.

One day a smart young town mouse went out for a stroll in the country and was caught in a shower of rain. He crept under a hedge to shelter, but raindrops trickled through the leaves and he got soaked and cold. And to make matters worse, he was hungry! He shivered and swore and sneezed, aachoo!

'Bless you,' said a soft little voice, and he turned around to see a little fieldmouse smiling at him.

'Come home with me,' she said, 'and you can dry out those wet clothes!'

In no time at all, the town mouse found himself warm and snug in the fieldmouse's little round house, which was cleverly thatched to keep the rain out.

'This is the life,' he sighed, as he tucked into fresh corn and nuts, apples, and honey. 'So healthy! So rural! So rustic!'

He liked it so much, he stayed for the whole weekend. The rain stopped, and he enjoyed several strolls in the fresh air, sunbathing in the garden, and even going to collect beechnuts in the woods. But he found it hard to sleep at night. There were so many noises, birds twittering, night animals rustling by, and once an owl screeching. And on the second day, he started getting a bit bored — there wasn't so much to do, or see — 'Not like the town,' he said to his hostess. 'There is always so much happening there! And so much food! You can pick and choose as much as you like. Really, my dear, you must come and visit. Town life is so exciting for a mouse these days!'

The fieldmouse had never been far from her field, and she found the town mouse strange and exciting. Finally she agreed to go back with him for a short visit. 'I can only spare a few days,' she said.

'Of course, my friend,' agreed the town mouse, 'but after you've tasted the delights of the town — who knows? You may well stay on and
on . . .'

The two hitched a ride on a farmer's lorry, and the fieldmouse watched, wide-eyed, through a crack in the floor. Cars, buses, houses, streets rushed by in a whirl of colours and lights. By the time they arrived at the town mouse's flat — down a ventilation shaft and under the floorboards of a big house — she was feeling slightly dazed and deafened, but very excited. It was like a palace down there — so big and comfortable.

'Now, what about a little snack?' said the town mouse.

The snack turned out to be a feast for the little fieldmouse, who had never seen even half the exotic foods which the town mouse piled onto the table. The little mouse ate till she thought she would burst. Afterwards some friends dropped in, on their way to the theatre, and the little fieldmouse listened in delight as they talked of films and plays and fashions. Then they all drank wine and danced to the sound of the record-player in the flat upstairs until finally the little mouse fell asleep on a pile of silken cushions.

But a few hours later she woke up, feeling thirsty and a bit sick. She longed for some fresh spring water but all she could find was wine. Then, suddenly, the whole house started shaking and rumbling like thunder. It was only a passing articulated lorry, but it seemed like an earthquake to the little mouse. After that she couldn't get back to sleep. Every car braking or door slamming made her jump. And when the people above got up and started walking around overhead, it was even worse. She soon had a throbbing headache. Next morning she couldn't face any of the special breakfast her friend had prepared. 'A little fresh air,' she muttered, 'I'll just have a little walk and I'll feel better.'

'Be careful,' warned the town mouse, but his words were drowned out by a police siren out in the street. The little fieldmouse crept out of the ventilation shaft, quite unprepared to meet an army of feet rushing up and down, as people hurried by. High heels, heavy boots, prams, bags and bicycles whizzed here and there, with the little mouse dodging in and out. But suddenly — GRR! Two huge dogs on the ends of leads came leaping at her and a cat appeared from behind a dustbin. In a panic she jumped into the road to escape. But just at that moment a farmer's lorry came rumbling slowly past and she leaped again . . .

As she clung for dear life to the bottom of the lorry, the little mouse whispered, 'The town is no place for a mouse!'

When his little friend did not return, the town mouse was sorry. 'She must have gone home,' he thought. 'What a shame! The countryside is no place for a mouse!'

And so they both lived happily ever after. But as to which one was right — well, what do you think?

Traditional story, retold by Helen East

The government said

The government said,
'Right now go over to Sheppey
and do up the roads.'
And so they came,
and put up the lights
which shone through the window
all through the night.
Then they dug up the footings
and laid down the pipes.
Then they laid down the roads
and now the lorries come whistling
along with their loads.

Julie Dewberry

Where are they?

Where have the flowers, the bees they fed
And the fieldmice gone
Now they've removed the hedges
And made four fields into one?

The long straight hedges
That stretched like streets of a town,
Where the spiders hung their webs
And made their home, are broken down.

Roaring monster machines
Make the land their own
Now the many trees are felled
And birds that nested there have flown.

Stanley Cook

Fact box 1

The following are very brief examples of how the lives of some indigenous peoples are being disrupted. To discuss the topic in more detail, you will need further information (see *Resources*, page 100).

Some Australian Aborigines who have lived more or less undisturbed until recent times are now under threat because minerals have been found on their land.

The Amazonian rainforest, where the Yanomami people live, is being destroyed for logging, ranching, farming, road building and mineral extraction.

In the Arab states, more and more marginal land is being settled by farmers. This means the more arid areas are overgrazed and Bedouin herders find it harder to follow their traditional way of life.

In Canada, the government encourages Inuits to live in permanent villages. They rarely hunt now because most animals avoid human settlements. There is little paid work for the Inuits to do, and alcoholism and depression are widespread.

continued

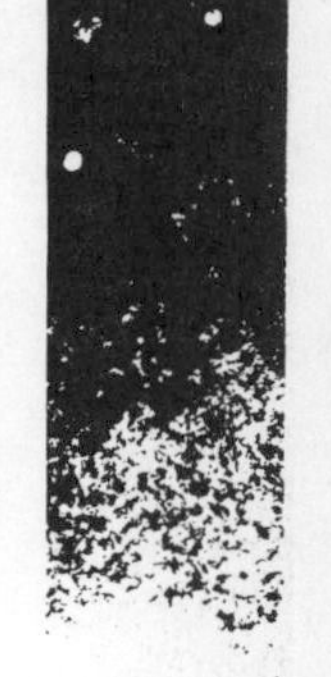

Fact box 2

Over 30 New Towns have been built in the countryside in Britain since World War II.

Since 1945, in Britain 95% of hay meadows have disappeared, as well as 80% of chalk downlands and 40% of native broadleaf forest.

In 1940 one in 100 people lived in cities of over 1 million; in 1980 it was one in 10.

In 1850 the population of London was about 1 million; in 1980 it was over 8 million, but now it is declining again.

Every night thousands of people sleep rough in London. Some build their own 'homes' out of cardboard boxes and old mattresses.

In Mexico City 1.5 million poor people (out of the city's total population of 17 million) live on a dry lake bed. In summer it is thick with flying dust; in winter it is a swamp.

Millions of people live in shanty towns on the edges of big cities, in homes built from scrap materials. They usually have no water, sewage or electricity. Without their labour, many Third World cities would grind to a halt.

In Dallas and Los Angeles half the land area is taken up by roads, car parks and garages, and petrol stations.

Discussion

- Encourage children to think about some of the issues behind changes in the local area. Why are they being made? Who benefits? Does anyone suffer? Does the environment suffer? Who makes the decisions? What would life be like if there were never any changes? Is life in the area better than it used to be, or worse?
- People who move to a new area may find it disturbing or exciting. What would the children miss most if they moved? How would they feel? How would they set about making themselves feel at home? Why do people move? Who makes the decisions?

I'm not going to be a bum

Victor Raul Quispe is 11 years old. He lives in a sprawling, over-populated, dusty shantytown on the edge of Lima, a big city in Peru. His family are very poor and they all have to work very hard to make a living. Victor often helps his mother selling potatoes in the nearby market, but he also has his own job, selling sweets to people in the street.

'I started working when I was seven,' says Victor. 'I work because I've got to eat. When I'm grown up, I'm not going to be a bum, see? I'll know how to make a living and have my own money. I don't like selling candy as much as I did when I was a little kid, but I like making money. I spend it on shoes and school supplies. I give what's left to my mother.'

Most of Victor's friends work as well. They work whenever they can — after school, at weekends and in the holidays. They clean car windscreens at the traffic lights, or sell candles, or work in the market. They do whatever work they can find.

The children belong to an organisation which sets out to help young people help themselves. Victor's group meets every Friday night at someone's house.

'We sing, and play and talk about our experiences,' he says. 'We look at the problems faced by the kids in the district, especially their health problems — there isn't enough money for medicine. And we talk about how we can get our bosses to respect us. We try to get lots of kids involved, because, that way, we will be stronger.'

Unfortunately, some employers do not treat the children very well. One boy hurt his back carrying heavy crates, and his group went to the employer and persuaded her to pay for his medical care. The children help each other a lot. This group decided to work even harder and gave the extra money they earned to the injured boy. Victor's group help another boy whose parents are away a lot, by organising a rota to take care of his little brothers and sisters. And they try to improve their lives in other ways. Where Victor lives, the streets are often filthy and he and his friends got their parents to pressurise the local council to improve the rubbish collection.

Despite his hard life, Victor is very hopeful. 'My dream is that other kids will not suffer hunger and misery. And adults won't just pity us, but show us affection and support. With support we can do anything!'

Mary Judith Ress

Motorway

Motorway — motorway — motorway,
Never stay — never stay — never stay,
Broad bridge ribbon overrides us,
Giant-strides us,
Manmade dinosaurus, dwarfs us.

Motor-metal fleas fly by,
Whining car horns grow and die,
Skim the giant's broad black back,
White line,
Sign post,
Motor track.

Listen in your sleep, dream deep,
Hear him stamp his giant feet,
Beating, beating, street on street,
Motorway — motorway — motorway.

Marion Lines

How can you buy or sell the sky, the warmth of the land? This idea is strange to us. If we do not own the freshness of the air and the sparkle of the water, how can you buy them? Every part of this earth is sacred to my people. Every shining pine needle, every sandy shore, every mist in the dark woods, every clearing and humming insect is holy in the memory and experience of my people.

Chief Seathl

Demolition

Families gone,
Boards in the windows,
Houses alone,
Waiting the end.
Ruin is near,
Street in its death-throes;
Leaving a scar
No one can mend.

Swing the hammer!
Fell the trees!
Bring the Crescent to its knees!

See where they fall,
Lintel and staircase.
Batter them all
Flat to the ground!
Chimneystacks tumbled,
Skylight and fireplace,
Houses are humbled —
Crescent is down.

Swing the hammer!
Fell the trees!
Bring the Crescent to its knees!

Marion Lines

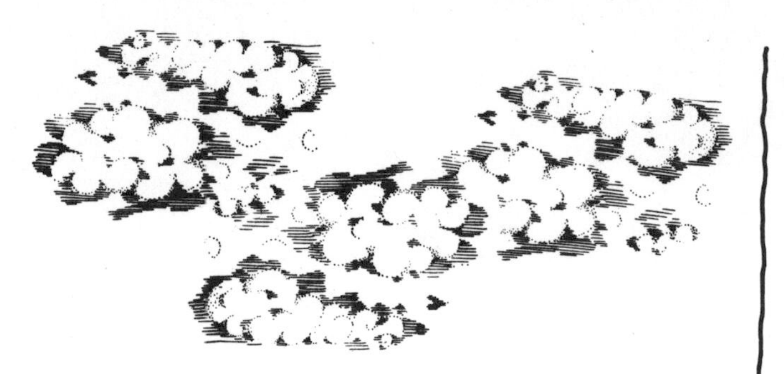

Building a skyscraper

They're building a skyscraper
Near our street.
Its height will be nearly
One thousand feet.

It covers completely
A city block.
They drilled its foundation
Through solid rock.

They made its framework
Of great steel beams
With riveted joints
And welded seams.

A swarm of workmen
Strain and strive,
Like busy bees
In a honeyed hive.

Building a skyscraper
Into the air
While crowds of people
Stand and stare.

Higher and higher
The tall towers rise
Like Jacob's ladder
Into the skies.

James S. Tippett

- You could go on to talk about the plight of some indigenous peoples whose homes and way of life are threatened by modern development and by the demands of other people. The particular facts will vary, but the issues are the same: whose rights take precedence? Can a compromise be reached?
- What is it like to live in the countryside? How is life affected by different seasons and weather? How do people get around? Is it good to live in a small community? What are the disadvantages of rural life? How could matters be improved?
- How should the countryside be used? Should the needs of commuters for housing and transport be met by building on open space? Or should it be for recreation – for walking, fishing, camping, skiing? Should factories be built in the country to bring employment? Or should the land all be used for growing crops? Or managed for wildlife? Who actually makes the decisions?
- Why are more and more people moving to towns? Talk about some of the 'pull' factors (lots to do, higher wages, easy public transport, shops nearby . . .) and the 'push' factors (increasing mechanisation of farms, drought . . .).
- How do cities cater for the needs of the inhabitants? How could life be improved? Ideas might range from easing traffic congestion to alleviating social problems such as the violence and racism that sometimes result from people living closely together. Does it matter that people in cities are out of touch with nature? How do they notice the passing seasons in the city? Could nature be brought more into towns?
- Children may have very negative images of people who live in shanty towns or the 'cardboard city' dwellers in developed countries. Encourage them to see that such homes are not a problem – they are people's own solutions to grinding poverty or other social evils. How can such people best be helped and who should be responsible?

continued

A poem for the rainforest

Song of the Xingu Indian

They have stolen my land;
the birds have flown,
my people gone.
My rainbow rises over sand;
my river falls on stone.

Amazonian Timbers, Inc.

This can go next —
here, let me draw the line.
That's roughly right,
give or take
a few square miles or so.
I'll list the ones we need.
No, burn the rest.
Only take the best,
we're not in this
for charity,
Replant? No —
you're new to this, I see!
There's plenty more
where that comes from,
no problem! Finish here —
and then move on.

Dusk

Butterfly, blinded
by smoke, drifts like torn paper
to the flames below.

Shadows

Spider,
last of her kind,
scuttles underground, safe;
prepares her nest for young ones. But
none come.

The Coming of Night

Sun sinks
behind the high canopy;
the iron men are silenced.

The moon rises,
the firefly wakes.
Death pauses for a night.

Song of the Forest

Our land has gone,
our people flown.
Sun scorches our earth,
our river weeps.

Judith Nicholls

My moccasins have not walked

My moccasins have not walked
Among the giant forest trees

My leggings have not brushed
Against the fern and berry bush

My medicine pouch has not been filled
with roots and herbs and sweetgrass

My hands have not fondled the spotted fawn

My eyes have not beheld
The golden rainbow of the north

My hair has not been adorned
With the eagle feather

Yet
My dreams are dreams of these
My heart is one with them
The scent of them caresses my soul

Duke Redbird

Activities

- ♦ What evidence can children find locally of life in times past? For example, coal-hole covers, horse troughs, street names . . .
- ♦ If there is a major change going on locally, children could investigate it – why is it happening? Who will benefit? What do local people think about it?
- ♦ Ask children to imagine that the local council are planning to pull down their home to make a new park. They plan to rehouse residents some distance away. Children can write a letter to a friend saying how they feel.
- ♦ Children could investigate further a particular instance of a threat to an indigenous people, and perhaps create a drama to present at a future assembly.
- ♦ Children can make two lists, of the advantages and disadvantages of living in towns. To what extent do the children agree amongst themselves? What do their parents think? A lot of work could be done including writing, map-making, models and pictures on how cities can be improved for the people living there.
- ♦ In pairs, children could choose a proposed development of some sort, and each write a biased newspaper article about it, one favourable, and the other opposed on environmental grounds.
- ♦ A web diagram could be made showing the effects of a single action such as axing a bus route or closing a village school. Encourage the children to think of alternative solutions, given the conditions which brought about the proposed change.

WHERE YOU LIVE

Purposes

1 To identify with the local area.
2 To celebrate the good things about it.
3 To consider how it could be improved.

Starting-points

■ Think of somewhere local which has a definite atmosphere and describe it for the children to guess – 'This place feels very unfriendly. There is a long wall along one side and office blocks on the other. I always hurry along this street.' Or, 'This is a very peaceful spot, with the sound of running water, where I like to sit on a bench and daydream.' Ask children to describe other places in the same way.

■ Have two large sheets of paper to write on, and ask the children to say alternately what they like and dislike about the area.

■ Children can prepare and read aloud one of the poems about weather. Does the weather or the time of day affect the children's feelings about where *they* live? How does it change the character of a place?

■ Choose some children to role-play a situation where one group are seen by another in the act of spraying graffiti on the school wall, or breaking glass at a bus stop. How might the scene differ if one group were adults?

continued

Hard cheese

The grown-ups are all safe,
Tucked up inside,
Where they belong.

They doze into the telly,
Bustle through the washing-up,
Snore into the fire,
Rustle through the paper.

They're all there,
Out of harm's way.

Now it's *our* street:
All the backyards,
All the gardens,
All the shadows,
All the dark corners,
All the privet-hedges,
All the lampposts,
All the doorways.

Here is an important
announcement:
The army of occupation
Is confined to barracks.
Hooray.

We're the natives.
We creep out at night,
Play everywhere,
Swing on *all* the lampposts,
Split your gizzard?

Then, about nine o'clock,
They send out search-parties.

We can hear them coming.
And we crouch
In the garden-sheds,
Behind the dustbins,

Up the alley-ways,
Inside the dustbins,
Or stand stock-still,
And pull ourselves in,
As thin as a pin,
Behind the lampposts.

And they stand still,
And peer into the dark,
They take a deep breath —
You can hear it for miles —
And, then, they bawl,
They shout, they caterwaul:
'J-i-i-i-i-mmeeee!'
'Timeforbed. D'youhearme?'
'M-a-a-a-a-reeee!'
'J-o-o-o-o-hnneeee!'
'S-a-a-a-a-mmeeee!'
'Mary!' 'Jimmy!'
'Johnny!' 'Sammy!'
Like cats. With very big mouths.

Then we give ourselves up,
Prisoners-of-war.
Till tomorrow night.

But just you wait.
One of these nights
We'll hold out,
We'll lie doggo,
And wait, and wait,
Till they just give up
And mumble
And go to bed.
You just wait.
They'll see!

Justin St John

Discussion

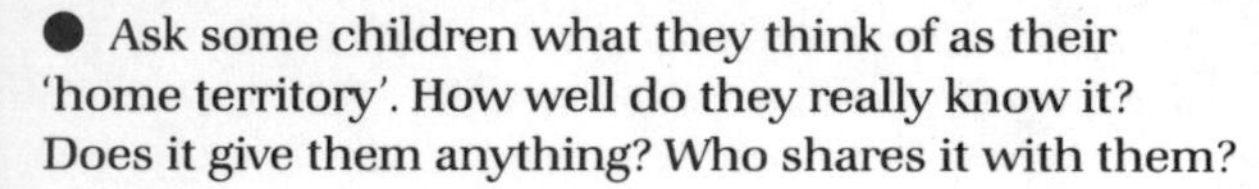

- Ask some children what they think of as their 'home territory'. How well do they really know it? Does it give them anything? Who shares it with them?
- When they are talking about places they like and dislike, encourage them to express why they like a place and what gives it its special atmosphere. Do they all feel the same way about certain places?
- How well does the area serve the needs of different local people – the children themselves, elderly people, people with and without cars . . .?
- If the children have mentioned a place they don't like, encourage them to think about how it could be improved. Who would be the best people to carry out the improvement? Would anyone suffer?
- If you are prepared to take it further, focus the discussion on something the children could take positive action about. (See 'Activities' below.)

Walking in autumn with Grandad

'There's a change in the air,' Grandad says,
'A chill in the breeze, now Autumn's come.
You can hear it too, if you listen,
listen to the leaves and their whisperings.'

Each evening now he calls and we trek
over the field towards the trees,
where rabbits play in the last of the sun
till Grandad claps his hands and they run for
cover.

Each time we find something special:
Velvet foot toadstools on tree trunks.
'Dangerous,' he says. 'Don't touch those.'
Or chestnuts to roast on gran's open range,
or jumbo size conkers that others have
missed.
'I always knew the best places,' he says.

We collect the seeds from sycamores
And flip them into the air.
He jokes how the spread of leaves on the
ground
looks a lot like our front room carpet,
then points to a squirrel, high in an oak,
And we watch as he gathers acorns
to store in some secret place.

An early gale has uprooted trees,
laid them low, like felled giants.
Grandad climbed them when he was a lad,
he and his mates, agile as monkeys,
till down they shinned to comb the hedge
for cobnuts or late blackberries.

Already new trees have been planted,
sturdy saplings that bend but won't break
if another gale comes thumping through.

Grandad says, 'Be off with you, run home
while I take it slow.' But I stick to his step
and guide his arm as he carefully climbs the
stile.
It wouldn't take much to knock *him* down,
now winter looks over his shoulder
and winds are poised to return.

Brian Moses

Going to school in town

A long walk,
half a mile or more,
over four noisy roads, before
I reach the high school wall,
covered with pictures in chalk,
and hear the playground bell call
us into our lines.
I go past twenty shops, a shellfish stall,
and through a smelly tunnel where
the sun never shines,
and then across the square,
around a corner by the old King's Head
and there must wait,
do what my teacher said,
for the green light to say
that I can cross the road;
bus after bus every day
and lorries each with a different load.
And then I am
dodging the factory where they make jam,
and at last run into school there,
ready for Mr Smith and morning prayer.

Leonard Clark

Blind alley

There's a turning I must pass
Often four times in a day,
Narrow, rather dark, with grass
Growing, a neglected way;

Two long walls, a tumbled shed,
Bushes shadowing each wall —
When I've wondered where it led;
People say, Nowhere at all.

But if that is true, oh why
Should this turning be at all?
Some time, in the daylight, I
Will creep up along the wall;

For it somehow makes you think,
It has such a secret air,
It might lead you to the brink
Of — oh well, of anywhere!

Some time I will go. And see,
Here's the turning just in sight,
Full of shadows beckoning me!
Some time, yes. But not tonight.

Eleanor Farjeon

Rain

A driv, a rav,
a murr, a hagger,
a rug, a dagg,
a hellyiefer.

Orkney names for rain

I like the town on rainy nights

I like the town on rainy nights
When everything is wet
When all the town is sparkling bright
And streets of shining jet

When all the rain about the town
Is like a looking-glass
And all the lights are upside down
Below me as I pass

In all the pools are cloudy skies
All down the dirty streets
But a fairy city gleams and lies
Below me at my feet

Jonathan Watson (aged 13)

London snow (extract)

When men were all asleep the snow came
flying,
In large white flakes falling on the city brown,
Stealthily and perpetually settling and loosely
lying,
Hushing the latest traffic of the drowsy town;
Deadening, muffling, stifling its murmurs
failing;
Lazily and incessantly floating down and
down;
Silently sifting and veiling road, roof and
railing;
Hiding difference, making unevenness even,
Into angles and crevices softly drifting and
sailing.

Robert Bridges

Activities

◆ Children could devise a scoresheet to be used in local streets. They could give marks out of ten, a grade from (A) to (E), or tick multiple-choice boxes for features such as amount of litter, number of broken paving slabs, number of trees, amount of open space . . .

◆ Ask the children to look for one new thing each day that they have never noticed before. Remind them to look up at the skyline, down at the ground, through holes in fences, over walls . . . Ask for some reports at subsequent assemblies.

◆ Organise an exhibition of children's photographs or drawings of the area, with categories such as 'interesting buildings', 'local wildlife' or 'eyesores'.

◆ A group could work together to write an 'anthem' for the area, or for the school, extolling its virtues. If they are not confident musically, they could write words to a familiar tune. This could be extended to planning a whole festival – perhaps another assembly – for your area, looking at symbols which might represent it, its history, and things to celebrate.

◆ Give the children a local map and ask them to work out a plan for improving the area.

◆ Perhaps the children can take some action to improve the school environment – making a mural to brighten up a dull corner, or painting markings on the playground for games. Larger-scale improvements might include tree planting, wildlife gardens or playground structures. The more the children are involved, the greater will be their sense of identification with the results.

◆ The school might also get involved in projects such as organising a local litter campaign, clearing a pond, or adopting a corner of the park. Where there is nothing practical the school or the children can do themselves, they could write to the relevant authorities with their suggestions.

◆ Encourage the children to look at the physical features of the area. Perhaps they could make up fantasy stories to explain the origin of certain hills, lakes, or woods . . .

The playground

In the playground
At the back of our house
There have been some changes.

They said the climbing frame was
NOT SAFE
So they sawed it down.

They said the paddling pool was
NOT SAFE
So they drained it dry.

They said the see-saw was
NOT SAFE
So they took it away.

They said the sandpit was
NOT SAFE
So they fenced it in.

They said the playground was
NOT SAFE
So they locked it up.

Sawn down
Drained dry
Taken away
Fenced in
Locked up

How do you feel?
Safe?

Michael Rosen

Sea fever

I must go down to the seas again, to the lonely sea and the sky,
And all I ask is a tall ship and a star to steer her by,
And the wheel's kick and the wind's song and the white sail's shaking,
And a grey mist on the sea's face, and a grey dawn breaking.

I must go down to the seas again, for the call of the running tide,
Is a wild call and clear call that may not be denied;
And all I ask is a windy day with the white clouds flying,
And the flung spray and the blown spume, and the sea-gulls crying.

I must go down to the seas again, to the vagrant gypsy life,
To the gull's way and the whale's way where the wind's like a whetted knife;
And all I ask is a merry yarn from a laughing fellow-rover,
And quiet sleep and a sweet dream when the long trick's over.

John Masefield

The conversion of Mr Bean

We used to be fond of the old village pond
but the pond wasn't there anymore —
just a battered old bed and some trolleys
instead
with some rubbish, and tins by the score.

Mrs Bean made a scene on the old village
green
and she marched to the tip with her son.
Then they heaved out the mess, but they're
potty, I guess
'cos they actually thought it was fun.

She wasn't a fool, for the new village pool
is enormous, and sparkles with life.
Now ducks dabble round it and children
surround it
and all of it thanks to my wife.

Now I sit there on guard and sometimes it's
hard
as I lounge with my rod and my line.
You can now catch a pike instead of a bike
and as for the view, it is fine.

Marian Swinger

My place

When I need a rest, do I sink into a chair,
Watch the tv, read a magazine?
No, I sit on my mountain way up in the sky,
And listen to silences floating by,
floating by.

When I need a change, do I hide myself away,
Shut the door and be alone?
No, I go to the seashore where the children play,
Building their castles on sunny days,
sunny days.

When I'm feeling sad, do I hang my head down low?
Sit and wait for it to pass?
No, I run through my green park fast as I can go,
Seeing the clouds swaying to and fro,
to and fro.

When I need to think, do I sit upon my bed?
Do I scratch my head and sigh?
No I walk in my city, through the busy streets,
Watching the buskers and feeling free,
feeling free.

Words and music: Niki Davies

FOOD

Food is essential to life: our bodies need energy foods to allow us to move, to keep warm and to keep our various internal organs working; we need protein to enable us to grow and to repair and replace cells; we need fibre for our digestive system, and vitamins and minerals to keep our bodies functioning smoothly.

Because it is so central to our lives, food has always played an important role in human society. The tradition of hospitality – offering food and drink to strangers – is very strong in some cultures, often those where food might be scarce. Symbolic food is associated with many religious festivals and great feasts often mark special occasions both religious and secular. In many religions, past and present, offerings of food are made to a deity, to give thanks or as a propitiation. At harvest festivals, it is the food itself which is the focus of the ceremonies, whether it is wheat, rice, or fish. People all over the world have felt the need to join together to celebrate the end of the season's hard work, the provision of food for the future and to thank their gods.

On a day-to-day level, obtaining, preparing and eating food have traditionally been communal activities. Hunters of bison or impala have found it more effective to band together; a rice paddy can be planted more efficiently by a group than by a single hand; pounding grain to a flour is both more enjoyable and easier when the task is shared. And when the food is ready, sitting down to eat with one's companions is for many people often the high spot of the day – a time to relax, to share news and stories and cement social bonds. In industrialised, so-called 'developed' countries, where life moves at a faster and faster pace, we may be in danger of losing some of this shared experience, along with any sense of identification with the natural cycles of growing food.

For many people in the poorer countries, sadly it is not time and inclination which is lacking, but the food itself. While obesity is prevalent in the 'developed' world, many people in Africa, Asia and South America do not get enough to eat. We hear about the major famines when thousands may die, but millions of people in the world are malnourished *all the time*, to an extent that they cannot function properly. Meanwhile, the 'developed' world over-produces food, which is sometimes left to rot. There are no easy answers. Politics, unequal trading, war, corruption, unfair land distribution, over-consumption by the richer nations and overpopulation play a bigger part than climate.

Science and technological farming methods have increased food production to an enormous extent and, until recently, it was theoretically possible for the world to produce enough food for everyone. But only now are we beginning to see that such advances bring their own problems which may, in the long run, prove disastrous. Animals are husbanded in ways which are not only cruel to them, but which carry increasing risks of disease to people who eat them. Pesticides build up in the soil and in the bodies of living things – including ourselves; nitrates poison our water supplies; and topsoil is disappearing at an alarming rate. Something has to change if future generations are to be fed.

PREPARING AND SHARING FOOD

Purposes

1 To think about sharing food as a social bond and as a way of celebrating.

2 To celebrate the wide diversity of food and ways of cooking.

Starting-points

■ Invite parents from a variety of cultural backgrounds to bring in the ingredients for a meal, and, as far as possible, demonstrate how it is prepared. Or children could describe a meal such as they have at home, perhaps with a big painting of it.

■ Set a table as if for a celebration meal, with napkins, glasses, flowers, candles . . . or perhaps for a typical children's birthday party, or a wedding, or a special meal connected with one of the religions represented in your school. Ask the children what it might be for, and introduce a discussion on celebratory meals.

■ Sharing food and celebration feasts play a part in most religions. Invite people from various religions to talk about the significance of food, and maybe fasting, if it is appropriate, in their traditions.

Fact box

The word 'companions' comes from the Latin *com* (with) and *panis* (bread). So companions are people who share a meal together.

continued

Baking bread

I love the
friday night
smell of
mammie baking
bread — creeping
up to me in
bed, and tho
zzzz I'll fall
asleep, before i
even get a
bite — when
morning come,
you can bet
I'll meet a
kitchen table
laden with
bread, still
warm and fresh
salt bread
sweet bread
crisp and brown
and best of all
coconut buns
THAT's why
I love the
friday night
smell of mammie
baking bread
putting me to
sleep, dreaming
of jumping from
the highest branch
of the jamoon tree
into the red water
creek
beating calton
run and catching
the biggest fish
in the world
plus, getting
the answers right
to every single
sum
that every day
in my dream
begins and ends
with the friday
night smell of
mammie baking
bread, and
coconut buns
of course.

Marc Matthews

Guinea corn

Guinea corn, I long to see you
Guinea corn, I long to plant you
Guinea corn, I long to mould you
Guinea corn, I long to weed you
Guinea corn, I long to hoe you
Guinea corn, I long to top you
Guinea corn, I long to cut you
Guinea corn, I long to dry you
Guinea corn, I long to beat you
Guinea corn, I long to trash you
Guinea corn, I long to parch you
Guinea corn, I long to grind you
Guinea corn, I long to turn you
Guinea corn, I long to eat you

Anon

Then let man look at his food

(and how we provide it):
For that we pour forth water in abundance,
And we split the earth in fragments,
And produce therein corn,
And grapes and nutritious plants,
And olives and dates,
And enclosed gardens, dense with lofty trees,
And fruits and fodder —
For use and convenience to you and your
cattle.

Islamic: from the Qur'an

Discussion

- What are the children's favourite foods? What would be a really typical meal in their family? What do they know about the kinds of foods eaten in other countries? Why should people from different countries, or even different areas of the same country, eat different foods? How willing are the children to try new foods?
- Who does the cooking at home? How long is spent on food preparation? What are the advantages and disadvantages of instant food? Does the whole family sit down together? Who does the clearing up?
- What celebratory meals do the children have? Who shares them? Does anything special happen? Is the food always the same? Do the various items have any special significance? Do the family join together in preparing it? Are there any traditions associated with the preparation? Why is food so often a part of celebrations?
- In what other ways is food important in religion? Why should it be so central to people's spiritual lives? You could have a general discussion, or take up any of the following questions in more detail.

Why do people say grace at mealtimes? Why do many Christians eat bread as part of a service? What is the significance of Pancake Day? Why do people give Easter eggs? Why do Hindus not eat beef, and people of many religions not eat pork? Why do Buddhists and Jains think it is wrong to eat meat at all? What is the significance of the Sikh *langar* – the communal meal at the end of every service? What is the feast of Passover? Why should fasting be an important part of many religions?

Sayings and graces

Some hae meat and canna eat,
And some wad eat that want it;
But we hae meat, and we can eat,
And sae the Lord be thankit.

The Selkirk Grace

Blessed are you, O Lord our God, King of the world, who gives food to all the creatures of the world. Blessed are you, O God, giver of food to all.

Jewish

O you who believe. Do not forbid yourselves those things which Allah has made it lawful for you to eat, and do not take more than you need.

Islamic: from the Qur'an

When eating bamboo sprouts,
remember the man who planted them.

Chinese

Once when Jesus was having a meal at someone's house, he said to his host, 'When you give a lunch or a dinner, don't ask your friends, relations and rich neighbours. They will be sure to invite you back, and then you will be paid for what you did. No, when you have a feast, invite the poor, the crippled, the lame and the blind; because they can't pay you back, you will be blessed.'

Christian

Baucis and Philemon

The importance of hospitality and sharing are demonstrated in this ancient Greek story from Ovid's Metamorphoses.

There came a time, long, long ago, when the gods decided to travel the earth. Zeus, the king of the gods, and Hermes, his messenger, came from their heavenly home on Mount Olympus. They made themselves look like ordinary men. They came to a place where there were good farms and fine houses, and the people clearly had plenty to eat and plenty of wine to drink. The gods thought that in a place where there was such plenty they would easily find someone to give them a meal and a bed for the night. So they went round, knocking on doors, asking for a simple meal and a place to sleep. But no one would give them so much as a crust of bread and a cup of water. They knocked on a hundred doors, but no one gave them anything.

At last they left that village, and walked towards a very small, poor-looking hut a little way away. In this hut lived an old man called Philemon, and an old woman called Baucis. They had been married since they were quite young, and had always lived together happy and contented, although they were very poor. They saw the two strangers coming, and they did not wait to be asked. They ran out and invited them into the hut, to have supper and spend the night. Baucis and Philemon did not have anything ready to give the strangers to eat, but they hurried round and began to prepare a meal. Philemon fetched vegetables from the garden, and Baucis began to cook them, fetching a small piece of bacon to flavour the stew. And as they worked, they made their guests sit down by the fire, and chatted with them to make them feel welcome and at home.

At last the meal was ready, and Baucis began to lay the table. They only had two rough wooden chairs, but Baucis covered them with some cloths she had woven herself. The table was old and did not stand steady, so Philemon fetched a tile to put under one of the legs to make it steadier. There was no fine china or glass, but Baucis fetched their best clay bowls for the stew, and Philemon brought two wooden cups for the wine.

Then they served the meal to their guests. There were olives and hard bread, and the vegetable stew, and fruit and honeycomb that they had stored, and one small clay jug of wine — all they had. The two gods sat down to this simple meal, and ate hungrily, and drank the wine eagerly. But after a while, Philemon and Baucis noticed a strange thing. Philemon kept pouring the wine from the jug, but no matter how much the strangers drank, there was always plenty more in the jug!

Then Philemon and Baucis realised that their guests must be gods in disguise. In terror they knelt down before Zeus and Hermes. 'Please forgive us,' they said. 'The meal we have given you is not worthy of gods, and we have given it to you on clay plates, with only old chairs to sit on. What can we give you that is a proper sacrifice for the gods?'

'Do not fear,' said Zeus. 'We did not come for sacrifices. We came to see if people on earth will welcome strangers and give them food. Your neighbours gave us nothing, but you have given us the best you had. They will have what they deserve, and so will you. Follow me.'

So Baucis and Philemon followed the gods out of their hut and up the steep hillside. When they got to the top, Zeus said, 'Look down.' They looked, and saw that where the village had been, there was nothing but a huge lake. On the shores of this lake stood their old hut. But as they watched, they saw it changing. Their old and shabby hut turned into a beautiful temple to the gods.

And Baucis and Philemon lived happily in the temple, taking care of it for the gods. And when they were both very old, they stood outside the door together, arm in arm, gazing at the lake. As they stood there, they were changed. At exactly the same moment, Baucis and Philemon changed into two trees, their branches entwined together.

And people say that you can still see those two trees today, standing by the lake.

from Ovid's Metamorphoses, *retold by Elizabeth Breuilly and Sandra Palmer*

The silver rain

The Silver Rain
The Shining Sun
The fields where scarlet poppies run
And all the ripples of the wheat
Are in the bread that I do eat
And when I sit for every meal
And say a grace I always feel
That I am eating rain and sun
The fields where scarlet poppies run

Yasmin Isaacs (aged 10)

Activities

♦ Many investigations can be done into the foods the children eat regularly, based on facts they gather from keeping a daily food diary, or from class surveys, or by simply listing all the food they eat. What foods are most common? Are there some that all the children eat? What foods are considered special treats?

♦ A class collage could be made from food and drink pictures, and perhaps large text, cut from magazines. Food is also an ideal subject for soft sculpture. Using felt or scrap material embellished with embroidery, papier mâché or clay, children can make vegeburgers, iced cakes, or whole meals.

♦ Children can write their own mealtime graces.

♦ Is there a way your school mealtime could be improved?

♦ Organise a multicultural social evening for parents and children where either the adults bring food, or the children cook it during the day.

♦ Children could collaborate to write a poem, maybe with music, on the theme, 'food, glorious food', about their favourite things to eat.

UNFAIR SHARES

Purposes

1 To begin to understand world food distribution.

2 To consider some of the reasons why people don't have enough to eat.

3 To consider the moral issue of greed.

Starting-points

■ Write Gandhi's famous saying 'There is enough food on this Earth for everyone's need, but not everyone's greed' on large frieze paper or wallpaper, and unroll it slowly for the children to read. Explain a little about who Gandhi was, and then use the quotation to introduce a discussion.

■ Bring in 24 cakes or apples, and cut them in quarters. Choose 24 children to come to the front and distribute the food at random, so that:

6 (25%) have nothing/crumbs
6 (25%) have 1 slice each
6 (25%) have 3 slices each
5 (21%) have 10 slices each
1 (4%) has 22 slices

■ Ask the children how they feel about their portions, and they may suggest sharing more fairly. Explain that these proportions reflect world-wide food distribution, but that sharing more fairly is not so simple in a world context. Point out that in some countries all five groups exist, while others have two or more of the groups. What do they think is the position in their own country?

■ Prepare a supermarket bag with items from different countries, and display it with a large world map or globe. Children can take turns to unpack an item and, using coloured wool, attach each food item to the place it comes from. Or the name of the food could be written on a label and stuck on the map.

Fact box

More than one in ten people on the planet do not get enough food to keep healthy.

The average American throws away ten rubbish bins of food a year.

The EEC produces more food than it needs or can sell. Food 'mountains' are sometimes left to rot or are thrown away.

The average daily calorie requirement for an adult is 2400. In the USA, on average, people get about 3658 calories, and in India about 1880.

One-third of British people are obese. About £250 million is spent annually on slimming aids.

The amount of food given to pets in France is equivalent to the quantity needed to feed 12 million children.

When food aid was sent by voluntary organisations to Ethiopia during a famine, some of the donated packets of lentils had 'Produce of Ethiopia' on the label.

One of the biggest exports from Honduras is bananas. Many people in Honduras do not get enough to eat, because they have no land on which to grow food and cannot earn enough on the banana plantations to buy it.

Meat for hamburgers in Britain usually comes from Europe, but the cattle are often fed on soya beans grown in Brazil on land that used to be rainforest.

An animal has to eat about 8kg of grain to produce 1kg of meat.

Discussion

● Children may not realise that many people are hungry all the time, not just when a major famine occurs. Ask them about their own experience of hunger. When they get home from school and say they are 'starving', is it really true?

● Why do we need food? Help them to realise that when people do not get enough to eat over long periods, it makes it harder for them to work, they are more likely to get ill, and children do not develop properly and may die from quite minor illnesses.

● The issues about world hunger are very complex but, using the fact box, you can introduce some of the ideas. Who is responsible? Is there anything *we* can or

Hunger

This is hunger. An animal
all fangs and eyes.
It cannot be distracted or deceived
It is not satisfied with one meal
It is not content
with a lunch or a dinner.
Always threatens blood.
Roars like a lion, squeezes like a boa,
thinks like a person.
The specimen before you
was captured in India (outskirts of Bombay)
but it exists in a more or less savage state
in many other places.
Please stand back.

Nicolas Guillen

Goha's guest

Goha invited a friend round to his house. He put a plate piled high with food in front of his friend and the man quickly ate it all up. Goha put another plate of food down. The man ate it all up. Again and again, Goha rushed off to fetch more beans, more rice, and more chick-peas. This food was what he had got ready for his own dinner and for the next day's dinner as well.

Finally there was nothing left to eat. Then this man said, 'I must go now — I'm on my way to the doctor because, you see, I've lost my appetite — I'm a bit off my food.'

You can imagine, Goha was horrified — so he said, 'Well, please, please, whatever you do, don't come back when you get your appetite back.'

Some people don't know just how greedy they are, do they?

An Egyptian tale

The lion's share

A lion, a tiger, a panther and a jackal once went out hunting together. They hunted for a long time and finally caught a gazelle, a wild boar and a hare. When the hunt was over, the lion said to the tiger, 'Now, tiger, you divide the booty between us!'

The tiger thought for a moment and then said, 'The lion will get the gazelle, I shall keep the wild boar, and the jackal and the panther can share the hare between them!'

When the lion heard this, he growled angrily and leapt at the tiger. With one blow he broke the tiger's leg, and then he said, 'Tiger, you don't know how to divide things. You try, jackal!'

The jackal picked up the gazelle and put it in front of the lion, and said, 'There, mighty lion, that's your breakfast!'

Then he took the wild boar, placed it in front of the lion too, and said, 'There, mighty lion, that's your dinner. The rest of us will be satisfied with the hare.'

'Excellent,' growled the lion, 'That's the kind of sharing I like. Tell me, jackal, where did you learn that?'

'From the tiger's broken leg, mighty lion!' answered the jackal.

Arabian story

Hard work

A Sikh story tells of the time that Guru Nanak stayed in a certain village with a poor carpenter called Lalo. A rich man called Bhago was offended that the Guru had decided to stay with the humble carpenter rather than with him. He invited Guru Nanak to a meal at his house. The Guru came, but did not eat any of the rich food that was put before him.

Angrily, Bhago asked him, 'Why do you eat the hard bread that Malik gives you, but won't eat the delicious food that I am offering?'

'I will show you,' said Guru Nanak.

He asked someone to fetch a piece of bread from Malik's house, and, taking hold of it, he squeezed it. Milk came out of the bread. Then he picked up some of the food from Bhago's table, and squeezed it. To everyone's horror, blood came out of it.

'Your food has been gained from the hardship of others,' said Guru Nanak, 'Malik's food has been gained by his own hard toil.'

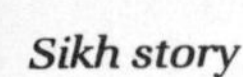

Sikh story

Starvation in de market-place

All kind o' breadfruit, pumpkin, potato and
melon,
Banana, mango, paw-paw and lemon;
Men drinking beer and stout;
Children running all about;
Women licking off duh mout';
And I hungry luk a dog.

Conkies, corn pone, sweet bread selling;
Pork chop, fish cake, souse and puddin';
Women licking off duh mout';
Men drinking beer and stout;
And I hungry luk a dog.

Raw food, cook food, all kind o' food;
Food enough for a multitude;
Women drinking beer and stout;
Men licking off duh mout';
Children running all about;
And I starving.

Glyne Walrond

should do? If one country sends surplus food, what will happen to the other country's farmers?

Should we stop buying food from poor countries? If we did, where would they get the money to buy foreign oil and machinery? Should we pay more? Eat less? All become vegetarian?

● Do the children ever overeat? Does it matter? Could our eating fewer sweets and biscuits help hungry children elsewhere? Is it wrong to leave food on your plate?

● Famine caused by drought is dealt with in *Water for plants* (page 14). With older children you might want to talk about some of the *un*natural causes of desertification – overgrazing, intensive farming, cutting down trees, diverting and damming rivers, etc.

● We often have the image of hungry people in the 'Third World' as hapless victims, unable to provide for themselves. Help the children to see that this is not true. People end up in the famine relief camps only when everything else they have tried has failed.

Activities

♦ A survey in a local shop or the food cupboard at home would show how much of our food comes from abroad – from both the developed and developing countries. Findings could be added to the world map or globe mentioned in the starting-point above.

♦ Parents and grandparents can be asked about foods which are available now that weren't when they were young. This will demonstrate how world food trade has increased in recent years.

♦ Make a 'feast or famine' display in which each child creates his or her favourite meal on a plate in clay, Plasticine or scrap materials. Put these next to a bowl of rice to show the stark difference between our diet and that of the hungry.

♦ Older children could design a poster or leaflet to encourage people to take some action which might help towards a long-term solution to hunger.

♦ The poem *Hunger* lends itself very well to illustration by a picture or model.

♦ Children could make a time-line or clock to show what they eat and when. How many times do they have unnecessary snacks?

FOOD PRODUCTION AND FARMING

Purposes

1 To understand that the production of food affects the environment and the habitats of other creatures.

2 To consider our moral responsibility to ensure food for the future.

Starting-points

- Display some toy or model farm machinery, such as tractors and combine harvesters, including perhaps a small aeroplane to represent crop-spraying. Find out what children know about them, and use them to introduce a discussion about modern arable farming.

- In the same way, use some traditional children's picture books or jigsaw puzzle pictures which depict romantic images of farm animals. Ask the children how realistic they think these images are, and then talk a bit about modern animal husbandry.

- Show a perfect 'supermarket' apple and a blemished, home-grown one, perhaps with a maggot hole. Cut them open. Talk about whether it matters if our food is not perfect.

Fact box

In 1990 there were 4500 million people living on the planet. Of those, 500 million did not get enough to eat. By the year 2000 there is likely to be a total of 6000 million.

Between 1945 and 1975 the 'green revolution' doubled the amount of food grown, by using large amounts of chemicals, and by producing new crop varieties.

Most farmers in the poorer countries cannot afford machinery and chemicals.

One vegetable may have had up to 46 doses of pesticide.

Nitrates from fertilisers, and pesticide residues, are increasingly being found in drinking water.

Intensive farming and the cutting down of forests for farm land are leading to a massive loss of topsoil. (See also *Planet Earth*, page 88).

Before the 'green revolution' 2000 varieties of rice were grown world-wide. Now there are only 25.

In Britain 200,000km of hedgerows have been uprooted since 1949. This is equivalent to five times around the equator. Twenty-one out of 28 British mammals breed in hedgerows.

Egg-laying hens are sometimes kept three to a cage, only 46cm x 51cm; many pigs are kept inside all year round; and calves are often removed from their mothers at only three days old.

Organically produced fruit and vegetables may not be insect-free, or a perfect shape, and they often cost more.

Song of the battery chicken

We can't grumble about accommodation:
we have a new concrete floor that's
always dry, four walls that are
painted white, and a sheet-iron roof
the rain drums on. A fan flows warm air
beneath our feet to disperse the smell
of chicken-shit and, on dull days,
fluorescent lighting sees us.

You can tell me: if you come by
the North door, I am in the twelfth pen
on the left-hand side of the third row
from the floor; and in that pen
I am usually the middle one of three.
But, even without directions, you'd
discover me. I have the same orange-
red comb, yellow beak and auburn
feathers, but as the door opens and you
hear above the electric fan a kind of
one-word wail, I am the one
who sounds loudest in my head.

Listen. Outside this house there's an
orchard with small moss-green apple
trees; beyond that, two fields of
cabbages; then, on the far side of
the road, a broiler house. Listen:
one cockerel grows out of there, as
tall and proud as the first hour of sun.
Sometimes I stop calling with the others
to listen, and wonder if he hears me.

The next time you come here, look for me.
Notice the way I sound inside my head.
God made us all quite differently,
and blessed us with this expensive home.

Edwin Brock

Cornfield on the Downs

Gold grain, from chalk downland
razed white, how shall we treat it —
far beyond reach
of the hungry who need it?
We've enough and to spare
why over-produce it?
Through our mindless
greed and haste
grain and downland
go to waste

Ian Serraillier

Fruit for tomorrow

A wise rabbi was walking along a road when he saw a man planting a tree. The rabbi asked him, 'How many years will it take for this tree to bear fruit?'

The man answered that it would take seventy years.

The rabbi asked, 'Are you so fit and strong that you expect to live that long and eat its fruit?'

The man answered, 'I found a fruitful world because my forefathers planted for me. So I will do the same for my children.'

Jewish story

You are what you eat

Bring back the regular seasons!
I hardly know where I am.
What with fridges and deep freezers,
I'm in a pickle — or a jam!

Lettuce, radish, and tomato,
Strawberries, raspberries, leeks,
You eat them now at any old time,
No need to wait round for weeks

For things actually to ripen,
For things to grow from seed —
Just grab an old can-opener,
Eat whatever whenever you need.

Slit open a vacuum-sealed chicken,
Twist open a vacuum-sealed jam,
Pull the tab on the sardine container,
Turn the key clockwise on spam.

No, you can't tell the seasons
By anything you eat.
We only have changes of weather
Down our street.

You don't need to wait for sunshine
Or fear the cold bleak rain.
Jump on the first jumbo jet you see
And chomp your chip butties in Spain.

Matt Simpson

Discussion

● Talk about some of the issues involved in finding a balance between feeding all the world's people as against the damage intensive farming can cause. Should we pay more for our food, if it would mean less harm was done? Would it help if we ate less? Why do people want perfectly shaped vegetables all the same size? Why should we mind if there are caterpillars in our lettuce? Have we the right to kill insect pests?

● Have we the right to regard animals as processing machines to turn grass into milk and meat? (See also *Living together*, page 36.) Again, should we pay more for less-intensively raised animals? Are we prepared to eat less meat and dairy produce and fewer eggs? How much room would the present 47 million battery hens need if they were free-range?

● Read *Fruit for tomorrow* and talk about how important it is that we think not only of our present food needs, but also of the needs of the generations to come.

Activities

♦ Take children on a visit to a farm. Ironically, they are more likely to see traditional methods in a city farm than a rural one.

♦ From their own research, the children could make a chart showing the points for and against intensive and organic farming.

♦ If there is a local shop selling organic food, the children could compare prices, and the appearance of the fruit and vegetables, and find out the opinions of people buying the produce.

♦ Some children might like to write or act their own moral tale about the importance of looking to the food needs of future generations.

HARVEST

Purposes

1 To appreciate the meaning of harvest festivals.
2 To celebrate harvest in an appropriate way.

Starting-points

You could use the starting-points and discussion to introduce the idea of harvest celebrations, and then devise a school harvest festival, as suggested in the activities below.

■ Individual children can read accounts of harvest celebrations in different cultures, using the ones given here or some they have written from their own experience or which they have found in books.
or
■ Invite people from the community to talk about harvest celebrations in their culture or religion.

Fact box

At harvest time in China people climb onto high places to look for a clear view of the full harvest moon to give thanks for their crops. They believe that a circle is the symbol of happiness and they eat round cakes to celebrate. Pictures are painted onto paper scrolls of the Moon Rabbit and the Moon Toad, who can grant health and wealth. At the end of the celebrations, the scrolls are burnt and the Moon Rabbit and the Moon Toad ride back on the smoke to their moon home.

The Christian Harvest Festival goes back to the time when everyone in the village helped with getting the crops in. Sometimes the person who cut the last stalk was cheered and put on top of the harvest wagon as the Lord of the Harvest. At the end of the day there was a great harvest supper. Churches were decorated with bundles of corn and a great display of fruit and vegetables, and a special harvest loaf was placed on the altar. After the thanksgiving service the food would be distributed to less fortunate people.

Manabozho and the maple trees

Manabozho sees that the relationship between the maple trees and people is not good. The people are taking the easy path and letting the trees feed them while they neglect their hunting, gathering and farming. So Manabozho thins the sap and makes it flow only during the late winter and early spring. This way it will be appreciated, and the people will have to hunt, fish, gather, and grow food to sustain themselves.

A long time ago, when the world was new, Gitchee Manitou made things so that life was very easy for the people. There was plenty of game and the weather was always good and the maple trees were filled with thick sweet syrup. Whenever anyone wanted to get maple syrup from the trees, all they had to do was break off a twig and collect it as it dripped out.

One day, Manabozho went walking around. 'I think I'll go see how my friends the Anishinabe are doing,' he said. So he went to a village of Indian people. But there was no one around. So Manabozho looked for the people. They were not fishing in the streams or the lake. They were not working in the fields hoeing their crops. They were not gathering berries. Finally he found them. They were in the grove of maple trees near the village. They were all just lying on their backs with their mouths open, letting the maple syrup drip into their mouths.

'This will not do,' Manabozho said. 'My people are all going to be fat and lazy if they keep on living this way.'

So Manabozho went down to the river. He took with him a big basket he had made of birch bark. With this basket he brought back many buckets of water. He went to the top of the maple trees and poured the water in so that it thinned out the syrup. Now thick maple syrup no longer dripped out of the broken twigs. Now what came out was thin and watery and just barely sweet to the taste.

'This is how it will be from now on,' Manabozho said. 'No longer will syrup drip from the maple trees. Now there will be only this watery sap. When people want to make maple syrup they will have to gather many buckets full of the sap in a birch-bark basket like mine. They will have to gather wood and make fires so they can heat stones to drop into the baskets. They will have to boil the water with the heated stones for a long time to make even a little maple syrup. Then my people will no longer grow fat and lazy. Then they will appreciate this maple syrup Gitchee Manitou made available to them. Not only that, this sap will drip from the trees only at a certain time of the year. Then it will not keep people from hunting and fishing and gathering and hoeing in the fields. This is how it is going to be,' Manabozho said.

And that it how it is to this day.

Native American story, retold by Joseph Bruchac

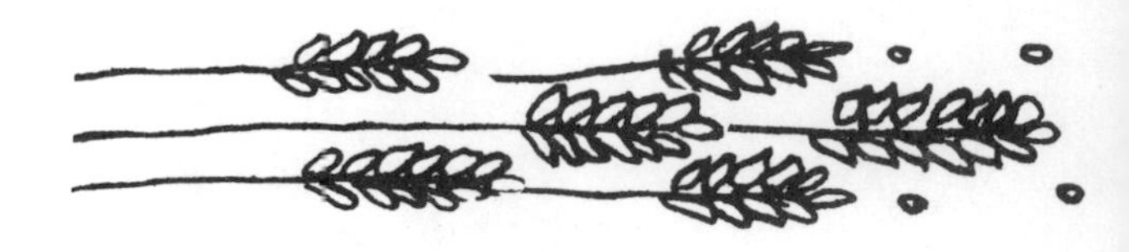

Bless this year for us,
O our God, and bless every species of its fruits for our benefit. Bestow a blessing upon the face of the earth, and satisfy us with Thy goodness; O bless our years, and make them good years for Thine honour and glory.

Polish-Jewish prayer

Old Quin Queeribus

Old Quin Queeribus —
He loved his garden so,
He wouldn't have a rake around,
A shovel or a hoe.

For each potato's eyes he bought
Fine spectacles of gold,
And mufflers for the corn, to keep
Its ears from getting cold.

On every head of lettuce green —
What do you think of that?
And every head of cabbage, too,
He tied a garden hat.

Old Quin Queeribus —
He loved his garden so,
He couldn't eat his growing things,
He only let them grow!

Nancy Byrd Turner

No more fruit

Long ago, there was a king-banyan tree, and the shade of its branches was cool and lovely. Its shadow spread far over the surrounding plain, and all could partake of its fruit. None guarded its fruit, and none hurt another for its fruit.

But then there came a man who ate his fill of fruit, broke a branch and went away. And the god living in the tree thought, 'How astonishing it is, that a man should be so evil as to break a branch off the tree, after eating his fill. Suppose the tree were to bear no more fruit.' And the tree bore no more fruit.

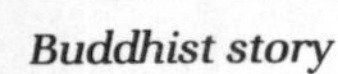

Buddhist story

Adam walked in the Garden

on the first day He smelled wonderful scents and enjoyed the beautiful sight. The aroma of the ripened fruit drew him to the trees. He reached for an apricot that hung from a branch. The fruit lifted itself so that he could not touch it. He reached for a pomegranate. The fruit evaded his hand. Then a voice spoke, 'Till the soil and care for the trees and then you may eat.'

Jewish: from the Midrash

The harvest beat

Reach up high, stand on your toes,
Pluck the fruit which on the branch grows.
Reach for the apple, reach for the pear,
Over here and over there.

Now bend down and look around,
Gather vegetables from the ground.
Pull the carrots, bend your knees,
Pluck tomatoes, beans, and peas.

Pick the grapes which grow on the vine,
Plump and juicy with sunshine.
Drop them in the bucket, stamp your feet,
Make grape juice with the harvest beat!

Do a somersault frontwards and back,
Lift that bale and carry that sack.
Swing that scythe from side to side,
Bounce up and down on the haywagon ride.

Stretch to your left, stretch to your right.
Harvest this food in the Autumn sunlight.
Twist and turn, kick up your heels,
Clap your hands and dance your reels!

Author unknown

In Melgara in Greece people celebrate a spring harvest festival of fish because that is their most important crop. During the festivities dancers imitate the actions of the fishermen pulling in the fishing nets.

The Jewish festival of Sukkoth mainly commemorates the time when the Israelites lived in temporary shelters in the wilderness, but it also celebrates the Earth's bounty. One feature of the festival is to wave a *lulav*, an arrangement of four different kinds of plants.

The Hindu festival of Diwali celebrates many things, but one element is harvest. Rangoli patterns made of foodstuffs are arranged outside the house door. They have a religious significance, but are also seen as a way of sharing harvest with the small animals which come and eat the grain.

Discussion

● Why was harvest such an important festival for people in times past? Why was it a celebration a whole community would share? Why was it often a time of fun and not just saying thank you? Is it important for us still to celebrate harvest, even if we buy most of our food in shops and most of it is not grown locally?

Activities

♦ A harvest celebration could take place at a time appropriate to any of the religions represented in your school. You could celebrate the world's harvest, with produce from many different countries.

– Or, they could invent their own forms of celebrations in song or dance or poetry or prayers, giving thanks for a particular crop, or for food world-wide.

– As so much of our food is processed and packaged, the assembly could feature the work of all the people who have had a hand in getting the foods to our store cupboards.

– If appropriate for your area, the children could devise a celebration especially for a local crop.

A handful of rice

Yams, aubergines, grapes and clementines,
Food from near and far away,
Pears, pomegranates, peppers and peanuts,
What shall we buy to eat today?
  How would it be if we just ate rice,
  Nothing but a handful of plain, boiled rice,
  Like the refugees or the people we see
  Staring out from a tv screen.
  They've no food at all
  When the rain won't fall,
  And the crops don't grow.
  So we all need to help any way we can
  When the crops won't grow.

Trout, tuna fish, hake and halibut,
Food from near and far away,
Clams, calamari, cockles and cod fish,
What shall we buy to eat today?
  How would it be if we just ate maize?
  Trying to make it last us for days and days,
  Like the refugees . . .

Ribs, shish kebab, chow mien, fish and chips,
Food from near and far away,
Beans, biriani, bangers and burgers,
What shall we buy to eat today?
  How would it be if we just didn't eat,
  Lying on the ground in the dust and heat,
  Like the refugees . . .

Words and music: David Moses

G Em Am D7
No-thing but a hand - ful of plain, boiled rice, Like the re - fu - gees or the
Bm Em Am F
peo-ple we see sta - ring out from a t v screen. They've
G C Am7 D7 G
no food at all when the rain won't fall and the crops don't grow. So we
C Am7 D7 G
D.C.
all need to help a - ny way we can when the crops won't grow.

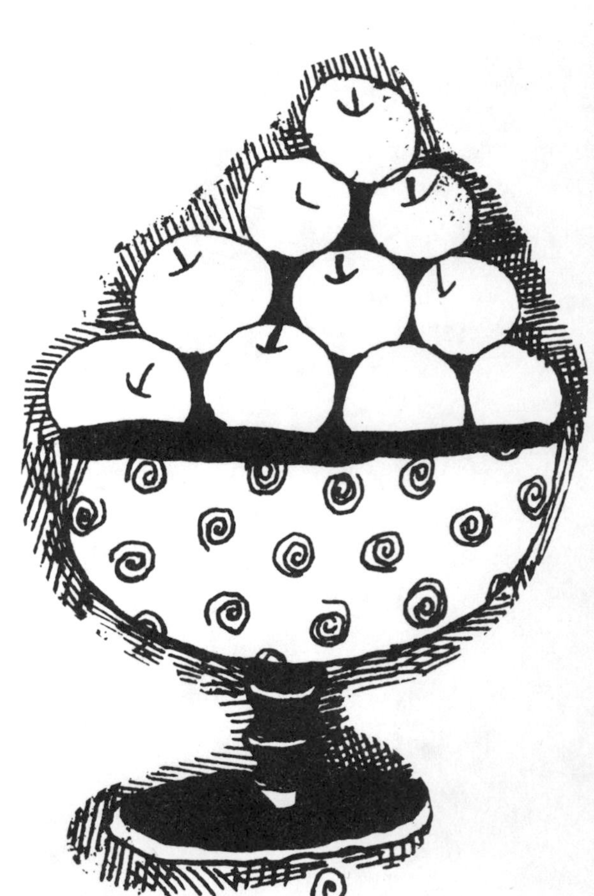

ENERGY AND WASTE

For millions of years people lived on the Earth in a more or less sustainable way. Their sources of energy were organic — either they or animals moved things; vegetable oil and wood were used for heat and light. Many societies used only organic materials for shelter and artefacts, and eventually these were naturally recycled. Where there was mining and quarrying for raw materials, it was usually on a very small scale.

Today the story is very different. We have a vastly increased world population using many more resources; from the Iron and Bronze Ages onwards, science and technology have opened the door to ways of using more and more of the Earth's raw materials. The Industrial Revolution of the 18th and 19th centuries speeded up the process enormously, and the coming of electricity has produced change at a phenomenal rate, at least in the 'developed' countries.

Life in these countries has become easier for most people: they have more leisure and things to do with that leisure time; they have continual access to new information and new ideas; they have a more varied diet; they can cook and keep warm efficiently; and they do not need an army of slaves to keep the wheels turning. But this increased production has brought its own danger to human life — pit disasters, oil-rig fires, Chernobyl, Bhopal . . . half the world is still living in grinding poverty, often as a direct result of the increased prosperity of the industrialised nations.

The good life has also been achieved at great cost to the Earth itself, and so at a cost to future generations. Extracting fossil fuels is, at best, unsightly, and accidents can cause enormous damage to wildlife. The fuels are likely to run out in the foreseeable future, and with them one of the main sources of plastics. Huge hydro-electric dams have flooded valuable farmland, and may be a cause of earthquakes. Nuclear power — thought to be the cheap, safe, non-polluting alternative — can have devastating effects on the land when it goes wrong. We are cutting down forests for furniture and paper, destroying huge areas of land to extract minerals, and denuding the seas of life to provide food and fertiliser.

We are producing unimaginable quantities of waste — paper, metals, plastic, glass — all of which have to be disposed of somewhere. Perhaps worse than this, we are producing harmful waste which we do not know how to dispose of. Burning fossil fuels causes acid rain, air pollution and global warming; pesticides build up in the food chain and cannot be eradicated; nuclear waste is sealed up in glass and concrete for future generations to deal with; chemicals are poured into rivers; and ships full of toxic waste roam the seas searching for a port which will accept their poisonous cargo.

We cannot return to a halcyon past. It did not exist. Life then, as it is now for millions of people, was short and hard, except for those rich enough to live off the labour of others. With more people alive now than have ever lived before, greater and greater resources are needed. Children need not be presented with the full horrifying story, but learning about even some of it should help them to see that the only real answers are these: we must use less, and we must recycle what we do use whenever possible.

A CLOSED SYSTEM

Purposes

1 To appreciate that the Earth is a closed system.

2 To examine the idea of renewable and non-renewable resources.

Starting-points

■ Tell the story *Paradise Island*, perhaps with a group of children acting it out. Between you, you may well be able to add to it. Ask the audience to decide what the end of the story should be.

Discussion

● What *should* the castaways have done? If they had known they wouldn't be rescued, how could they have planned for the future?

● What should they have done with their rubbish? Could they have used any of it again? What else might they have been throwing away and what could it have been used for? What could they do when the tents eventually fell apart?

● What would have happened if they *had* cut down all the corn? What use could they have made of the power of the stream? If they were very careful, would they be able to manage until they died of old age? What would happen if they had children?

● Finally, ask to what extent the children think the Earth is like the island. What lessons does it give us about how we should treat the Earth? Who are the only people who can rescue us?

Activities

⧫ Suppose another ship did arrive years later. Children could write an entry for the captain's logbook about what he found on this previously beautiful island.

⧫ Ask children to list things on the island which should have been *renewable* – trees, corn, fish, squabbits – and those which were not – tents, tins, bottles . . . They can do the same with the energy resources – sun, stream, and themselves; and matches, oil and the torch batteries.

Paradise island

Once upon a time, some explorers went to investigate a tiny, remote island which no one had ever visited before. They landed their boat on a flawless beach of dazzling white sand, with a clear, sparkling stream bubbling down from the one big hill. It was the most beautiful, unspoilt place they had ever seen.

They set off to explore. It didn't take long, because the island was very small. They found several kinds of fruit trees, some wild cereal, like wheat, and some furry animals that seemed to be a cross between a rabbit and a squirrel. They decided to call them squabbits.

They found a perfect place to set up camp, just at the foot of the hill, on a flat piece of ground by the stream. They landed some supplies from their boat and settled down happily for the night.

Towards morning, they were woken by a terrific storm. To their horror, they watched as the huge waves dashed their little boat against the rocks. 'Never mind,' they said, 'someone will rescue us.'

So they lit their little oil stoves, comforted themselves with a hot breakfast of tinned baked beans on toast and drank their tea by the light of their electric torches. They tossed the empty tins and milk bottles on the ground and in the stream. But no one came to rescue them.

After a week, the tins of food were all gone. 'Never mind,' they said, 'someone will soon rescue us. We can catch the squabbits and cook them.' Now the squabbits weren't a bit afraid, and were caught very easily, and for several weeks the people ate enormous quantities of squabbit stew. Because they thought they would soon be leaving, they didn't bother too much about where they threw the bones and fur. But no one came to rescue them.

Then one day, they suddenly realised there weren't any more squabbits. 'Never mind,' they said, 'someone will soon rescue us. We still have our fishing rods. We can catch fish.' So they cooked and ate fish and threw the bones and heads in the stream. And still no one came to rescue them.

Soon, the supplies of camping gas for their stove ran out. 'Never mind, they said, 'someone will soon rescue us. We can chop down trees for firewood.'

Several weeks later they started to feel unwell, and one of them said, 'We need some fruit and vegetables to vary our diet.' But they had chopped down all the fruit trees for firewood.

They tried to grind some corn using big stones, but they were too weak from lack of food.

'Never mind,' they said, 'we can live on water for weeks, and someone will soon rescue us.' But the water by now was too polluted to drink – it was so choked up with empty tins, gas cylinders, squabbit and fish remains, and the people felt too ill to clear it. The stream was still clear higher up in the rocks, but only two of them were strong enough to climb. One of them cut his feet badly on some broken milk bottle glass and couldn't go on. The other made it, but couldn't bring any water down to her friends. 'Oh dear,' she said, 'I have nothing to carry the water in.'

So there was nothing for it, but just to lie around waiting for someone to rescue them. To their enormous relief and delight, a few days later, they saw a ship in the distance.

'Hurrah!' they shouted, 'Rescue at last.' They grabbed their torches to signal with. But the batteries had run out . . .

Jill Brand

THE ENERGY WE USE

Purposes

1 To appreciate how much our lives are enhanced by using energy sources other than that of our own bodies.

2 To understand a little about where different types of energy come from.

Starting-points

■ One person starts to describe his or her day, and the audience call out 'stop' each time they think that something electric might have been used. For example, 'I woke up at 7.30 . . .' 'Stop! Did you have an electric alarm clock?' 'I went into the bathroom . . .' 'Stop! Did you put the light on?', and so on. Make a list, with perhaps a separate one for gas, oil and solid fuel.

After a while stop and recap, but this time considering what other uses of energy were involved: how was the alarm clock produced? How were the original materials obtained? How did it get to the shop? Introduce the idea of human energy as well.

■ Read the poem, *This is the bike*, and use it to introduce a discussion about what energy is and where it comes from. You will need to explain briefly that the sun does more than 'warm' the seed: once the seedling is above ground, the sun provides energy for the plant to grow, through the process of photosynthesis.

Sun

Thermo-nuclear heart,
you throb at the centre
of the solar system,
our giver of warmth,
light.

Your atomic blaze of energy
seems endless, infinite.
At evening you are crimson faced;
in high summer — blinding
white.

Golden mouth, thirstily you gulp
puddle, pool, pond and river.
Kindly you warm the cold Moon
on a freezing December
night.

Burning bonfire of the skies
we bask in your beams.
Always be there, Sun, always rise,
ever glowing, ever gleaming
bright.

Wes Magee

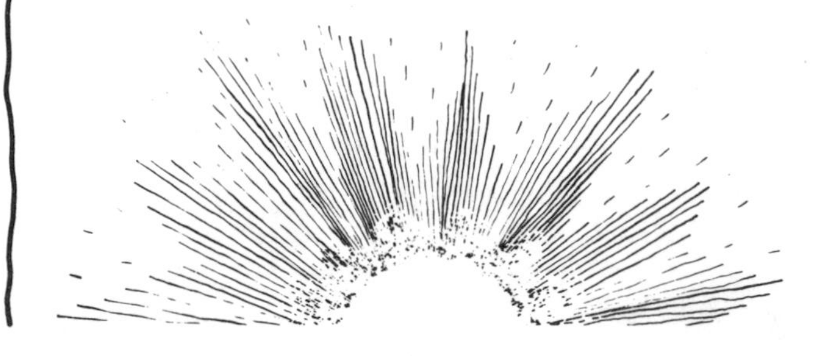

Why the monkey and the turtle are cold at night

One rainy evening a monkey and a turtle were squatting beneath a tree and complaining of the cold.

'Brrrr!' said the monkey, shivering with cold.

'Achoo, achoo!' sneezed the turtle. Finally they both agreed that the following day, early in the morning, they would chop down a tree and make themselves warm coats from its bark. But in the morning the sun began to shine, and it warmed them so nicely that the monkey climbed to the very top of a palm tree to make the best of it, and the turtle sunned himself in his favourite clearing.

At about noon the monkey climbed down from the tree to his friend the turtle and said:

'Hey there, old thing, how are you getting on?'

'Very well indeed; excellently,' answered the turtle with satisfaction.

'But, listen, what about the coats? Are we going to make them, as we said we would yesterday evening?' asked the monkey.

'What an idea! Don't mention coats to me,' replied the turtle. 'What do we need them for? We're warm enough, aren't we?'

And so they peacefully sunned themselves the whole day long. But, unfortunately, the day passed, and the moment the sun went down it began raining again. As before, the monkey and the turtle squatted beneath a tree and complained of the cold.

'Brrrr!' shivered the monkey.

'Achoo, achoo!' sneezed the turtle. And they again agreed that the following day, early in the morning, they would chop down a tree and make warm coats from its bark. But in the morning the sun began shining again, and it warmed them so nicely that the turtle said:

'What an idea! Don't mention coats to me. What do we need them for? We're warm enough, aren't we?' And the monkey agreed.

So that was what the lazy animals did, day after day, and are still doing to this very moment. When it rains in the evening, they shiver with cold under a tree, complain and sneeze, and resolve to make themselves warm coats the next day; and when morning comes, with the sun and the warmth, they are lazy again and do nothing.

Traditional

The secret of the machines

We were taken from the ore-bed and the mine,
  We were melted in the furnace and the pit —
We were cast and wrought and hammered to design,
  We were cut and filed and tooled and gauged to fit.
Some water, coal, and oil is all we ask,
  And a thousandth of an inch to give us play:
And now, if you will set us to our task,
  We will serve you four and twenty hours a day!

We can pull and haul and push and lift and drive,
We can print and plough and weave and heat and light,
We can run and race and swim and fly and dive,
We can see and hear and count and read and write!

Rudyard Kipling

Electric antics

In the morning
The toaster
Ate my bread

In the afternoon
The radio
Wanted ME to sing

In the evening
The table lamp
Asked for a light

So it was early
When I went to bed

But then . . .
The electric blanket
Spoke. 'Brrr! I'm cold,' it said.

And then . . .
The clock
Told me to remind it
When to ring!

The last straw was when
The burglar alarm
Broke down and confessed
That it got scared at night!

I daren't go out:
The street lamps
Might get me.

Trevor Millum

Fact box

Oil supplies about half of the world's energy use. Coal supplies about one-third, largely to produce electricity. Natural gas accounts for about one-fifth.

In some poorer countries 90% of the fuel used is wood.

There are about 400 nuclear reactors in 36 countries.

A rubbish incineration plant near Coventry supplies heat to a nearby factory.

On some Mediterranean islands nearly every roof has solar panels to supply hot water.

Electricity for homes in Fair Isle is provided by a giant wind turbine.

At night, some of the water from Niagara Falls is diverted to produce hydro-electric power.

In Cornwall an experiment is being run to make use of the heat from rocks 6km underground.

In Brazil a fuel for cars is made from sugar cane.

In Norway a small power plant produces electricity from waves.

In 1989 six tidal power stations were in operation in different parts of the world.

continued

This is the bike . . .

This is the bike I rode to school.

These are the legs that pushed the pedals
On the bike I rode to school.

This is the body that drove the legs
That pushed the pedals
On the bike I rode to school.

This is the bread that fuelled the body
That drove the legs
That pushed the pedals
On the bike I rode to school.

This is the corn that made the bread
That fuelled the body
That drove the legs
That pushed the pedals
On the bike I rode to school.

This is the sun that warmed the seeds
That grew the corn
That made the bread
That fuelled the body
That drove the legs
That pushed the pedals
On the bike I rode to school.

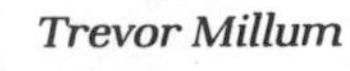

Trevor Millum

Acrostics

Whenever the wind blows
I see the giant sails turning,
Never stopping till the wind stops,
Dominating the landscape.

Can you imagine that
Over a million years ago
A tree died and now it
Lights up our homes.

Jill Brand

Windmills

I see a windmill turning,
bringing energy from the air.
I see a windmill turning
and I like to see it there.

I'd like to see a lot more,
turning, turning, side by side.
I'd like to see machines to use
the power of the tide.

I'd like to see us utilize
the sun's rays pouring down,
and bicycles and non-polluting
motors in the town,

and factories that do not poison
seas and trees and grass.
And I think that one day, even,
all these things may come to pass.

Charles Thomson

Discussion

● How are our lives improved by electricity, gas and petrol? Who benefits most from technology in transport, in school, in the workplace, and at home? What are the greatest benefits for the children and the world in general? If time is saved, what do people do with it? Why do people like camping holidays? Although older people often talk about 'the good old days', were they really so good?

● Detailed work on energy resources will best be done in the classroom, but children need to understand that in the developed world most of our energy comes from fossil fuels. Talk about people's ingenuity in utilising other energy sources, drawing on the children's own knowledge and using the information in the fact box and other sources where necessary.

● Many children may not realise where the energy in fossil fuels actually comes from. For older children you could explain that, because of a chain of natural events, we are able to use the energy produced by the sun millions of years ago. You could help them build up a flow diagram: sun shines →
trees photosynthesise and grow →
trees die and form coal →
coal burns →
water turns to steam →
steam turns turbines →
turbines produce electricity →
electricity turns food processor blades/heats iron/
heats element to produce light etc.

Activities

♦ Taking an activity such as going to the cinema, or making toast, children can list all the ways energy has been involved and what kind it is.

♦ Children could write, or role-play, a real or imaginary account of what happened when there was a power cut; or they could write a description of how someone spent his or her day 200 years ago.

♦ A class might write a collection of acrostics about energy.

SAVING ENERGY

Purposes

1 To understand that every form of energy has some cost – human, environmental or financial.

2 To appreciate the need to conserve energy, and consider how it can be done.

Starting-points

■ Read *How the people got fire*. Use it to introduce a discussion about energy production – the need for it, the precious nature of energy, the human and environmental cost of producing it. (This is a long story and you may like to read it in two instalments.)

■ With older children, you might make a large card label for various energy sources – oil, nuclear, wave, hydro-electric, natural gas . . . Prepare other cards giving the advantages and disadvantages in simple terms.

Give out all the cards, line up the children with the resource cards, and then ask the children with the other cards to come and stand by the appropriate resource card.

continued

How the people got fire

Through the brave and determined efforts of a small boy and a fox, fire is brought to the people.

Long ago, the people had no fire. At first, without fire, their lives were not bad. However, the Earth began to grow colder, and the people saw they would have to do something or they would die. So they called a council meeting.

'We have heard,' the elders said, 'that there is a thing called fire. It is a dangerous thing, but it can keep us warm.'

'Where can we find this fire?' the younger people said.

'We have heard,' said the elders, 'that fire is kept in a cave by an old woman and her two daughters. They guard the fire from anyone who would steal it and they will give fire to no one. They kill anyone they catch trying to take fire. It will be hard, but someone must go and steal fire or we will not survive. Who is brave enough to go and bring back fire?'

No one spoke. Everyone was afraid. Fox had been listening from the forest near the council circle. He crawled closer until he was next to a small boy sitting at the edge of the crowd.

'Little Brother,' Fox whispered, 'tell the people that you will get the fire.'

The boy looked at the Fox, surprised that he had spoken. Then the boy shook his head. 'I cannot do it,' the boy said.

'Little Brother,' Fox whispered, 'I will help you. With my help, you will surely succeed.'

After hearing that, the boy decided. He stood up and stepped forward into the council circle.

'I will go and get fire,' he said.

Everyone looked at him and the elders shook their heads. 'Will no one else go and get fire for the people?' No one else volunteered. So, even though they did not think he could do it, they told the boy to go and try.

'First,' said Fox, 'you must lay dry sticks together to make a bed for the fire when it is brought back. Then you must get two pairs of good snowshoes. Put one pair on and hang the other about your neck. Then you must run fast and keep running until you can run no more. That is the only way to reach the cave of fire keepers. I will show you the way to go.'

The boy did all that the fox had told him and when he was ready the fox said, 'Run in that direction. I will be right behind you.'

The boy began to run. He ran as fast as he could. He ran and ran until he thought he could run no more. But as soon as he started to slow up, fox began to snap at his ankles.

'Run on, Little Brother, run on!' Fox said and the boy kept running. He ran for a long time, but again began to tire. As soon as he slowed down, Fox nipped at his ankles again.

'Run on, Little Brother, run on!' Fox said and then darted in front of the boy. The boy was angry now at Fox. He began to chase him, but Fox stayed just ahead, leading him on. Four times the boy slowed down and four times Fox nipped at his ankles and kept him running.

Finally, the boy could run no more. His snowshoes were worn out. He stopped at the bank of a river. His legs could no longer hold him up and he sank to his knees in the snow.

The Fox came up to him and placed four dry twigs on the ground. 'Little Brother,' he said, 'you have done well. The cave of the keepers of fire is just a little further down this river. Now you must do as I say. Leave your second pair of snowshoes here. Hide these

Fact box

(See the section *Air*, pages 24–25, for information about acid rain and global warming.)

Oil is likely to run out by the year 2030, natural gas by 2045 and coal by 2240.

The developed countries use 40 times as much fossil fuel as the poorer countries.

If each home in Britain cut its energy use by 20%, it would reduce the annual emission by 16 million tonnes of CO_2.

It takes less energy to recycle most metals than to mine and process new stocks. The same goes for glass.

Gas cookers are more energy-efficient than electric ones.

It can take 50 times more energy to produce a battery than the battery itself produces.

A compact fluorescent light bulb lasts about eight times as long as a conventional one, and uses much less electricity.

An uninsulated house loses a lot of heat – 25% through the roof, 10% through windows, 35% through walls, 15% through draughts, 15% through the floor.

Discussion

- Detailed work on different energy sources would be done in the classroom, but children need to understand that fossil fuels are like a once-only gift which we mustn't squander, and that the other sources, for a variety of reasons, cannot yet supply the lack (except, perhaps, nuclear power, which has other major drawbacks).
- What will happen when the fossil fuels run out? Why shouldn't people in the poorer countries have the same facilities as those in the richer countries? (At present women and children have to walk great distances to gather firewood, and great forests are being destroyed for fuel.)

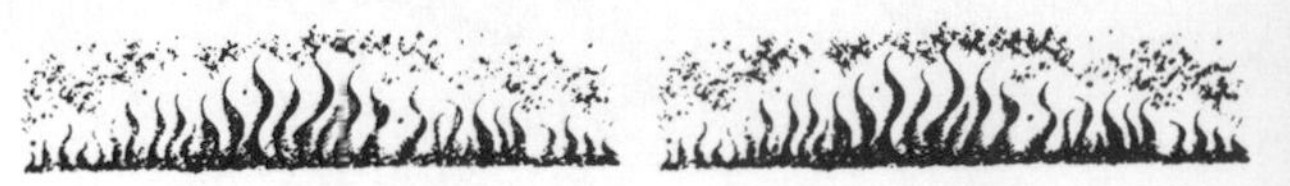

four twigs inside your clothing where they will stay dry. When the keepers of the fire are asleep, light those twigs. After you have done that, stomp out the fire and run back here to your snowshoes. The fire keepers will chase you, but if you do as I say, you will escape.'

'I will do as you say,' said the boy 'but how will I get into the cave where they keep the fire? Is it not true that the fire keepers kill anyone who tries to get close?'

'Turn yourself into a rabbit,' the Fox said. 'It is something you can do.'

The boy turned himself into a rabbit.

'Now,' Fox said, 'because you are a rabbit, you must try to escape from me.'

The boy who was now a rabbit tried to run away, but Fox was in front of him every way he ran. Finally, because there was no other way to go, he jumped into the river and began to float downstream, struggling in the water. He floated past the cave where the old woman and her two daughters kept the fire.

'A rabbit is drowning,' one of the sisters said. 'Pull him out,' said the other. 'We will dry him off by our fire.'

Soon, the boy who was now a rabbit was dry and warm by the fire. He watched the two sisters and the old woman as they tended the fire.

When night came the old woman said, 'Keep watch on the fire; I can feel that there are thieves nearby.' Then she went to sleep.

The two sisters were tired, too. After a time, the older of the two sisters decided she could watch no longer.

'Keep watch on the fire,' she said to the younger sister. Then she, too, went to sleep.

The boy who was disguised as a rabbit began to hum a sleep song. The younger sister's eyelids grew heavier and heavier. Finally she, too, could stay awake no longer.

'You,' she said to the rabbit, 'keep watch on the fire while I sleep.'

The boy who was disguised as a rabbit waited for a time to make sure all three of the fire keepers were really asleep. Then he changed back into his own shape. He took the first of the four dry sticks and lit it in the fire. Then he stomped on the fire, putting it out. As soon as the fire was out, the old woman and her daughters woke.

'He is stealing the fire!' the old woman shouted. 'Stop him.'

The boy ran outside the cave with the three following him. When he reached his snowshoes, he jumped onto them, tied them quickly and began to run. With his snowshoes it was easier for him to run than the fire keepers, but they still kept following. Fox ran alongside him. Now the younger of the two sisters was very close.

'Light the second stick!' Fox shouted.

The boy lit the second dry stick from the first one, which had almost burnt out. Then he threw the first stick into the snow to one side. The younger sister stopped to pick it up and the boy kept running. He ran and ran without stopping. Now the older of the two sisters was close behind and almost ready to grab him.

'Light the third stick!' Fox shouted.

The boy lit the third dry stick from the second one and threw the second one behind him in the snow. The older sister stopped to pick it up and the boy kept running. He ran and ran without stopping and Fox ran along beside him. The old woman was very close to him now. He could feel her breath on his neck and she reached for him with her long arms.

'Light the fourth stick!' Fox shouted.

Before the old woman could grab him, the boy lit the fourth dry stick and threw the third one behind him. Just like her daughters, the old woman stopped to pick up the stick. Now the boy was getting close to his village. The fourth stick was still burning, but it was very short. The boy was so tired that he could hardly move his legs. He tripped and fell in the snow. Fox, who had been following him, jumped out and grabbed what little was left of the fourth stick in his mouth. It was still burning and it was so short that it burnt Fox's mouth. To this day all foxes have black mouths because of that. Fox ran to the place where the sticks were placed to make a bed for the fire. He dropped the ember onto it. The fire blossomed up and all the people came and gathered around.

That was how the people got fire.

Native American (Penobscot) tale, retold by Joseph Bruchac

The peasant's address to his ox

O Ox, our goodly puller of the plough
Please humour us by pulling straight, and
kindly
Do not get the furrows crossed.
Lead the way, O leader, gee-up!
We stooped for days on end to harvest your
fodder.
Allow yourself to try just a little, dearest
provider.
While you are eating, do not fret about the
furrows: eat!
For your stall, O protector of the family
We carried the tons of timber by hand. We
Sleep in the damp, you in the dry. Yesterday
You had a cough, beloved pacemaker.
We were beside ourselves. You won't
Peg out before the sowing, will you, you dog?

Bertolt Brecht, from an Egyptian peasant's song, 1400 BC

Person-power

Our car drinks lead-free petrol,
it's a user-friendly fuel.
But I prefer to use my legs
to get me safe to school!

Our house is all-electric,
gas is what cookers like,
but I have lots of energy
so I pedal my red bike!

The sun heats solar panels,
the windmill likes the breeze,
the waves have awesome power
but I need none of these.

Just give me my strong muscles
a skateboard, bike or skates,
and I'll use person-power
in the park to race my mates!

John Rice

● Use the facts in the fact box to help children think about how we can save power in our day-to-day lives, without causing real privation. Do we need the thermostat so high, or could we wear warmer clothes? Are lights left on unnecessarily? What happens if doors are left open? What are the most energy-efficient ways to cook? Do we use the car too much? Could school times be changed to save heating and lighting?

● Should we use power for seaside illuminations or Christmas street lights? What about neon advertising? Floodlighting historic buildings or sports grounds? Heated swimming pools? . . .

Activities

♦ A huge collage or mural could be made, featuring different kinds of energy source – power station, wind turbine plant, gasworks, dam . . .

♦ Who comes to school by car? How much petrol does that represent? Are there alternatives? If so, why aren't they used? How do members of the family travel to work? Can the children devise a transport scheme for your area? Or make posters to encourage people to share cars, walk or cycle?

♦ The school could be surveyed to discover how energy-efficient it is, and then a campaign started to save energy. Let children see the bills, and see whether a significant financial saving can be made.

♦ The discussion about energy saving at home could be extended by further research, and lists of suggestions made. Children who are really interested could design an energy-efficient house of the future.

COSTING THE EARTH

Purposes

1 To consider the moral issue of taking more than we need.

2 To understand a little about some of the environmental impact of obtaining raw materials and manufacturing more and more goods.

3 To appreciate the problems caused by the enormous quantities of waste we throw away.

4 To think of ways we can all help.

Starting-points

■ Read *Dora the storer*. Why did she surround herself with so many things? Where did they all come from? Why had people thrown them away when they were still usable? Why did Dora like to collect things? Why did she feel good at the end of the jumble sale?

■ Read *Why the sky is far away*. Why was the sky so angry? In what ways do *we* not respect the 'gifts of nature'? What might happen if we go on plundering the Earth?

■ Arrange for the rubbish from one class to be kept for a week. Tip it all out on a table. You could focus on: items which could have had a use (such as the trimmings from a paper cutter); items not fully used (such as paper with only a few lines of writing on it); or items which shouldn't have been used in the first place (such as excessive packaging).

Why the sky is far away

Waste not want not is the moral of this African story in which the people's careless attitude to the sky's gift of plentiful food finally brings disaster and a future of endless hard work.

In the beginning the sky was very close to the earth. In that time men and women did not have to sow crops and harvest them or prepare soup and cook rice. Anybody who was hungry just cut a piece of the sky off and ate it. It was delicious, too. Sometimes the sky tasted like meat stew, sometimes like roasted corn and sometimes like ripe pineapple.

There was very little work to do and so people spent their time weaving beautiful cloth, carving handsome statues and retelling tales of adventure.

The king of the land was called the Oba and his court was magnificent. At the royal court there was a team of servants whose only work was to cut and shape the sky for ordinary meals and for special ceremonies.

But the sky was growing angry because people were wasteful. Very often they cut off more than they could possibly eat and threw the leftovers on the garbage heap.

'I am tired of seeing myself soured and spoiled on every garbage heap in the land,' brooded the sky.

One morning at sunrise, the sky turned very dark. Thick black clouds gathered over the Oba's palace and a great voice boomed out from above:

Oba! Mighty one! Your people have wasted my gift. I am tired of seeing myself on heaps of garbage everywhere. I warn you. Do not waste my gift any longer, or it will no longer be yours.'

The Oba, in terror, sent messengers carrying the sky's warning to every corner of the land. People tried to be more careful.

Now there was a woman in this kingdom who was never satisfied. She could barely move when she wore all the weighty coral necklaces her husband had bought her but she craved more necklaces. She had eleven children of her own but she felt her house was empty. And most of all, Adese loved to eat.

Once during a grand celebration Adese and her husband were invited to the Oba's palace, where they danced and ate past midnight.

'What an evening it was,' she thought later, standing in her own garden again. 'How I wish I could relive it tonight — the drumming I heard, the riches I saw, the food I ate!' She looked up at the sky and, as if to recapture her earlier pleasure, cut a huge piece off to eat. She had only finished one-third of it when she found she could swallow no more and realised what she had done.

'Wake the children!' screamed Adese. Now the children had enjoyed a masquerade and a party after their dinner, and most of them were still too full even to nibble at their mother's piece of sky.

The neighbours were called and the neighbours' neighbours were called but all were too full after the feasting. Adese still held in her hand a big chunk of sky. 'What does it matter?' she said, 'One more piece on the rubbish heap.' And she threw the leftovers on the rubbish pile behind her house.

The ground shook with thunder. Lightning creased the sky above the Oba's palace but no rain fell.

'Oba! Mighty one!' boomed a voice from above. 'Your people have not treated me with respect. Now I will leave you and move far away. Now you must learn how to plough the land and gather crops and hunt in the forests. Perhaps through your own labour you will learn not to waste the gifts of nature.'

No one slept very well that night. The rising sun uncovered the heads of men and women and children peering over rooftops and through windows, straining to see if the sky had really left them. It truly had. It had sailed upwards, far out of their reach.

From that day onwards, men had to grow their own food. They tilled the land and planted crops and harvested them. And far above them rested the sky, distant and blue.

Nigerian folk tale, retold by Mary-Joan Gerson

Man's best friend

What uses petrol,
Rubber and oil?
Uses tons of iron
From under the soil?
Why, cars! Yes, cars! Oh, lovely cars!
Cars are man's best friend by far!

What clogs the streets
And clogs the roads,
Crushes the hedgehogs,
Frogs and toads?
Why, cars! Yes, cars! Oh, lovely cars!
Cars are man's best friend by far!

What are shiny and sleek
and fast and whizzy,
And keep the doctors
And nurses busy?
Why, cars! Yes, cars! Oh, lovely cars!
Cars are man's best friend by far!

What gives out fumes
To rot our brains?
What gives us lovely
Acid rain?
Why, the car! The car! Oh, lovely cars!
Cars are man's best friend by far!

So build more highways,
Knock more trees down,
Make a dual carriageway
Through the middle of town:
For cars, for cars, for lovely cars!
Because cars are man's best friend by far!

Trevor Millum

Fact box 1

Each year people in Britain
- consume roughly 130 million trees' worth of paper;
- use roughly 25,000kg of steel;
- buy 2 million *new* cars.

One person gets through, on average: 90 drink cans, 70 food cans, 107 bottles and jars, and 45kg of plastic.

We use over 50 types of plastic, mostly made from oil, coal and natural gas. All these resources are likely to run out (see page 78).

It takes 4 tonnes of bauxite to make 1 tonne of aluminium.

Although only one tree in 20 in a rainforest may be cut down for use, two-thirds of the others will be damaged beyond recovery in the process.

One-quarter of the world's population uses four-fifths of the Earth's resources.

In 1988 seven times more goods were manufactured world-wide than in 1950. The figure is increasing all the time.

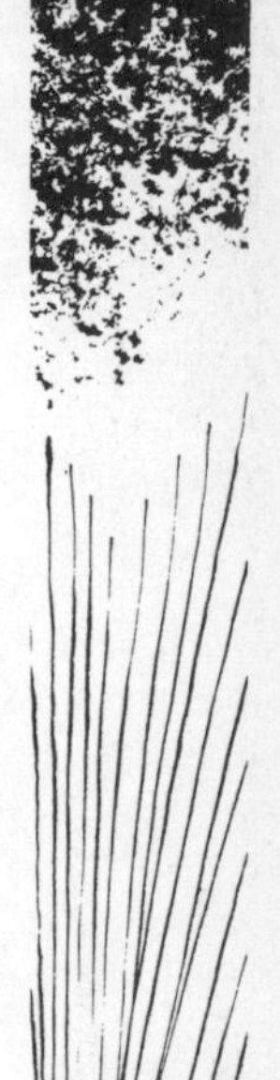

continued

Fact box 2

Each day the amount of domestic rubbish thrown away in Britain would fill Trafalgar Square up to the top of Nelson's Column.

Each person in a 'developed' country throws away 10 times his or her own body weight of rubbish each year.

About one-third of domestic waste is packaging. Nearly a quarter is vegetable waste.

Most waste is disposed of by filling in large holes, or making mounds and covering them with soil. Chemicals leach out and may get into the water supply.

Some waste is incinerated, but this can produce toxic fumes and add to the problem of acid rain.

Recycling aluminium cans uses one-fifth of the energy needed to produce new ones. Only three or four out of a hundred are recycled.

The state of Oregon in the USA reduces taxes for businesses involved in recycling.

Discussion

- Why are we called the 'consumer society'? Does having more make people happier? Or better? Why do some people deliberately choose a very simple way of life? Do people really need so many things? Why do people change their cars so often, and buy more clothes just to be in fashion?

- Is it fair that the richer countries use so much more of the world's resources than the poorer countries? What does the maxim, 'Live more simply, that others may simply live', mean? How would it help if we cut down our own consumption? What materials do we get from poor countries? What will happen as poor countries develop?

Dora the storer

Dora was a storer. She liked things. All kinds of things found a home in her house. She didn't go out looking, but somehow she always spotted them, lost or thrown away, just the very things she knew would come in useful one day. 'Finders, Keepers,' Dora would say, as she loaded up her pram.

Birdcages and bookcases, bicycles and balls, boxes, books and biscuit tins, Dora found and kept them all. The one thing that Dora did not have was *space*.

Dora had *no* space to put things. Dora had *no* space to cook things. Dora had *no* space to sit, or knit, or eat, or even sleep. 'I must find more space,' she said as she clambered carefully out of bed.

Later that morning a slip of paper squeezed in through the letter box. Dora finally found her glasses, and this is what she read:

Dora rushed round the house gathering up things she did not want too much.

But when she looked around her at the things that remained, there was still so much there that Dora felt ashamed. 'I must be generous,' she said. 'I must take *everything*. It is for a very good cause.'

Hour after hour Dora pushed her pram to and from the Jumble Sale hall.

But as time went on, it got harder and harder to part with her precious finds. She could not help sniffing when she said goodbye to the bicycles, and she cried as she wheeled away the crystal chandeliers.

At last the final load was delivered. Dora had almost reached home when she realised — she still had her pram. 'I suppose even you had better go,' she said with a sigh.

So she wheeled it slowly back to the Jumble Sale hall and left it parked outside.

Dora was exhausted when she got home. But when she looked around her house, she was pleased to see that there was so much space. There was also a lovely carpet on the floor that she hadn't seen for years.

But all that night, Dora couldn't get to sleep. She lay in the empty darkness thinking of all her precious things. She was sure they must be feeling unloved and unwanted. She could almost hear them calling to her, 'Come back and save us!'

When the sun came up, Dora dressed quickly and raced up to the hall. She could see her things through the window waiting to be sold. 'I'll get them back,' said Dora, 'if I have to buy them all. At least I'm first in the queue.'

Six hours later, Dora was still waiting. 'Hello,' said a voice. 'Have you been here long?' Dora turned to see a woman with a little boy smiling up at her. 'I want to look too,' said the boy, so Dora lifted him up. 'Ooh, Mum!' he shouted, 'There's a bike in there.'

Then, an old man hurried up and peered in through the window too. 'Look at those chandeliers!' he cried. 'Just what I always wanted.' More and more people joined the queue and peeped in through the window. They *all* saw things they wanted. 'How useful! How beautiful! How elegant!' they cried. Dora said nothing but she began to smile.

When the doors were opened and everyone rushed in, Dora was the first inside — but she didn't buy a thing.

She just watched and she smiled as all her things were sold and proudly pushed and carried off to their new homes.

It was late and dark when Dora set off home herself. She almost missed the shopping trolley dumped in the ditch — all battered and unwanted and in need of a good home. Dora couldn't bear to leave it lying there alone.

The trolley rattled along the road and Dora danced behind. There was room in that trolley for a hundred brand-new finds. So although she wasn't looking, Dora could not help spotting, lost or thrown away, just a few things that she knew would come in useful one day. 'After all,' said Dora the storer, 'Finders, Keepers!'

Helen East

Where's me shirt?

Inside a plastic carrier bag,
wrapped in a brown paper parcel,
there's this cardboard box
with the lid on back to front.

Inside the box
under swish tissue paper
aha! a shirt
all hoity-toity and tight-lipped
in another plastic bag,

folded, creased, and pinned
with eleven pins – be sure
your fingers pincer them out!

Hang on, there's more!
there's a cardboard backbone
and a plastic lock on the collar.

Matt Simpson

- What kind of damage is done to the landscape and to wildlife habitats through the extraction of raw materials? Are there any local examples? What can be done to minimise the effects?
- Many plastics and fabrics are made from oil and coal; what will happen when they run out? What are the advantages and disadvantages of using more animal and plant resources?
- Children may think that, as trees are renewable, there is no harm in using plenty of paper. Point out that paper forests are unsightly and a very poor wildlife habitat, and that making paper produces poisonous wastes and uses lots of energy.
- Why is waste disposal a problem?
- How can waste be cut down in school? Could some things be reused or put to a new use? Could paint cloths be washed instead of thrown away? Are there things which were really not needed in the first place?
- What about waste at home? An important issue is over-packaging and the over-use of disposable bags. What examples do the children know of? Is there anything they and their families could do about it? What could the shops and manufacturers do?
- What materials can be recycled? Ensure that children realise the advantages of recycling – it saves raw materials, it solves the problem of waste disposal and it saves energy. How could people be encouraged to recycle more? Whose responsibility is it? What facilities are provided in your area?
- What can be done with old clothes, toys, furniture, cars . . . ?

continued

Everything in the Universe belongs to the Lord –
you should therefore only take what is really necessary for yourself, which is set aside for you. You should not take anything else, because you know to whom it belongs.

from the Hindu scriptures

Surely life means more than food,
and the body more than clothing! Look at the birds in the sky. They do not sow or reap or gather into barns; yet your heavenly Father feeds them. Are you not worth much more than they are? Can any of you, for all his worrying, add one single cubit to his span of life? And why worry about clothing? Think of the flowers growing in the fields; they never have to work or spin; yet I assure you that not even Solomon in all his regalia was robed like one of these.

from the Bible

Observed

He parks by the kerb,
outside the butcher's.
His wife goes into the shop.
There's a bit of a queue.
While he's waiting for her to return
what do you think he'll do?

Perhaps he'll
(a) Hum along with whatever's on the radio?
(b) Pick his nose?
(c) Daydream?
(d) Tap his fingers impatiently?

Please answer (a), (b), (c) or (d)——

You were wrong:
he doesn't pick, dream, tap or hum along.

He spring-cleans his car.

He holds his door ajar
and throws out an empty can, sweet papers,
a cigarette packet, a grubby envelope
with his name on it

and on top of this
he empties his ashtray

and then his wife appears
and they drive away,
leaving

an empty can, sweet papers,
a cigarette packet, an envelope,

a heap of cigarette ends

and they drive back to their home:
to their house with the garden,
the garage, the three bedrooms,
the bathroom, the dining room,
the kitchen and the lounge

and the half-empty dustbin
that they keep
by the backdoor.

Bernard Young

Activities

- Let the children see inside the stock cupboards! Are there lots of things which are never used? They can investigate why, and, maybe, with teachers, devise a guide to be used when the school is going to order new equipment or materials.
- Start a school campaign to cut down on waste, particularly of paper. Children could find out exactly how much rubbish the school throws away each week, and then do another survey when the scheme has been operating for a few weeks.
- Your school cook could talk about how much food is thrown away each week. You could start a compost bin for the school garden or for the use of local gardeners.
- Have a school competition to find the most inventive use of scrap materials.
- Ask the children to check their own possessions. Do they have things they never use? Is it because they don't like them or have grown out of them? Have they forgotten about them? Are they broken? Is that because the children mistreated them or because they were badly made?
- They could make a similar survey of the rest of the house. Are there kitchen or DIY gadgets that never get used? Do people in the family buy magazines they don't read? Do they buy lots of new clothes?
- Children can do a survey of their rubbish bins at home, and perhaps start their own family campaign.
- The school could organise a local litter campaign – not just to urge people not to drop litter, but to encourage them not to produce so much to start with. This would need some research into the use of packaging and how much of it is really necessary. Perhaps local shops could be persuaded not to use so many bags.

Make it new again

What'll we do with an old tin can?
What'll we do with an old tin can?
Clean it out and squash it in,
Melt it down to sheets of tin –
Re-use it as you will.
  All the things that we can buy
  Can be recycled if we try,
  Clean it out and squash it in,
  Melt it down to sheets of tin,
  Take it, use it, don't you lose it,
  Make it new again.

What'll we do with the old newspaper?
What'll we do with the old newspaper?
We'll tie it up and send it where
A big machine will munch and tear –
Re-use it as you will.
  All the things that we can buy
  Can be recycled if we try,
  We'll tie it up and send it where
  A big machine will munch and tear,
  Clean it out and squash it in,
  Melt it down to sheets of tin,
  Take it, use it, don't you lose it,
  Make it new again.

What'll we do with these old green beans?
What'll we do with these old green beans?
Rot them down to fertilise
A brand new crop of bumper size –
Reuse them as you will.
  All the things that we can buy
  Can be recycled if we try,
  Rot them down to fertilize
  A brand new crop of bumper size . . .

Words: Janet Russell
Melody: traditional

PLANET EARTH

This section concerns our attitudes and behaviour to the planet as a whole. It is arranged in a different way from the rest of the book, and is not divided into topics. It could be used as a *culmination* of all the previous activities and assemblies about the environment, in which the various threads are brought together; or it could be an *introduction* to a school focus on environmental issues. The section could also be used *on its own*, perhaps at an appropriate time of year, such as the Jewish New Year, traditionally regarded as the world's birthday; or it might be triggered by events in the news; or by a decision to improve the school environment.

It is suggested that you have a special assembly, or even a week of assemblies, with the general theme of 'caring for the planet'. It could be a time of both celebration and dedication. The whole school could contribute and it would be an ideal opportunity to invite parents and other people from the local community to participate.

The *Ideas for Assembly* take the place of the *Starting-points* and *Discussion*, and are simply suggestions for some elements which might be included, or ways of providing a structure or focus. For ease of reference, the ideas are grouped under general headings. You might decide to use the ideas from a single group, but it is more likely that for any one assembly you would select suggestions from more than one group. The poems, stories and quotations are arranged according to the same headings, but there is inevitably considerable overlap between them.

The Earth and Space concerns the Earth as a body in space, as a solid structure whose actual mass can be damaged. (Most of the information in the *Fact box* relates to this heading.)

A sense of wonder explores and celebrates the beauty and bounty of the Earth. Most people, whether or not they adhere to a particular religion, are awed at times by the miracle of the Earth's very existence.

The suggestions and resources in *Interdependence* encourage children to see that the Earth is a complete ecosystem: anything we do to one part, whether for good or evil, will have inevitable consequences for other parts.

Attitudes to the Earth is closely related to the previous grouping. It explores the way people of widely different cultures regard the Earth – as a precious entity, with an integrity all its own, which must be respected.

The need to care is self-explanatory: given that the Earth is such an intricate web of related parts, that it is irreplaceable and that humankind has already done so much to upset its delicate balance, it is vital that we start to care and to act *now* before it is too late.

Finally, in *Celebrations* there are some examples of success stories, where people acting together have been able to improve the quality of their own lives, the lives of other living things and the health of the planet itself. Maybe your school could star in its own success story.

PLANET EARTH

This section is arranged differently from the rest of the book, as explained on page 86.

Purposes

1 To understand a little about the Earth as a planet.

2 To learn a little about how different people regard the Earth, and consider our own attitudes to it.

3 To understand that all things on the planet, both living and non-living, are interdependent.

4 To celebrate the beauty of the Earth.

5 To realise that human activity is having a marked and damaging effect on the planet and on the balance of nature.

6 To think about how we should change our behaviour and what positive steps we can take to protect the planet, both as groups and as individuals.

7 To have a chance to make a personal commitment to caring for the planet.

continued

The Earth and space

The rocks

I press my hand
flat upon the ground
and know that underneath it are
the great rocks of the earth,
blackened and brown
clay and sand;
as at their birth,
when earth was a cooling star,
they lie band upon band,
huge ribs of solid stone
with fossil of plant and bone.
And when I stand
alone upon this steadfast ground
I wonder why it was all planned
and how the earth was drowned
and whether the sea was once all land,
the land all sea.

Leonard Clarke

The spinning earth

The earth, they say,
spins round and round.
It doesn't look it
from the ground,
and never makes
a spinning sound.

And water never
swirls and swishes
from oceans full
of dizzy fishes,
and shelves don't lose
their pans and dishes.

And houses don't go whirling by,
or puppies swirl around the sky
or robins spin instead of fly.

It may be true
what people say
about one spinning
night and day . . .

but I keep wondering, anyway.

Aileen Fisher

Building site

From granite rock to shattered brick
Great jaws devour; the hinges thick
With clinging mud, and groaning loud,
They stoop for more, the steel neck bowed
In sharp descent. From teeth to gut
The cables stretch with piston, nut
Controlled by one — one man alone
Has power to chew up earth and stone.

With levers at his hands he has
The strength of twenty men, and as
The iron head tears up the ground,
It piles the innards in a mound,
The gaping wound begins to seep
With muddy blood. 'Tis now we weep
For once this graveyard, rubble-strewn,
Was peaceful field; now ripped and hewn.

Emma-Louise Jones (aged 16)

Fact box

The planets, in order of distance from the sun, are Mercury, Venus, Earth, Mars, Jupiter, Saturn, Uranus, Neptune and Pluto (although once every 228 years Pluto comes nearer the sun than is Neptune).

Scientists think that the Earth and the planets are about 4,600,000,000 years old.

The Earth is 150,000,000km from the sun.

Our galaxy, the Milky Way, contains about 100,000,000,000 stars, of which our sun is one.

Topsoil takes 200–120,000 years to develop, but can be lost in a matter of months.

Each year 75 billion tonnes of topsoil is lost.

The worst soil erosion is in China. Americans know when the Chinese start ploughing because of the dust over Hawaii.

Two-thirds of the countries of the world are threatened by desertification.

The deserts of Lebanon were fertile and thickly wooded in biblical times, and the Mongolian desert was lush grassland only 800 years ago.

In the mid-nineteenth century there were 170 million hectares of forest in the USA. Now there are 10 million.

The richer countries of the world have destroyed most of their forests, and now they are doing the same to those of the poorer countries.

To build 1 kilometre of road, 10 metres wide, over 500 lorry loads of materials (including rock) are needed.

Battle for the earth

Hiranayaksha was the first demon on earth. Millions of years ago he upset the balance of the planet, making it fall from its orbit. Hinduism has always known that the earth is round and that it floats in space as if it were weightless. It explains this weightlessness as being due to a delicate balance of liquids and minerals inside the globe. Today's industrialists, who are so busy tunnelling under the earth's surface, should perhaps take heed.

Hiranayaksha was the greatest demon who ever walked the planet. His body was so big and strong that it blocked the view in all directions just like a mountain, and the crest of his crown seemed to kiss the sky and cover the sun. When he walked, the earth shook and even the demigods hid themselves in fear of him. He was frightened of no one and wandered all over the earth searching for someone strong enough to fight him.

But despite his huge strength, Hiranayaksha was a slave to one thing — he loved gold. He covered himself in it — golden anklets, a golden girdle, golden bracelets, golden armour and a crown of gold. Wherever he found gold he took it, but he was never satisfied. He wanted more and more. Driven by his greed, he began to mine the earth. Because he was so powerful and everyone feared him he considered the earth his property to do with as he wished. Deeper and deeper he mined.

At last Hiranayaksha had taken so much gold from the earth that the internal balance of the planet was upset and it fell from its orbit in space. Plunging into the depths, it came to rest in the primeval waters of destruction at the very base of the universe. There it lay, helpless.

Hiranayaksha was no ordinary being. He had the power to travel anywhere in space. So he abandoned the earth, lost in the darkness, and set off with his gold in search of a fight. Full of pent-up anger, he roamed about the universe looking for someone who would dare to accept his challenge.

Just at this time, Vishnu, the supreme lord who is always watching over and protecting the universe, heard of the terrible catastrophe that had befallen the earth and entered the universe to rescue the planet. As he was lifting it up, the demon came upon him and challenged him: 'That's mine,' he roared, 'Fight me for it if you want it!'

Vishnu responded to his challenge and a great battle was fought for the sake of the earth. At last Vishnu killed the demon. Gently he lifted up the earth, restored its weightlessness and carefully put it back in its orbit.

Hindu story

Whatever I dig of you,
O Earth, may you of that have quick replenishment! O purifying One, may my spade thrust never reach right into your heart!

from the Hindu scriptures

Air is the Guru,
Water the father, Earth is the great Mother, Day and night, male and female nurses, in whose laps the whole world plays.

Sikh: from the Guru Granth Sahib

The bossy young tree

'Fallen leaves,' said the tree,
'Are merely debris.
Do ask the wind
To blow them away.'
'Before a year can pass
They will rot into me,
So don't be an ass,'
Said the grass.
'Bah!' said the tree,
'They are still debris,
So do ask the wind
To blow them away.'
'Don't be so vicious,
They are quite nutritious,
As you will soon see
When they rot into me.'
'They're keeping you warm,'
said the tree,
'And you want them to stay
Because they're covering you
Like a double duvet.'
'They're keeping me damp,'
said the grass,
'And I'm bound to get cramp
But I think they should stay
And rot the natural way.'
'I insist,' said the tree,
'I do not want debris
Littering the ground
In front of me.'
'It's ecologically sound
To have leaves on the ground.
With them you'll thrive,
But without won't survive.'
'Are you sure?' said the tree.
'Yes,' said the grass.
'Then let it pass,' said the tree,
'I was being an ass.'
'Did you call?' said the wind.
'Oh no,' said the tree,
'I was merely admiring
this lovely debris.'

Brian Patten

A sense of wonder

And my heart soars

The beauty of the trees,
the softness of the air,
the fragrance of the grass,
speak to me.

The summit of the mountain,
The thunder of the sky,
the rhythm of the sea,
speak to me.

The faintness of the stars,
the freshness of the morning,
the dewdrop on the flower,
speak to me.

The strength of fire,
the taste of salmon,
the trail of the sun,
and the life that never goes away,
They speak to me.

And my heart soars.

Chief Dan George

Ideas for assembly

The Earth and space

○ With the room darkened, shine a torch or spotlight on a large globe or picture of the Earth from space (see page 101).

– Different children could be spotlighted while they read a selection of poems and prose, from here or from other sections of the book.

or

– Children could read out the statistics about the Earth in the fact box, plus others they have researched themselves.

or

– Children could read some stories of how the world was created (see *Resources*, page 101).

or

– Read the first three verses of the Bible and on the words, 'Let there be light', have all the lights switched on.

○ Some children might like to devise a dramatic movement or dance sequence to music, based on the opening chapter of Genesis, or on another creation story (see *Resources*, page 101). Suitable music might be Holst's *Planets* suite (although there isn't actually a piece about Earth), Haydn's *Creation*, Richard Strauss's *Thus spake Zarathustra* or Bach's *Toccata and fugue in D minor*.

○ Explain that one of the first astronauts to circle Earth described it as being 'like a blue pearl in space'. Ask the children for their ideas about how others might describe the Earth. For example, a scientist, a priest, a painter, an alien . . . What are the children's own ideas about what the Earth is like?

Ideas for assembly *continued*

A sense of wonder

○ Arrange a slide show (using slides from teachers, parents or commercial sources) on the theme 'Our beautiful Earth'. Accompany it with suitable taped music, such as Vivaldi's *Four seasons*, Britten's *Spring symphony*, Beethoven's *Pastoral symphony* or one of the pieces mentioned above. This is something a group of children would enjoy putting together.

○ Focus on why the Earth is special – it is the only planet which, as far as we know, supports life. What does life on Earth depend on? (Air, water, sunlight, minerals.) Without all these, in the right amounts, we could not exist.

○ What do the children find beautiful or special to themselves in the world? This is quite a hard question for children, so perhaps teachers could contribute to start them off – a tree, a sunset, their pet hamster, the Antarctic, a rainbow . . . They could include manufactured things – a necklace, the family car, the bedroom wallpaper . . . The children could present their ideas as pictures, photographs, poems and other writings, or 'thank you' prayers.

○ For *Maui slows down the sun*, a large cut-out sun could be mounted on a stick and carried by one child, with others acting out the parts of Maui and his brothers. At the end, emphasise 'having time to notice', perhaps leading into a section about the beauties of the world, as above.

Attitudes to the Earth

○ Focus on the ways people of various cultures regard the planet. Perhaps a number of classes could each research a particular group (see *People everywhere*, pages 47-49) and present their findings in their own way – through prose and poetry, pictures, drama, music, readings . . .

They could find out about the teachings of the world religions – many of which lay particular emphasis on our relationship with the planet and the natural world – and perhaps invite speakers from the community.

Maui slows down the sun

Once long ago, the sun rose and set again immediately each day. There was only time for work — and certainly no time to enjoy the beauties of the Earth. The Maoris tell how this was all changed.

Maui the trickster felt bothered. He felt as though he was always in a hurry. He wanted to stop for a while and enjoy all the beauties of the world around him, but there was no time to do it.

'One minute the sun rises, next minute down it goes, and it's time for bed! I never get anything finished — and look at the poor fishermen and the women, trying to keep up with all their work! I've had enough of the lazy sun! Time there was a change!'

Maui had a think. To make the sun slow down, they had better catch him first. They tried three times.

First, they tried rope made of coconut fibre. Maui and his brothers plaited it. Then they dragged it out to the horizon, tied it in a noose, and laid it round the edge of the pit where the sun hides at night. They crouched down to wait.

Wham! Out flew the sun, and the rope snapped like a strand of cobweb.

'Mmm. I thought that would happen,' said Maui. 'Luckily, I've got another plan.'

The second time, they tried more coconut rope: a rope as thick as a tree, plaited out of all the coconuts in the island.

Wham! Out flew the sun, the noose tightened, Maui and his brothers held on like madmen, the sun shuddered and strained for a moment . . . but the ropes shrivelled in the heat. The sun shot on across the sky; Maui and his brothers fell in a heap.

'Hmmm. I had a feeling we were wrong in sticking to coconut rope. Luckily, I've got a better idea.'

The third time, Maui needed his sister, Hina, to help. She cut off all her magic hair for him.

'This should do the trick!' said Maui, plaiting busily.

They put the noose around the pit, and lay in wait for the dawn.

Wham! Out flew the sun, the noose tightened, Maui and his brothers held on like demons, and the sun shuddered and strained and struggled and twisted about and screamed . . .

'Listen to me!' shouted Maui. 'I'll let you go — if you promise to slow down and give us more hours in the day.'

The sun wriggled and writhed, and the sweat flew off Maui and his brothers, but they held on.

'Aaagh! I will! I promise!' yelled the sun at last.

Maui and his brothers let go, and fell in a heap.

Up soared the sun into the morning sky.

'I told you it would work!' said Maui.

'We'd better go off fishing before it gets dark,' said the others.

'There's no hurry,' said Maui. 'We've got plenty of time now. Sit down, take a rest.'

But the others couldn't get used to it and off they went. Maui stretched out on a sandbank, and lay thinking happily all the long, long day. And when the sun did set at last, there were the hair ropes, still trailing from it into the sea!

'How pretty!' thought Maui. 'How nice to have time to notice.'

Traditional Maori story

Seeds of meaning

The Earth is full of miracles

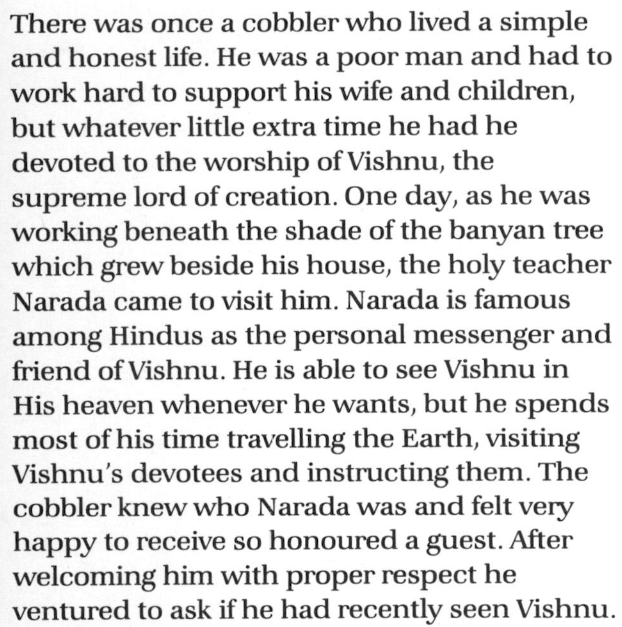

There was once a cobbler who lived a simple and honest life. He was a poor man and had to work hard to support his wife and children, but whatever little extra time he had he devoted to the worship of Vishnu, the supreme lord of creation. One day, as he was working beneath the shade of the banyan tree which grew beside his house, the holy teacher Narada came to visit him. Narada is famous among Hindus as the personal messenger and friend of Vishnu. He is able to see Vishnu in His heaven whenever he wants, but he spends most of his time travelling the Earth, visiting Vishnu's devotees and instructing them. The cobbler knew who Narada was and felt very happy to receive so honoured a guest. After welcoming him with proper respect he ventured to ask if he had recently seen Vishnu.

'Yes,' replied Narada, 'I have just been with Him and He has sent me to see you.'

The cobbler was thrilled to hear that Vishnu had sent Narada to him. After some time he asked, out of curiosity, 'What was Vishnu doing when you saw Him?'

Now Vishnu knew that the cobbler was a very special person and, wanting to teach Narada a lesson, had told him what to tell the cobbler when he asked his question.

'He was threading an elephant through the eye of a needle,' Narada replied mysteriously.

'Threading an elephant through the eye of a needle? That's amazing. Only Vishnu could do that!'

'Surely you don't believe me.' Narada laughed in amusement at the cobbler's simplicity. He had given this answer merely to test the cobbler and did not expect him to believe his story so readily. 'I don't think even Vishnu could do that. It's impossible.'

'Nothing's impossible for Vishnu,' argued the cobbler, who was not as simple as he appeared. 'This world is full of His miracles. He makes the sun rise each day. He makes the rivers run and the trees grow.'

'Look at this,' he went on as he reached to the ground and picked up a seed from beneath the banyan tree. 'Inside this seed is a banyan tree as big as the one above us. It's just waiting to come out. If Vishnu can squeeze a whole banyan tree into such a tiny seed, surely he can thread an elephant through the eye of a needle!'

Hindu story retold by Ranchor Prime

Viewed from the distance of the moon, the astonishing thing about the Earth, catching the breath, is that it is alive. The photographs show the dry pounded surface of the moon in the foreground, dead as an old bone. Aloft, floating free beneath the moist, gleaming membrane of bright blue sky, is the rising Earth, the only exuberant thing in this part of the cosmos. If you could look long enough, you would see the swirling of the great drifts of white cloud, covering and uncovering the half-hidden masses of land. If you had been looking for a very long, geologic time, you could have seen the continents themselves in motion, drifting apart on their crystal plates, held afloat by the fire beneath. It has the organised, self-contained look of a live creature.

Lewis Thomas

They could also investigate groups such as the peoples of the world's rainforests who so carefully nurture their environment and feel themselves to be part of it; the Aborigines of Australia and the Native Americans, neither of whom had a concept of owning land before the coming of white settlers; the traditional Chinese, with the idea of yin and yang balancing each other and the science of geomancy (Feng Shui) in which humans must develop an area in harmony with the forces already there; and the Inuits of the Arctic, who can live in such harsh conditions only by having a respect for the land and its creatures.

Interdependence

○ A group of children could work out a way to illustrate the idea of the interdependence of all things on the Earth, and how the actions of humans can set off chains of events.

For example: writing on a piece of paper → the bleach used in the processing of the paper pollutes rivers → fish and other creatures die. The paper comes from a tree which was grown on land that used to have a lot of wildlife – the wildlife has gone. The tree was cut down with a chainsaw that runs on petrol → the petrol fumes add to acid rain, which then kills the other trees. The petrol came in a big tanker which not only caused acid rain, but also damaged the buildings in a small village it passed through . . .

The children could make short drama sequences with a linking narrative; they could build up a web diagram on a large sheet of paper or even make a physical web with string linking various elements of the story around the room; or they could write their own poems based on *This is the house that Jack built* (page 9).

This might be an opportunity to talk about the idea of Gaia: that life on Earth is a single, self-regulating organism (the biomass), with the air, the seas and the soil a part of life itself.

○ One of the stories here could be dramatised. For example, if your assembly takes place in a hall with wall bars, *The heaviest burden* could be acted out, with children at different heights of a huge 'tree'.

The need to care

○ Children can make their own commitment to caring for the planet by joining in a 'pledging session'. Jointly, you might produce a list of 'ten ways to help the Earth', which the children then read together. Or individual children could recite their own special pledge. A special ceremony could be devised, perhaps in conjunction with the Rainbow Threads idea, below.

Celebrating

○ Adapt the idea of the Rainbow Threads symbol, in which seven different coloured threads or ribbons are woven together to form a single strand. This was first introduced in Winchester Cathedral at the Harvest Festival in 1987.

In Judaism and Christianity the rainbow is the reminder of God's covenant with his people after the flood. According to Muslim tradition, God made humans from seven different coloured soils. The seven colours could also represent seven èlements of creation, for example, water, air, soil, plants, animals, light and fire; or the seven days of the biblical creation story; or the continents – Africa, North America, South and Central America, Antarctica, Asia, Australasia and Europe.

The weaving together of the different colours can symbolise a number of ideas: the unity of all creation; the need for all peoples to work together; the oneness of all the countries of the world . . . It could be done by using long ribbons, and devising a twisting dance, or a maypole-type dance; or children could make individual bracelets from coloured thread. Originally, these were threaded through small cardboard discs, rather like a watch face, on which people had drawn their own personal symbol for the environment or conservation. If enough of these are made, they could be given in a special ceremony to everyone present, including guests, to take home as a reminder of the assembly.

Attitudes to the Earth

One who neglects or disregards

the existence of earth, air, fire, water and vegetation disregards his own existence which is entwined with them.

from the Jain writings

In the heaven of Indra,

there is said to be a network of pearls, arranged so that if you look at one you see all the others reflected in it. In the same way each object in the world is not merely itself but involves every other object, and in fact *is* every other object.

from The Flower Garland Sutra, *Hindu writings*

Whatever befalls the earth

befalls the sons of the earth. If men spit upon the ground, they spit on themselves. This we know — the earth does not belong to man, man belongs to the earth. All things are connected like the blood which unites one family. Whatever befalls the earth befalls the sons of the earth. Man did not weave the web of life; he is merely a strand in it. Whatever he does to the web he does to himself.

Chief Seathl

As I looked down,

I saw a large river meandering slowly along for miles, passing from one country to another without stopping. I also saw huge forests, extending across several borders. Two words leapt to mind: commonality and interdependence. We are one world.

John-David Bartoe, US astronaut

Who's there?

Who's there?
Who's that hiding behind the brown trees,
lurking among the green undergrowth of the
woodland?
It's we — the Tree-Elves and the Moss-People
and we are watching you
breaking branches without permission.

Who's there?
Who's that gliding over the wet rocks,
dancing and splashing at the sea's edge?
It's us — the Rock Sirens and Mermen
and we are watching you
pouring poison in our watery home.

Who's there?
Who's that drifting through the sparkling mist,
flying across bright skies, bursting out of
clouds?
It's us — the Alven, we who travel in bubbles
of air
and we are watching you
filling our palace of sky with dust and dirt.

Who's there?
Who's that running over mountains,
wading through cold rivers, striding over
forests?
It's us — the Kelpies and Glashans,
the powerful beasts of the wiser world,
and we are watching you
wasting these waters and hurting this land.

John Rice

Interdependence

The heaviest burden

Each part of the beautiful mango tree believed it had the most important job to do.

There was once a beautiful mango tree, tall proud and healthy, and laden with luscious fruit every year. It seemed a tree amongst trees.

But one night a babble of complaining voices burst up through the earth from the roots beneath the tree.

'We roots do all the work around here!' they cried. 'We suck up water for all, and hold the whole tree up, trunk and branches, leaves and fruit. Our burden is so heavy we are sunk deep into the soil, and we cannot even rise above the ground to see the life on earth. We never feel the fresh air, or see the sun or moon. We suffer day and night so the others can take it easy. Look at the trunk — what an easy life it has, resting lazily and enjoying the air. Why can't we do that?'

'Huh!' boomed the trunk. 'What nonsense! I work harder than anyone else. I hold the whole tree together, fighting against the strong winds, because if I were to break, the whole tree would die. On top of that, I have to pass food up and down to everyone all the time — I never have any rest. As for suffering — you don't know what it's like! Animals tear at my bark and people chop branches off for firewood — ouch! The wind turns and twists my body — it's no fun at all. It is not I who have an easy time — it's the leaves. Look at them dancing lightly in the sunshine. Why can't I be like them?'

'Rubbish!' hissed the leaves angrily. 'We don't have an easy time at all. All day we draw energy from the sun and give it to the whole tree. Night and day we shelter you all from the worst of the rain and the scorching sun. But no one appreciates us. No one cares that the winds and rains tear us down and fling us here and there. Some of us are eaten by animals, or burnt by people. Do you know how that feels? Oh, if only we were the fruit growing fat and ripe, and doing nothing for it.'

The fruit bounced up and down with anger at this. 'Lies!' they cried. 'You leaves know nothing! We do far more than everyone else, for we give ourselves up to be eaten — and that is why the tree is valued, and why we are allowed to grow. Do you think people would want this tree without us? If we weren't sweet and tasty, it would soon be chopped down for firewood. And do you think it is pleasant to be eaten by insects and birds and by people and animals? We are picked — often before we are even ripe and ready. We are bitten and trodden on, sliced and pickled, baked and burnt. We have the worst life of all!'

'It is the stone that has the best time — it just rests embedded in us while we are busy ripening, and when we get eaten the stone is safe, and can sink into the earth to sleep and grow. What a lovely life!'

'Sh!' said the mango stone, lying, hairy and forgotten at the foot of the tree. 'Don't argue, my friends, it weakens us all. Anyway — there is nothing to argue about. You roots, and trunk, leaves, and fruit — you all work hard to make me — but think of what I must go through. I must crack open and let the seed inside me grow and remake you, all of you, roots and trunk and leaves and fruit. That is surely the hardest job of all!'

Now just at that moment a woman came to pick mangoes, and so the tree fell quiet. So I don't know whether the rest of the tree agreed with the seed or not. What do you think?

Indonesian story, retold by Helen East

Classroom activities

- Ask children to imagine that they are space travellers arriving on Earth after travelling many light years, and to write an account of what sort of world they find. They could set the time at millions of years ago or in the present or even in the future.
- Using reference books, a group could make scale models of the planets. These could range from paper cut-outs to models made of Plasticine, papier mâché or even old footballs, table tennis balls or hockey balls.
- Start a collection of newspaper and magazine articles which relate to the future. Display them, or make a book of cuttings, and encourage the children to add to it.
- A class could make up their own newspaper for 20 or 50 years from now. There could be two versions – one where everything feared by environmentalists has happened and one for a world in which people have heeded the warnings.
- With the children, organise a 'green audit' of the school, with questions such as, *How much recycled paper do we use? How energy efficient are we? Do we recycle materials? Do we waste materials?* When the survey is complete, discuss with the children, staff, governors and parents how things could be improved.
- A class or the whole school could get involved in, or even initiate, some direct action to improve the environment – dig a pond, adopt a hedge, make a birdhouse, start a recycling scheme, make presents from scrap materials . . .
- Encourage children to join local or national groups concerned with conservation and the environment.

The need to care

Treat the Earth well

It was not given to you by your parents
It was loaned to you by your children

Classroom globe

We strung our globe from the rafters
then watched how the continents span.
We were dizzy with faraway places,
they swam before our eyes.
Everyone wanted to take a swipe at
the planet, to roll the world, to cause
global chaos. We laughed at the
notion of some great hand, sweeping down
avalanches, rolling earthquakes round
Africa, knocking elephants off their feet.
Then reasons were found for leaving seats,
to touch, or tilt, or hit heads on the planet,
squaring up to the world like March hares.
We talked of how the Earth had been damaged,
leaving it bruised, sore from neglect,
and Jenny who feels sorry for anyone and
anything, lent her brow against the planet
and felt the sorrow and pain of Earth
in a cold hard globe.

Brian Moses

Before I flew

I was already aware of how small and vulnerable our planet is; but only when I saw it from space, in all its ineffable beauty and fragility, did I realise that humankind's most urgent task is to cherish and preserve it for future generations.

US astronaut

The monkey gardeners

Caring for the Earth means educating ourselves

A large festival was being celebrated in the kingdom of Banaras. The king's gardener wished to join the merrymakers so he asked the monkeys who lived in the garden to look after it while he was away. 'Today I will go and enjoy the festivities,' he said. 'While I am away, please water all the plants.'

The monkeys took hold of the watering cans and discussed how they should go about the task.

'We must not waste the precious water,' said one.

'No,' said another, 'You are right. Let us pull out each plant and examine the roots. We'll give more water to the bigger roots and less to the smaller.'

The monkeys did just that.

When the gardener returned, he was greatly shocked to see the dead plants. 'Why have you pulled out the plants?' he cried.

'We wanted to save the water for you,' said the monkeys.

The gardener could blame only himself for having left the garden in charge of the monkeys, who knew nothing of that kind of work. Though they had meant to do good, the monkeys had done a great deal of harm.

Buddhist story

The Earth is too important

for its future to be left to the politicians — or for that matter to the ecologists. It is for all of us.

Sir Peter Scott

Problems

A voice was saying on Breakfast TV
how we really should be taking more care
of our planet; and I thought between bites
of toast and jam, how it really must
get untidy sometimes. I wondered
if God ever shouted out loud,
like Mum when my room's in a dreadful state:
'Hey, you lot, isn't it about time
you set to work and tidied your planet?'
Then another voice said, *'This world*
is sick,' and I wondered how he knew.
You could hardly feel its nose,
like a dog, or shove a thermometer
under its tongue. Such problems were
far too complicated and I needed
expert advice, but my teacher
didn't know when I asked and joked
that she only knew where to look when
answers came out of a book. She told me
instead that my maths was a mess
and my handwriting wasn't tidy.
She didn't seem to understand
I had bigger problems weighting my mind.

Brian Moses

How I see it

Some say the world's
A hopeless case:
A speck of dust
In all that space
It's certainly
A scruffy place

Just one hope
For the human race
That I can see:
Me, I'm
ACE!

Kit Wright

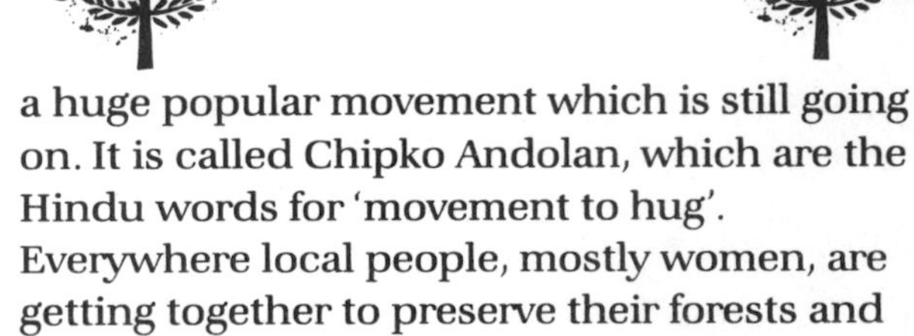

The Chipko Movement

Some years ago, in northern India, there was a company which made sports goods. Some of the things they made needed a special kind of wood, and they heard about a forest hundreds of kilometres away where lots of these ash trees grew. The forest didn't belong to anyone, but the government said that only people who paid money for a licence were allowed to cut down the trees. The sports goods company decided it would be worth paying a lot of money to get that licence, so that only they could have the trees.

They hired a contractor and, one day in March 1973, some of the loggers arrived in the Gopeshwar forest to start felling ten of the trees. Much to their surprise, they were met by a group of local people who had come, not to welcome them, but to try to persuade them not to cut the trees down. The trees, said the villagers, belonged to everyone. For hundreds of years, the forest had provided the local people with shelter, firewood, food for themselves and their animals, medicines, and wood for their simple furniture and farming tools. Without the forest, they said, they couldn't live. The villagers also explained that the trees played a vital part in stopping the rivers from flooding in the rainy season, and helping to store water in times of drought.

But the loggers wouldn't listen to any of it. 'Our bosses have paid the government a lot of money to be allowed to cut down these trees,' they said. 'You haven't paid anything, so you can't stop us. You'd better go back to your village and let us get on with the job.' But then the loggers got their second big surprise. The villagers didn't go away — they walked quietly to the trees which had been marked, and threw their arms around them! And there they stayed, hugging the trees, and daring the loggers to strike with their axes.

Of course, the loggers didn't want to injure the brave villagers, so they went back and told their bosses what had happened. It seemed for a while that the local people had won, but a few weeks later, they heard that the company were now going to chop down trees near another village, Rampur Phata, eighty kilometres away. At once, the people of Gopeshwar gathered together and set out to walk all the way to Rampur Phata. On the way, they sang and beat their drums, and all along their route people left their work and joined the march. When they arrived, they united with the local people and they all hugged the trees again.

This time the contractor's men didn't give up so easily. But the villagers were also determined, and the women in particular argued and protested for many months. Finally the contractor did give in, and to the great joy of all the local people, the loggers left.

That was not the end of the story. In fact, you could say it was the middle, because for many years before that, villagers in different parts of India had been struggling against their rulers and big business to save their trees. But these two particular incidents were the start of a huge popular movement which is still going on. It is called Chipko Andolan, which are the Hindu words for 'movement to hug'. Everywhere local people, mostly women, are getting together to preserve their forests and their way of life. This is how one elderly woman described how she felt:

These trees are our heart.
These trees are our life.
One who will fell these trees will also cut us.

The one who will saw these trees
will saw us instead of tree.
That's all.

Jill Brand

Even if there is only one tree
full of flowers and fruit in a village, that place becomes worthy of worship and respect.

from the Mahabharata, one of the Hindu scriptures

A Celtic benediction

Deep peace of the running wave to you.
Deep peace of the flowing air to you.
Deep peace of the quiet earth to you.
Deep peace of the shining stars to you.
Deep peace of the Son of Peace to you.

Traditional

The story of Bolshaw Wild Area

The children at Bolshaw Primary School have been very busy over the last two years, working hard to change a corner of their playing field into a thriving nature reserve.

In the autumn of 1988 the children at Bolshaw began to plan their nature reserve. They wanted to provide as many different habitats for mammals, birds and insects as possible, and as many different wild flowers as they could. They had lots of ideas — that was easy! Logs and stone piles for minibeasts, ditches and long grass for frogs and toads, birdboxes, hedges, compost heaps, marshy areas, and, most exciting of all, a pond!

All this meant that they couldn't just let a bit of the field go wild; they had to plan and manage the area very carefully. After a lot of thought they chose a corner of the field, with a few trees already there. A fence could be built across the corner, making a secure triangle which would not be disturbed too much. The fence would also keep small children away from the pond, a very important safety consideration. After asking the grounds staff for advice, and with the help of their teachers they made a plan, and sent it with an application for a grant to the Nature Conservancy Council.

Work started in February 1989, with the help of children, parents and teachers.

'We marked it out with string; then we started to dig. There were lots of grownups and children there . . .' Matthew Eyre

Several very muddy weekends later, we had an empty hole in the ground and a ditch with a bank running alongside it. A few weeks later the bank had a mixed hedge planted in it, and the fire brigade had filled our pond with water. It began to look a bit less like a building site. Then the real work started. Every child planted wild flower seeds into a peat pot, later to be transplanted to the Wild Area. Some children built a marshy area out of polythene and peat, and sowed it with marsh seeds. Other children planted wild flowers into the bank behind the pond. Some grew oak trees from acorns, and then planted them into the hedge. Parents made birdboxes, a birdtable, and a sign that said

The grass began to grow; ordinary playing-field grass reached waist height and began to flower. As if by magic, the pond began to come to life. All the time children, parents and teachers were planting seeds and flowers, building log piles and stone heaps, and planting more hedging.

The first year saw a big change in that corner of the field. The work still goes on, planting, topping the pond up with buckets in the summer, collecting the litter, clearing the pond and cutting the hedge. Now, though, all the children in the school use the area for study, dipping the pond, drawing the flowers, hunting minibeasts, watching the area change from spring to autumn.

'Once, in the corner of our field there was nothing much to see, just a bit of grass and an old oak tree . . .' Rachel Feargrieve

'Once we went on a ladybird hunt; it was fun . . .' Stephen Ladley

The Wild Area is a special place for wild things. The pond is full of life for much of the year; martins and woodpeckers, goldfinches and herons, redwings and fieldfares, bluetits and starlings all visit the area. More and more flowers are creeping in — foxgloves, marsh orchids, bluebells and great mullein, as well as dandelions, buttercups and thistles. Each year brings greater variety and more to watch. Each person in the school feels that the Wild Area is special, that it belongs to them a little bit.

'The best thing was when David fell in the pond . . .' Richard Broughton

'I think it is a good thing that we have the Wild Area because it teaches us to care for animals and protect the places where they live . . .' Kate Edwards

'And it still carries on . . . Maybe the Butterfly Garden that we are creating this year will be like that. Both areas are there for a reason . . .' Katie Anderson

'I feel that it is a very special place . . .' Anthony Parlane

'We have realised that we need to care more about our planet; once we have spoiled it we can never have another one . . .' Rachel Feargrieve

'It'll never be finished . . .' Anousha Karragah

Paul Wright

The green umbrella

They left us a stream with the banks choked
  with litter,
A beach turning black with the oil and the tar,
Air full of dust and the sky is grown cloudy,
Smoke from their factories, fumes from
  their cars.
What can we do? said the girl to the teacher.
What can we do? said the boy to the girl.
We're going to lift up a big green umbrella –
The world is our shelter; we'll shelter the world.
  And today, today, the children are singing,
  Praise to the sun and the sky and the Earth,
  We're going to raise a big green umbrella,
  Care for the world now we know what it's
    worth,
  And the children are singing today.

Be still for a moment and look at a tall tree,
See how her fingertips reach for the sky,
Be still for a moment you might hear her
  whisper,
Murmuring gently her green lullaby.
Basking in sunlight she draws on the water,
Pushing her roots down so dark and so deep,
She needs clear air and clear water to live in,
We need her murmur to sing us to sleep.
  And today, today, the children are singing,
  Praise to the sun and the sky and the Earth,
  We're going to raise a big green umbrella,
  Care for the world now we know what it's
    worth,
  And the children are singing today.

We want a world where the skies are wide open,
We want clear seas where the bright fishes play,
We want a moment to gaze at the sunset,
We'll make it happen, we're starting today!
This is the Earth, it spins through the heavens,
This is the Earth, it's yours and it's mine,
We 're going to lift up our big green umbrella,
This is the Earth, it's a gift for all time –

And today, today, the children are singing,
Praise to the sun and the sky and the Earth,
We're going to raise a big green umbrella,
Care for the world now we know what it's worth,
And the children are singing today.

Words and music: Nick Keir

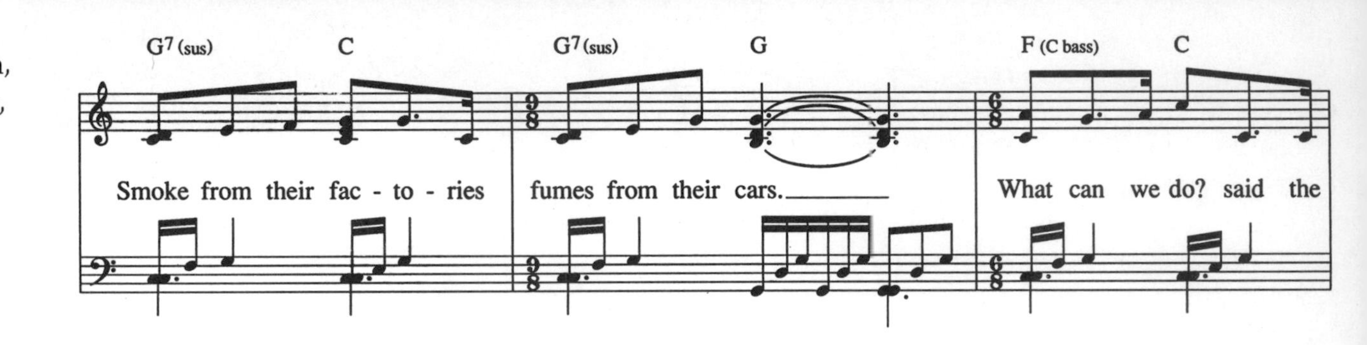

C (Cmaj7) F(C bass) G C (Cmaj7)
Praise to the sun and the sky and the Earth, We're going to raise a
F(C bass) G C G7 G
big green um - brel - la, Care for the world now we know what it's worth And the
D.S. Last time
F G7 C (Cmaj7)
child - ren are sing - ing to - day.
F C G7(sus) C G7 C

BIBLIOGRAPHY AND ADDRESSES

Books for teachers

Battle for the planet, Andre Singer, Pan/Channel 4 1987, ISBN 0 330 29891 7
Comprehensive, but very readable, this book is full of disturbing facts. It gives informative historical background to the present state of affairs, and has suggestions for how matters might be improved, given the political will.

Blueprint for a green planet, John Seymour and Herbert Girardet, Dorling Kindersley, 1987, ISBN 0 86318 178 3
One of the best of the many books on the market which both sets out the problems and suggests how we as individuals can help to solve them by changing our behaviour and by more careful shopping.

Earthrights: education as if the planet really mattered, Sue Greig, Graham Pike & David Selby, WWF/Kogan Page 1987, reprinted 1990, ISBN 1 85091 453 2 (Kogan Page), ISBN 1 947613 02 1 (WWF)
A compendium of ideas, facts, quotations, reports, discussions, school case studies and activities. It makes links with human rights, peace and development studies and stresses that the school itself and its ways of working should reflect the ideals, encouraging personal growth and self esteem.

Faith and nature, compiled by ICOREC, Ed. Martin Palmer, Anne Nash and Ivan Hattingh, Century/WWF, 1987, ISBN 0 7126 1921 6
In 1986, in Assissi, leading figures from the major religions met together to discuss the global environmental crisis. This book contains the declarations made at that time, as well as relevant scriptural readings, poems and stories.

Green facts, Michael Allaby, Hamlyn 1986, revised 1989, ISBN 0 600 566 188
This book presents scientific 'facts' for the layperson in a very clear and readable way. The author argues that many current fears are not well-founded, although some of his conclusions, for example about the longer term effects of Chernobyl, have since been demonstrated to be wrong.

Our common future: a reader's guide, Don Hinrichsen, IIED/Earthscan 1986, reprinted 1989
This is a shortened version of the report by the World Commission on Environment and Development – the 'Bruntland Report'. It presents the stark facts about how environmental degradation and unfair trading between rich and poor affects the lives of people throughout the world, and the Commissions recommendations are also given.

Shap calendar of religious festivals, Commission for Racial Equality, Elliot House, 10–12 Allington Street, London SW1E 5EH. Published annually
A booklet for teachers with a very comprehensive list of dates and brief descriptions of festivals from thirteen world religions.

Journals

Green teacher, Machynlleth, Powys, Wales SY20 8DN, UK
An international non-profit-making magazine, published six times a year, which includes discussion articles, ideas for classroom work, reports of good practice, and news of resources, and acts as a 'network centre'.

Resurgence, Salem Cottage, Trelill, Bodmin, Cornwall PL30 3HZ
This is a friendly magazine covering environmental matters, development, education, peace and related issues, concentrating on the positive side of things and emphasising the human scale.

Books for children

The ***Green guide to children's books***, published annually by Books for Keeps, 6 Brightfield Road, Lee, London SE12 8QF, Tel. 081 852 4953, is a comprehensive guide to children's books on environmental and related themes. It is strongly recommended. The books listed below are some of those particularly useful for the purposes of school assemblies.

The Blue Peter Green Book, Lewis Bronze, Nick Heathcote and Peter Brown, BBC/Sainsbury's 1990, ISBN 0 563 20886 4

Caring for Planet Earth, Barbara Holland and Hazel Lucas, Lion Publishing plc, 1990, ISBN 0 7459 1350 4

Environmentally yours, Puffin Books 1991, ISBN 0 14 034324 5

Friends of the Earth Yearbook, Grandreams 1990, ISBN 0 86227 7930

The young green consumer guide, John Elkington and Julia Hailes, Victor Gollancz 1990, ISBN 0 575 04722 4

Most educational publishers have series about specific conservation, wildlife and environmental issues. A few are listed in the relevant sections below, but there are many more and it is worth looking at current catalogues, because new titles are appearing all the time.

Other materials

The ***Council for Environmental Education*** publishes very useful resource sheets on a large number of topics, each including references to books, packs, posters, AV material and software. A full list of topics can be obtained from the address below.

Two major sources of classroom materials on relevant issues are ***World Wide Fund for Nature*** and ***Oxfam***. They publish games, activity packs, information sheets and books on most of the topics in this book. It is well worth sending for their catalogues – addresses below.

A catalogue of audiovisual materials about the environment can be obtained from:
International Centre for Conservation Education
Greenfield House, Guiting Power, Cheltenham, Gloucestershire GL54 5TZ

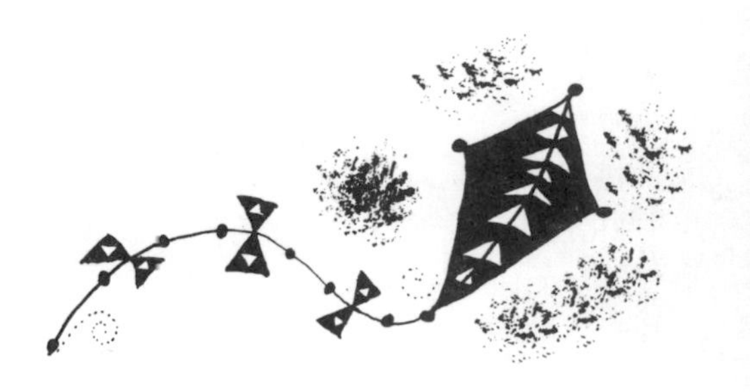

Organisations, United Kingdom

Ark Trust, 498–500 Harrow Road, London W9 3QA
Ark aims to help people change their own behaviour as well as campaigning to influence governments and organisations. They produce information leaflets, a video suitable for children, and a book giving basic information about the major issues.

Council for Environmental Education, School of Education, University of Reading, London Road, Reading RG1 5AQ
CEE coordinates and promotes environmental education in England, Wales and Northern Ireland. They have a wide range of publications.

Friends of the Earth, 26–28 Underwood Street, London N1 7JQ
One of the major national campaigning organisations with groups which also work on local issues. They have a wide range of publications, including information sheets for children. By joining a scheme called 'School Friends' teachers can receive regular information, a 20% discount on materials, and a starter pack which includes a number of project sheets.

Living Earth Foundation, 10 Upper Grosvenor St, London W1X 9PA
Specialises in environmental education, both in the UK and, increasingly, in developing countries. They publish an excellent rainforest pack, and will be producing more materials in time. Send a large s.a.e. for information.

International Consultancy on Religion, Education and Culture, Didsbury College, Wilmslow Road, Manchester M20 8RR
ICOREC works with all major religions in countries around the world, helping them develop environmental education action programmes. They have a large selection of educational and general materials on religious perspectives on the environment, as well as a free magazine on religion and ecology published six times a year.

Oxfam, 272 Banbury Road, Oxford OX2 7DZ
As well as raising money for urgent relief programmes and long term development, Oxfam promotes public awareness of the links between the environmental degradation and world poverty.

Watch Trust for Environmental Education, The Green, Witham Park, Waterside South, Lincoln LN5 7JR
WATCH is the junior section of the RSNC Wildlife Trusts Partnership. It offers a great deal to both teachers and individual child members and encourages active participation in local and national conservation projects.

World Wide Fund for Nature, Panda House, Godalming, Surrey GU7 1XR
As well as their fundraising and campaigning work, WWF has a very active education department. There is a teacher membership scheme which entitles members to a number of regular publications and a large discount on the many educational materials they publish.

Young People's Trust for the Environment and Nature Conservation, 95 Woodbridge Road, Guildford, Surrey GU1 4PY
The trust encourages active participation by young people. They run courses, holidays, and expeditions, publish fact sheets and a newsletter and will answer all kinds of queries if a stamped addressed envelope is sent.

Organisations (non-UK)

Australian Association for Environmental Education, GPO Box 112, Canberra ACT 2601

Friends of the Earth *(Australia)*, National Liaison Office, 366 Smith Street, Collingwood, Victoria 3065

Friends of the Earth *(Canada)*, Suite 53, 54 Queen Street, Ottawa KP5CS

Friends of the Earth *(New Zealand)*, Nagal House, Courthouse Lane, PO Box 39/065, Auckland West

Friends of the Earth *(USA)*, 218 D Street SE, Washington, DC 20003

WWF (Australia), Level 10, 8–12 Bridge Street, GPO Box 528, Sydney NSW 2001

WWF (Canada), 90 Eglinton Avenue East, Suite 504, Toronto, Ontario M4P 227

WWF (USA), 1250 Twenty-fourth St NW, Washington DC 20037

US Environmental Protection Agency, 401 M Street, SW, Washington, DC 20460

PLANET EARTH

Publications

Most of the materials in the general section, above, are applicable here.

Worlds of difference, Martin Palmer and Esther Bisset, WWF/Blackie, new edition 1989, ISBN 0 216 92922 9
A beautifully presented book of nine different creation stories, including those of the Jews, Christians, Muslims and Hindus and the humanists. Each one is backed up with information about the particular culture, showing how the story reflects their general beliefs and way of life.

The third planet: the Earth from space, see above, under 'Water'.

WATER

Publications

Clean water – a right for all, UNICEF, 55 Lincoln's Inn Fields, London WC2A 3NB
A project book suitable for 7–11 year-olds.

Focus on water, Christian Aid, PO Box 100, London SE1 7RT
A classroom pack containing information about water projects in developing countries, posters, photographs and suggestions for activities.

The third planet: the Earth from space, National Remote Sensing Centre. Available from: Publications, British Museum (Natural History), Cromwell Road, London SW7 5BD
A beautiful glossy photograph reproduced poster-size, featuring Africa and the Atlantic.

Water, Brighton Development Education Group, Brighthelm Centre, North Road, Brighton BN1 3LA
A pack for younger juniors which introduces world issues about water.

Words on water: *an anthology of poems entered for the Young Observer National Children's Poetry Competition*, Puffin 1987

Organisations

Greenpeace, Canonbury Villas, London N1 2PN
Very much a campaigning and direct action group, Greenpeace has always laid particular emphasis on the pollution of the seas and the plight of sea mammals.

Marine Conservation Society, 9 Gloucester Road, Ross-on-Wye, Herefordshire HR9 5BU
Campaigns to conserve the oceans and all that live in them.

The National Rivers Authority, Rivers House, 30–34 Albert Embankment, London SE1 7LT
For information about water pollution and the environment.

The Water Authorities Association, 1 Queen Anne's Gate, London SW1H 9BT
For details about the local water authorities in England and Wales. Many of them supply educational or information materials.

AIR

Publications

Acid rain, John Baines, 'Conserving our world' series, Wayland 1989, ISBN 1 85210 694
Beautifully photographed, with clear explanations and diagrams, and instructions for some experiments. There are quotes from individual people affected, which gives it immediacy.

City sounds, Rebecca Emberley, Little, Brown and Co, 1990
A beautiful picture book with no words except the imitated sounds of the city.

Organisations

National Society for Clean Air, 136 North Street, Brighton BN1 1RG
This promotes public awareness on all issues about air pollution, including noise, and also other environmental matters. They publish a number of leaflets, although not much specifically for schools.

Noise Abatement Society, PO Box 8 Bromley, Kent BR2 0UH
Please send a stamped, addressed envelope for information and a list of publications.

LIVING THINGS

Publications

Animal rights and wrongs, Lesley Newson, 'Currents' series, A & C Black 1989, ISBN 0 7136 2927 4
A well balanced book, with case studies presented by people directly concerned in the issues, giving both sides of the arguments. A clear readable text with black and white illustrations.

Let's discuss animal rights, P J Allison, Wayland 1986, ISBN 0 85078 871 4
Presents a very strong case on the side of the animals, but with discussion boxes to encourage children to make up their own minds.

Gardening for Wildlife, The Urban Trust, Unit 213, Jubilee Trades Centre, 130 Pershore Street, Birmingham, B5 6ND
A step-by-step guide to creating a garden which will attract wildlife.

Nature area management planner, The Urban Trust, (details above)
A wall chart year planner, showing how and when to manage different areas of a nature garden.

Organisations

There are an enormous number of organisations dealing with animal welfare and nature conservation. Details about *World Wide Fund for Nature, Friends of the Earth, The Young People's Trust for Environment and Nature Conservation* and *Watch* are above, in the general section. Other useful addresses for schools include:

British Union for the Abolition of Vivisection (BUAV), 16a Crane Grove, London N7 8LB

Beauty Without Cruelty International, 57 King Henry's Walk, London N1 4NX

Captive Animals Protection Society, 17 Raphael Road, Hove, Sussex BN3 5QP

Compassion in World Farming, 20 Lavant Street, Petersfield, Hampshire GU32 3EW

The League against Cruel Sports, 83–87 Union Street, London SE1 1SG

Lynx, PO Box 509, Dunmow, Essex CM6 1UH

Marine Conservation Society, 9 Gloucester Road, Ross on Wye, Herefordshire HR9 5BU

The National Anti-Vivisection Society, 51 Harley Street, London W1N 1DD

Royal Society for the Prevention of Cruelty to Animals *(RSPCA)*, Causeway, Horsham, West Sussex RH12 1HG
They have a junior membership department.

The Royal Society for the Protection of Birds, *The Young Ornithologists Club (YOC)*, The Lodge, Sandy, Bedfordshire SG19 2DL

The Vegetarian Society, 53 Marloes Road, London W8 6LA

World Society for the Protection of Animals, Park Place, 10 Lawn Lane, London SW8 1UD

Zoo Check, Cherry Tree Cottage, Coldharbour, Nr. Dorking, Surrey RH5 6HA

PEOPLE AND PLACES

Publications

Pressures on the countryside, Derrick Golland, Dryad Press Ltd 1986, ISBN 0 8521 9625 3
A book for older children, illustrated with black and white photographs. Gives a clear account of the facts and presents the problems, recognising that some development is necessary.

Utopia, Colin Ward, Penguin Education 1974, ISBN 0 14 08 1236 9
A book for older pupils, but teachers of younger children will find many useful suggestions and case studies. There is a lot of information about other people's dream homes and cities, and many thought-provoking ideas to discuss.

Vanishing tribes, 'Survival' series, Franklin Watts
Beautifully photographed, with clear accounts of threatened peoples throughout the world.

A rainforest child and ***An Arctic child***, Greenlight Publications 1990, Ty Bryn, Coomb Gardens, Llangynog, Carmarthen, Dyfed SA33 5AY
Two excellent packs of classroom materials with teacher's book, for the 8–13 age range.

Exploring your neighbourhood, Harcourt Brace Jovanovich
Four packs of materials, including videocassettes, activity cards and comprehensive teacher's book, to encourage primary-age children to investigate their local area. Some components of the packs are available separately.

Ways of living, Ben Burt, WWF UK 1984, ISBN 0 947613 00 5
This large poster gives information about some traditional ways of life and how they are threatened; the teacher's book explains in more detail, and has suggestions for classroom work and discussion.

Organisations

The Civic Trust Education Group, 17 Carlton House Terrace, London SW1Y 5AW
Actively engaged in promoting a caring attitude to the built environment in schools and colleges.

The Open Spaces Society, 25A Bell Street, Henley-on-Thames, Oxon RG9 2BA
As well as campaigning to protect both rural and urban open space for public use, the OSS publishes a number of information leaflets and books.

Survival International, 310 Edgeware Road, London W2 1DY
A campaigning organisation which aims to help tribal people secure their rights. They have useful educational material and will arrange talks in schools.

FOOD

Publications

Aid in action, Alistair Ross, A & C Black, ISBN 0 7136 2926 6
This discusses causes of disasters, including famine, and explains how aid helps people to help themselves.

'Celebrations' series, A & C Black
Titles include: *Eid ul-Fitr, Harvest Festival, Sam's Passover, Diwali,* and *Wedding*
Photographic books for young children showing how a festival is celebrated at home and school.

Famine in Africa, Lloyd Timberlake, 'Issues' series, Franklin Watts 1985
A book for older juniors, well illustrated with colour photos and diagrams. It explains some of the human causes of famine, and tries to give a note of hope about how things might change.

Festivals and celebrations, Rowland Purkin, Basil Blackwell 1982, ISBN 0 631 91570 2
This book for adults has a very useful chapter about harvests celebrations from different cultures and religions.

Food for life, Olivia Bennett, Macmillan Education in Association with the Save the Children Fund and The Commonwealth Institute, 1982, ISBN 0 333 31197 3
Packed with colour photos, this discusses the social implications of food throughout the world, as well as detailing the relationship between food and health.

Food for the world, Anna Sproule, 'Science world' series, Cambridge University Press 1987, ISBN 0 521 33240 0
Concentrates on the more technical side, about exactly what we eat, what is grown where, farming methods and food production. The information is easily accessible and illustrated with colour photographs and diagrams.

Organisations

Catholic Association for Overseas Development *(CAFOD)*, 2 Garden Close, Stockwell Road, London SW9 9TY
Publish relevant materials for both teachers and children. Catholic schools receive a regular newsletter.

Christian Aid, 35 Lower Marsh, London SE1 7TL
As well as their fundraising and development work, they publish a large number of educational materials, many of them about food.

Compassion in World Farming, 20 Lavant Street, Petersfield, Hampshire GU32 3EW
Aims to increase public awareness of the cruelty involved in factory farming, and campaigns to prevent it.

The Farm and Food Society, 4 Willfield Way, London NW11 7XT
Campaigns to end the cruelty of factory farming and to inform the public about the health and environmental hazards involved.

Soil Association, 86–88 Colston Street, Bristol, Avon BS1 5BB
Promotes organic farming and acts as a consumer watchdog on food quality issues. They publish educational materials, some of which are suitable for primary schools.

ENERGY AND WASTE

Publications

The DIY guide to combatting global warming, Ark Trust, (address above)
A leaflet for the general public with '101 hot tips to cool the Earth'.

Energy, power sources and electricity, Philip Neal, Dryad Press 1989, ISBN 0 85219 776 4
For older children, a comprehensive book with clear explanations of how different forms of energy are produced, their advantages and disadvantages, and information about new developments.

Scraps of wraps, Vicki Cobb, A & C Black ISBN 0 7136 2993 2
A light-hearted book for young children introducing the science behind common packaging materials, and suggesting simple experiments.

Waste and recycling, Barbara James, 'Conserving our world' series, Wayland ISBN 1 85210697 2
Another book for older children with clear explanations and case studies, well illustrated with photographs and diagrams.

The dustbin pack, Waste Watch, 1990. Available from the Department of Trade and Industry, the Environment Unit, Room 1016 Ashdown House, 123 Victoria Street, London SW1E 6RB
This pack for 7–11 year-olds consists of teachers' notes, a wallchart and well-presented classroom activity cards about waste reduction and recycling.

Most of the organisations listed below also produce materials suitable for schools.

Organisations

Aluminium Can Recycling Association, I–MEX House, 52 Blucher Street, Birmingham B1 1QU

British Coal Schools Service, Public Relations Department, Room 339, Hobart House, Grosvenor Place, London SW1X 7AE

British Gas Education Service, PO Box 46, Hounslow, Middlesex TW4 6NF

Energy Efficiency Office, Department of Energy, Thames House South, Mill Bank, London SW1P 4QJ

Glass Manufacturers Federation, Northumberland Road, Sheffield, Yorks S10 2UA (encourages reuse and recycling)

Phillips Petroleum Film Library, 15 Beaconsfield Road, London NW10 1YD

Save-a-can, Elm House, 19 Elmshott Lane, Cippenham, Slough, Berks SL1 5QS Tel: (06286) 66658
Provides support for can collecting competitions, a video, an annual school children's competition, and a pack of information about can manufacture and recycling called *Save-a-can teacher's pack*.

Shell Education Service, Shell–Mex House, Strand, London WC2R 0DX

Tidy Britain Group, The Pier, Wigan, Lancashire WN3 4EX

Waste Watch, National Council for Voluntary Organisations, 26 Bedford Square, London WC1B 3HU
Organises community-based recycling and reclamation schemes. Write for details about your area.

ACKNOWLEDGEMENTS

The authors and publishers would like to express their particular gratitude to Brian Moses, poetry consultant, Helen East, story consultant, Elizabeth Brieully and Sandra Palmer of the International Consultancy on Religion Education and Culture (ICOREC) for their advice on religious matters and contributions of religious material, Marilyn Stevens for general help and advice and to Alison Manners of WWF.

Grateful acknowledgement is made to the following for their permission to use poems and stories:
Harper Collins Publishers for *Calendar of cloud* by **Moira Andrew**; **Zoë Bailey** for *Flying* and *Voices*; **Nick Bartlett** for *Storm*; Hamish Hamilton Children's Books for *Workings of the Wind* by **James Berry** © 1988; **Ann Bonner** for *Summer drought*; Harper Collins Publishers for *Hanuman* by **Elizabeth Brieully** and **Sandra Palmer** from *Religion, Education and Life*; David Higham Associates for *Song of the battery hen* by **Edwin Brock**; **Joseph Bruchac** for *Birdfoot's Grandpa, Manabozho and the maple trees, How the people got fire* (we are grateful to Joseph Bruchac for donating his fee to WWF); Cadbury Ltd for *Tree* by **Patricia Cope** from *Cadbury's Seventh Book of Children's Poetry*, for *Building site* by **Emma Louise Jones**, and for *Silver rain* by **Yasmin Isaacs** from *Cadbury's First Book of Children's Verse*; **Dave Calder** for *An experiment*; **Raymond Chatlani** for *The stream and the desert*; **Stanley Cook** for *Where are they?*; **Nigel Cox** for *Jetsam*; **Leo Carey** for *Water*; Dobson Books Limited for *Fog in November* by **Leonard Clark** from *Four Seasons*; **Leonard Clark** for *The rocks* from *Good Company*, and for *Going to school in town*; Crabtree Publishing Company for *The harvest beat* from *We Celebrate Harvest*; Caxton Press for *A Fly* by **Ruth Dallas**; **Godfrey Tuup Duncan** for *The sorcerer's apprentice*; Harper Collins Publishers for the foreword by **Gerald Durrell** to *The Enchanted Canopy, Secrets from the Rainforest Roof* by Andrew M Mitchell; **Helen East** for *The Heaviest burden, Be quiet down there, The price of water, The town mouse and the country mouse, Why monkey and turtle are cold at night, Dora the storer, The greedy heron*; East African Publishing House for *The magnificent bull, a Dinka praise song* in *African Poetry for Schools*; **Gavin Ewart** for *The weather*; David Higham Associates for *Blind alley* by **Eleanor Farjeon**; **Aileen Fisher** for *My puppy* and *The spinning earth*; **John Foster** for *Facts about air*, and *Graveyard scene* from *Another Fifth Poetry Book* published by Oxford University Press, and *The circus elephants* from *Another First Poetry Book* published by Oxford University Press; Panmacmillan Children's Books for *The gift of the Sacred Dog*; by **Paul Gable**; Harcourt Brace Jovanovich for *Why the sky is far away* a Nigerian Folk Tale retold by **Mary Joan Gerson**; Hancock House Publishing Ltd for *And my heart soars* by **Chief Dan George**; **Kevin Graal** for *The house that Jack built*; Instituto Cubano del Libro for *Hunger* by **Nicholas Guillen**; Cambridge University Press for *Yhi brings the earth to life* by **Eric and Tessa Hadley** from *Legends of Earth, Air, Fire and Water* and *Maui slows down the sun* from *Legends of the Sun and Moon*; Harcourt Brace Jovanovich, Inc for *Fueled* by **Marcie Hans** from *Serve me a Slice of Moon* © 1965 by Marcie Hans; **Alan Howe** for *Owl and Hurricane*; **ICOREC** for *Ari and the chickens, Battle for the Earth, Fruit for tomorrow, Hard work, No more fruit, Seeds of meaning, Shiva and the Ganges, The monkey gardeners*; The Watts Group for *Demolition* and *Motorway* by **Marion Lines**; **Wes Magee** for *Sun*; The Society of Authors for *The Pool in the Rock* by **Walter de la Mare** and for *Sea Fever* by **John Masefield**; **Trevor Millum** for *Man's Best Friend, This is the bike* and *Electric Antics*; **Brian Moses** for *Problems, The classroom globe*, and *Walking in Autumn with Grandad*; The National Trust for *The secret of the machines* by **Rudyard Kipling**; **Judith Nicholls** for *Why?*; Faber & Faber Limited for *A poem for the rainforest* and *What on Earth?* by **Judith Nicholls**; **Grace Nicholls** for *I'm a parrot*; **Leslie Norris** for *Tiger*; Panos Institute (9 White Lion Street, London N1) for *The long walk is over* by **Winnie Ogano**; Heinemann Publishers (Oxford) Ltd for *Prayer for Rain* by **H Palmer** from *Preludes: Weather* ed R Jones; **Brian Patten** for *The Bossy Young Tree*; Penguin Books Ltd for *The river's story* by **Brian Patten**; **Irene Rawnsley** for *If only elephants* and *The greedy monster*; Stoddart Publishing for My moccasins have not walked by **Duke Redbird** from *Red on White: Biography of Duke Redbird*; **Mary Judith Ress**/New Internationalist for *I'm not going to be a bum;* **John Rice** for *Person power* and *Who's There?*; Faber and Faber Limited for and Doubleday, a division of Bantam Doubleday Dell Publishing Group Inc, for *Moss gathering*, by **Theodore Roethke**, © 1946 by Editorial Publications Inc from *The Collected Poems of Theodore Roethke*; **Michael Rosen** for *The Playground*; **Ian Serraillier** for *Cornfield on the Downs*; **Matt Simpson** for *Seal, Where's me shirt, You are what you eat* and *The moon and gravity*; Three Trees Press for *Every morning* by **George Swede** from *Time Flies* ; **Marian Swinger** for *A plea for clean water* and *Children watching the seagulls*; Oxford University Press for *Viewed from the distance of the moon* from *The Wonderful Mistake: Notes of a Biology Watcher* by **Lewis Thomas**; Harper & Row for *Building a skyscraper* by **James S Tippett**; **Charles Thomson** for *Air* and *The fish leave the sea*; Faber & Faber Ltd for *Old Quin Queerbus* by **Nancy Bird Turner** from *Funny Folk* ed Robert Fisher; Penguin Books Ltd for *How I see it* by **Kit Wright**; **Bernard Young** for *Observed*.

Songs:
Niki Davies for *Ocean of mystery* and *My place*; **Nick Keir** for *The green umbrella* and *Nowhere else to go;* **David Moses** for *A handful of rice*; **Leon Rosselson** for *Air is the world that we all of us share*; **Janet Russell** for *Make it new again*.

Every effort has been made to trace and acknowledge copyright owners. Unfortunately it has not been possible to trace some items and the publishers offer their apologies to the copyright holders. Following notification, full acknowledgement will be made in subsequent editions.

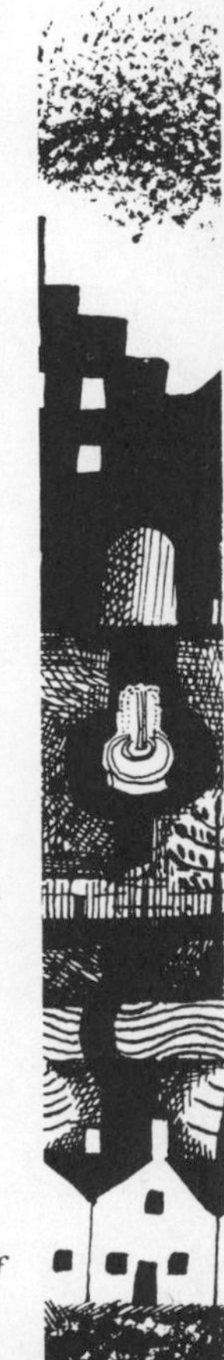

INDEX

Poems – titles and first lines

Stories and readings

More books about the environment from A & C Black

Earthwatch
A fascinating series which explains how human activities affect our Earth. Each book starts with investigations and suggestions to help children explore and improve their local environment and extends these to look at larger, global questions.

Clean air dirty air
0 7136 3325 5

Food for thought
0 7136 3328 X

Trees for tomorrow
0 7136 3327 1

Waste and recycling
0 7136 3326 3

Birds and Beasts
Songs, games and activities which explore animal life through seven themes – appearance, habitat, movement, communication, defences, winter, animals and people. 'A beautifully researched and presented collection of delightful songs.' *TES*

A selection of our most popular children's information books available in paperback:

Stopwatch series

Bird's Nest
0 7136 3494 4

Broad Bean
0 7136 3495 2

Bumble Bee
0 7136 3496 0

Hamster
0 7136 3497 9

Snail
0 7136 3498 7

Spider's Web
0 7136 3499 5

Threads series

Bread
0 7136 3500 2

Paper
0 7136 3502 9

Plastics
0 7136 3503 7

Water
0 7136 3504 5

Wood
0 7136 3505 3

For details of these and a complete list of our books on nature and the environment please write to
A & C Black, Howard Road, Eaton Socon, Cambs PE19 3EZ

About WWF

WWF is an international environmental organisation with national groups around the world. WWF's Environmental Education Programme was initiated in 1981 in response to the World Conservation Strategy. This document specifically called for changes in the attitude and behaviour of human societies so that people might live in harmony with the natural world on which they depend for their survival and well-being.

As part of its comprehensive education programme, WWF-UK is committed to the production of resource materials that enable teachers to bring environmental issues into everyday classroom teaching at all levels of education. The materials are designed to give young people knowledge and experience that allows them to make informed personal judgements about environmental issues. Resources are being developed for most subjects of the school curriculum including religious education, making use of the inherent qualities of each subject to develop specific aspects of environmental understanding and sensitivity. In addition, WWF-UK has in progress projects designed to help teachers plan, implement and evaluate effective cross-curricular environmental education.

It is hoped that The Green Umbrella will encourage all faiths to explore their relationship with the environment and to develop an understanding of the importance of caring for the world we all share.